The
Keeners

Maura D. Shaw

The Keeners

Maura D. Shaw

PLATINUM IMPRINT
MEDALLION PRESS, INC.
FLORIDA, USA

Published by Medallion Press, Inc.
225 Seabreeze Ave.
Palm Beach, FL 33480

Printed in the United States of America

Library of Congress Cataloging-in-Publication Data

Shaw, Maura D.
  The keeners / Maura D. Shaw.
      p. cm.
  ISBN 1-932815-15-5
  1. Irish American women--Fiction. 2. Women--Ireland--Fiction. 3. Clare
(Ireland)--Fiction. 4. Troy (N.Y.)--Fiction. 5. Famines--Fiction. I. Title.
  PS3619.H394K44 2004
  813'.6--dc22
                                    2004022667

To my sisters, Kerry and Erin, and my niece Clare.

PROLOGUE
1905

I DID NOT SET OUT to become a keener for the dead. But as a young girl in Ireland I took up with an old keener named Nuala Lynch. Or maybe she chose me. Out in the green fields of Clare I learned those terrible shrieking laments to sing at the sides of corpses.

It's an art I haven't practiced since I left the West of Ireland so many years ago. Even our language—the Irish in which we poured out our rage and our grief—is gone. Here in America no one wants to hear an old woman cry out to the world beyond this one. No one sings for the death of a good man. And it is their loss. When we left Ireland, we left a country desolate and silent. Not a dog was alive to howl. But we brought the hatreds with us, and the sorrows—without a way to heal them.

PART I

1846

CHAPTER 1

THE SUN HAD ALREADY SET on May Eve as I walked down the lane. The night was damp, carrying a breeze from the sea, and I tugged my shawl tight around my shoulders. I was in a hurry to reach the Duffy house, where the fiddlers and pipers and singers and storytellers gathered in the sweetness of peat smoke. I had waited as long as I could for Tom Riordan, near the foggy crossroads where he might come through. He'd said he'd see me at the *ceili* tonight. But I couldn't wait any longer. Kitty had gone ahead without me an hour ago.

The Beltane fire sent up arrows of sparks on the hilltop above Duffy's cottage. Maybe tonight Tom would take my hand and leap with me over the flames, a sign that he truly loved me. Or maybe he wouldn't show up at all. I ran my fingers through my black hair to untangle the curls and pushed the door open into the music.

The room was filled to bursting with people along the walls and the musicians on low stools in front of the hearth. Pat Maloney's fiddle began the notes of a hornpipe, and three lads stepped into the center of the room. Their heavy bare feet thumped on the dirt floor, steps intricate, legs pumping energy.

I watched for a moment and then squeezed myself into a space along the far wall, next to Kitty Dooley. Her brother Michael was the star of the dancers, a great lad with a bright face.

I was surprised to see him, since he and Tom were each other's shadows.

"Where's Tom, then, Margaret?" Kitty asked.

"Fighting to free all Ireland. Again and still."

"On Beltane Eve? Does he ever give it a rest?"

Kitty's hair was stuck all over with white flowers, wilting blossoms woven into the coppery strands. A faery queen, waiting for a human lover to fall under her bewitching spell.

"So tonight you're going to jump over the fire and go off into the woods with some fellow?" I whispered to Kitty.

"My brother says he'll murder me if I do. He says Father Martin is out there carrying his great cross, ready to swing at you before you can reach the trees."

"But you're supposed to do it, to fertilize the fields," I told her. "Granny said the lads and girls were always falling into the ditches together the whole month of May."

"Your granny? I never thought—"

I couldn't imagine it either. Was Granny ever sixteen, waiting for the right lad to look at her twice?

"She meant the ancient ones. The ones who were here before the British came. Back when things were right," I explained.

"I don't see how it could be right to go out in the ditches and fornicate." Kitty's brown eyes were open in disbelief.

"Politically, I mean. As Tom says, before the people of Ireland were oppressed by the foreign invader."

I could recite the words by heart.

"And our Tom wouldn't turn down the chance at a ditch, would he?" Kitty pinched me at the side of my waist, my most ticklish spot. She'd been doing that all my life.

"How should I know? He wouldn't find me in it, or you either."

"You're in a black mood of a sudden, aren't you?"

Kitty knew me all too well. Free Ireland was the beauty Tom Riordan longed for. The first time a *ceili* had been held in weeks and Tom hadn't even shown up. The place was full of men old and young, but not the one who mattered most.

"Maybe I'll jump over the bonfire myself and see what's on the other side," said Kitty.

"It's only for couples." It was just like Kitty to ignore the basic rules, pagan or not.

"Then come with me. Just to see. Not to jump."

Kitty cast a glance toward her brother Michael, who was still in thrall to the fiddle.

Once we were outside, the bonfire, now barely alive at the top of a rise above the vegetable patch, seemed hardly worth the trouble. Kitty's flowers glimmered as she moved up the slope. I took my usual place, ever following the impetuous Kitty, always trying to see ahead for the both of us.

The gunshot took us by surprise. A booming roar from the woods that drove us both to the ground, and a tearing clattering noise as a man on a huge beast crashed through the brush. I pulled Kitty toward me, away from the hooves thundering too near our heads.

A man lodged his shotgun against his saddle and swung down off the horse. He stumbled as his boots met the dirt, swayed and cursed. As he lurched toward the fire, I saw that it was Mr. Speke, the English landlord's agent who collects the rents and oversees the property. The worse for drink, he muttered and fiddled with the front of his trousers. Then, disgusting creature, he stood up and aimed a stream of piss at the smoldering fire.

"Bloody pagan papists, all of you. Can't stop your pagan whoring all over the land—see what good it will do you when you've nowhere to go but hell!"

His English voice was ugly. He belched.

Sweet Jesus, let him not see us here three feet away.

"Damn poachers. Shoot the bastards, I will. Got one tonight, God blast his hide."

Speke's stream ran dry. He kicked some clods of dirt toward

the fire and cursed all the Irish again.

Got one tonight. The gunshot. Somebody was out there bleeding in the dark. Please God, don't let him die. It could be Tom.

The dust made its way around the fire. Kitty coughed.

Speke swung toward the sound, ever alert for a man with a gun. These were troubled times in Ireland. I saw him blink both eyes and focus on Kitty, a woman lying on the ground. *A May gift, female, open to him at the pagan fire. A vision, a faery queen.*

"Run, Kitty! Go!" My shove propelled Kitty down the hill, into the cabbage sprouts, and kept her going toward the light.

A vision of white flowers dancing in the dark. Edward Speke stared after it with slack mouth and stiffening cock. Then he spit a great gob on the fire and hauled himself up on his horse. *The faeries were out doing mischief tonight. Best to leave it at one dead Paddy and go home.*

I was already pounding up the hill to the woods. A man lay bleeding his life away. Not Tom, never Tom. Please never Tom.

The single blast from Speke's gun had seemed so close, but I was far into the dark trees before I heard a moan. Pale moonlight picked out the black blood that oozed from the man lying curled on the cold earth.

Down on my knees beside him. His hair was dark, not fair like Tom's, and I felt ashamed at my relief. I leaned closer and saw the white thin face of young Conor Maloney, eyes squeezed tight. Oh dear sweet Mother, that lovely boy. Not more than thirteen but tall, a man for someone looking to shoot. The son of the fiddler.

I peeled back the shreds of cloth on his upper arm. He had been hit just below the shoulder. Bone gleamed ghostly in the dim light filtering through the trees.

Staunch the bleeding first, I heard my granny say. Pressure, pressure, keep the blood in where it's needed.

The hem of my red flannel skirt tore easily. I folded the bandage onto the wound and pressed down hard, though it made the boy cry out in pain.

"Hush, Conor, my man, be a brave one. We're going to get you home soon enough."

Maybe not soon enough. The boy's eyes rolled back in their sockets. I kept my hands on the bandage, until they ached with the pressing, until the cloth was soaked through, scarlet seeming black.

However will I get him down to his father? How can he walk? I'm not a good enough healer to save his life by myself. I'll have to be singing a keen for him instead. The bones of the arm beneath my hands were shifting fragments, blown to pieces by the blast of Speke's rage.

I sent all my thoughts of healing into that mangled wound, begging the blood to thicken and clot, begging the body to defend itself. Speke's hoofbeats had long died away. I heard men's voices coming through the trees, calling my name.

"Here! Over here! We're here!"

"Christ Jesus," said Tom Riordan, standing over me. His blond hair shone in the moonlight, his face angled in shadows.

I looked up at him without moving my fingers from the bloody cloth.

"Conor's bad. Speke shot him for poaching. His arm is smashed."

"We've got to move him." Tom turned to the lads with him.

"Hugh—can you get both your arms under his right shoulder? Cradle the arm, there. And Michael, the other one? I'll take his feet. Poor lad doesn't weigh six stone."

On the count of three, they lifted the boy in their arms. I crowded in next to Hugh Sweeney, keeping the pressure firmly on the wound. In the dim light Conor's face was white. He was only a boy, like my brother Jimmy, who was home safe and sound, thank God. Hungry, but safe.

The people in the cottage broke into murmured prayers and angry curses when we brought the boy in. Kitty put her hands to her mouth.

Michael Dooley was tender as he placed him on the floor near the hearth. He supported the wounded arm until Mrs. Duffy wedged a scrap of wool blanket under the boy. Michael sighed as he let Conor's weight sag to the floor.

He wiped the blood from his hands and forearms on his trouser legs. The coppery hairs on his arm were matted together.

"This is no way to run a country. A young lad's life taken for hunting a rabbit or two."

"The rabbit is more welcome here than we are," said Tom. "That devil Speke sits awake nights with his gun to keep us off the land."

I heard the familiar anger in Tom's voice. I crouched at Conor's one side, Mrs. Duffy at the other. Pat Maloney stood stiff and silent, watching his boy's future drip onto the dirt.

"Do you think we should go for the doctor?" asked Willie Duffy.

"We should go for the bailiff and have Speke arrested for brutal murder," said Tom.

"You know it won't stick, Tommy. And the only witnesses being the two girls, Margaret Meehan and my sister Kitty—Speke will be out the door of the jail before he's ever gone in." Michael Dooley shook his head.

"The doctor won't come from Kilfenora at this time of night," said John Sweeney, Hugh's father. "Maybe the priest will make a better showing."

I spoke up loudly, so the boy could hear if he was conscious. "We don't need the priest. The doctor can take the shot out tomorrow, and Conor will heal up fit as a fiddle."

I prayed that I was right. The wound was a mass of ugly fragments. But the bleeding had slowed, and if he was kept warm, maybe the shock would wear off. I didn't sense the hand of death hovering over the boy, ready to snatch him as soon as my back was turned.

In the morning one of the men could ask the loan of a horse and cart from Ned Geary, a local farmer, to bring the boy into Kilfenora. Like the rest of the families in our small *clachan* of Kilvarna—three dozen or so tenant cottages—the Maloneys had no money to pay the doctor and nothing to trade. Even the laying hens were eaten, after the blight on the potato crop last year left us hungry. But the doctor was a kind man and often stopped to listen to Pat's fiddle at the market days in town. Surely he wouldn't turn away a wounded boy from his door.

"I'll stay if you need me," I offered to Mrs. Duffy.

"Ah no, darling, I'll watch him like my own. If the pain gets too bad, I'll see if Mr. Duffy has a bit of poteen in the jug for him. I know he's been hoarding the last of it. Go on, your Tom's leaving. Walk out with him."

Tom leaned against the wall near the door. I could sense his edginess from here.

"Sit with him by the bonfire for a little. You could do with a few minutes of May Eve cuddling."

"I will, then." My voice sounded uncertain, even to my own ears. Then I saw Tom glance in my direction. I lifted my chin and nodded.

"We'll meet in the morning, lads. Tell the others," I heard him say to Hugh and Michael.

Another girl might have asked Tom what he was meeting for, but I knew better. What Tom kept to himself was less of a danger to everybody.

The night was black and starless as we walked up to the bonfire, a mere heap of glowing embers now. A shudder ran through me at the memory of Speke's words, and Tom put his arm around my shoulders.

I let myself relax against him, ever so slightly.

"Speke was after Kitty," I whispered. "After he shot poor Colin. I shoved her down the hill."

"A lot of boys would be after Kitty on May Eve," said Tom.

His voice turned cold. "But I would kill Speke if he touched her."

A chill of fear shook me again. The hatred ran so deep, like a river coursing through Tom's soul. Not just for Speke himself, but for all the British who kept the Irish people in poverty and hunger. I bit back the words that would tell him I was afraid for him, afraid of the rage and the violence. Instead I reached for his hand and held it tight in both of mine.

"It's May Eve, Tom. Let's not bring the darkness nearer."

I squeezed his hand and the heat flowed between us. I wanted to be young.

"Come on!" I pulled him along with me and together we ran straight at the embers, leaping at the last possible moment over the fire, sailing awkwardly above the warmth into the dark damp earth. I laughed, and then Tom leaned over and kissed me, a sweet, lingering, tingling kiss. I closed my eyes against the dizzy feeling.

"Now we go into the fields, my girl. It's our ancient duty to make the flowers grow."

"Just because I study the old ways doesn't mean I practice them," I said, but I didn't move from his arms. "It's one thing to learn the keens for the dead and quite another to do what you're suggesting, Tommy."

His long fingers were deep in my black hair, holding my face close to his. He kissed me again while we had the chance. Our time alone together was neither frequent nor long.

"Maybe next year," he said.

"Hope dies hard. Who knows what may happen on May Eve next?"

"I thought you had the Second Sight, Margaret Meehan. That's what the old biddies say."

"It's not like that at all," I said.

CHAPTER 2

KITTY AND I HAD BEEN friends since we were born. Together we weeded the patches, helped our mothers, sold eggs at the market day fairs, and collected herbs on rambles with my granny. We went to Mass each Sunday and giggled at the boys. When my granny died, I fell in with Nuala Lynch and started learning to keen. I knew Kitty thought it peculiar, but I did it anyway. Life went on in Kilvarna. And then last fall the potatoes rotted in the ground, turned to blackened slime by the blight.

In May 1846, most of us in the west of Ireland were hungry. Many families ate their seed potatoes and had nothing to plant for the future. Those who couldn't pay the rent were evicted, and landlords turned the small patches into grazing pastures for beef cattle, whose flesh was more valuable than ours. The towns were invaded by thousands of the evicted, living in shacks along alleyways, fever-infested invitations to death. The infirmaries and workhouses were filled. And the pestilence and horror began to seep out into the countryside, into the beautiful soft air of Clare.

On a sunny afternoon, after our work was done, Kitty and I walked across the fields and through the meadows to the sea. We didn't go down to the sandy coast, where the men set off in their fishing boats, but instead went out to our favorite place on the headlands at Moher, where the cliffs drop seven hundred feet to the blue-green water below and stretch for five miles along the coast. At the top of the headland we could see O'Brien's Tower perched high on a rise. It was black against the sky, looking like one of the old castle ruins that molder away on the fields here in Clare. It wasn't a real castle, though. The landowner built it himself to attract wealthy visitors who were touring the West. We saw them in their carriages, with their servants and their fine clothes. But I don't think they ever saw us.

We heard the cries of the gulls and the peregrines that nested in the rocky ledges, but Kitty and I had agreed beforehand that no matter how hungry, we were not going to be tempted by visions of eggs. Brave and foolhardy boys climbed down those ledges. Some came back with prizes cradled gently in their shirts. Others were smashed like eggshells themselves.

The sight of the massive expanse of rock always took my breath away and gave me an odd fluttering in my middle. The surf foamed at the bottom of the cliffs, so far down. Here and there a small ledge jutted out, just the place where a nest might be found tucked inside a crevice. I swallowed. If the wind were behind me just right, I could fly off the face of the earth and soar.

The cliffs curved against the deep, green gleam of the ocean. Kitty leaned to see more clearly over the edge. The breeze riffled her red-brown hair and whipped the edges of her shawl. I imagined her being swept off the edge into the nothingness of the long drop.

"Get back, Kitty!" Of course she strained forward instead.

"But I see something. Down on that ledge. Do you see it? A scrap of blue?"

I gritted my teeth together and looked. About a hundred feet down the cliff face, I saw a spot of blue. It could have been a boy, or it could have been a piece of cloth snagged on a rock.

I took a step back and hauled Kitty with me.

"I don't think it's anything. But I don't know."

A horse-drawn carriage appeared on the road behind us. It had the Harris estate crest on the door. God forbid it was that disgusting Mr. Speke out to take in the view.

But another man and three women were seated in the carriage, all ruffles and hats and shades against the sun. English gentry. The horses continued up the dirt road to the top of the long hill.

"They might have a spyglass at the tower," said Kitty. "Then they could see."

I did not want to tangle with the gentry at the tower. I knelt on all fours, flattened myself on the ground at the edge of the cliff, and stuck my head over. Feeling sick at the sight of the drop below, I squinted my eyes to look at the blue rag. I couldn't see anything for sure. I backed away from the edge and stood up to brush the grass from my skirt.

"I guess we'd better ask, just in case."

I made my brother swear he wouldn't come here for eggs, but Jimmy didn't always listen.

It was a long walk uphill. Even from the ground, the view of the sea and the cliffs made my heart soar. Treacherous and unforgiving to some, but so achingly beautiful. I could see why Mr. O'Brien built his tower here

The wooden door at the foot of the tower was ajar. We could hear female voices, excited and exclaiming in their English tones.

When I rapped on the door, the voices abruptly stopped.

A gentleman opened the door just wide enough to see our faces.

"Be off with you! We've nothing for you here." He slammed the door shut with his boot.

We heard him through the barred slit window.

"The beggars are everywhere. My apologies, ladies. Shall we go up to the observation deck?"

We were no beggars.

Kitty turned her back to the door and banged it hard with her heel, so as not to break her bare toes. The kicks made a continuing, satisfying, thunking boom.

I stood below the open window and called up in my best English.

"Please! We've come for help. A lad may be trapped on the ledge below."

From inside the tower, the sound of a man's voice drifted out.

"And what would they expect us to do? Climb down the cliffs on a rope? To haul up one of their Irish brats? Really. This is too much."

I could feel my face turning red with humiliation. Or maybe it was rage.

Another, softer voice replied.

"So sorry . . . apologize . . . rarely see the native people—except working in the fields or whatever . . . keep to themselves . . ."

Kitty banged on the door without cease. I shouted out my frustration.

"Look through the spyglass, that's all we're asking! See if a boy is down there!"

In a moment the door opened. A slight, little woman with beautifully coiled chestnut hair under her bonnet looked at us, her eyes filled with anxiety.

"Young woman, whatever is the matter? It's not begging that is causing all this distress."

I liked the gentle wave of her voice. I inclined my head respectfully but did not soften my tone.

"My friend and I saw a bit of blue cloth on a ledge about a hundred feet down the cliff over there. It may be a boy gone for eggs that can't get back. We need someone to help."

"Oh, gracious. I don't know that my guests are in any position . . ." She looked behind her as if she was afraid of the people she'd invited up to the tower.

"Perhaps you could use the glass to see and then decide," I suggested.

Kitty bent over to rub her heel, which was sore from kicking the door.

"I'd like to see through the spyglass," she said.

The lady blinked in surprise.

"I'm afraid that's not at all possible. Please wait here and I'll see what I can discover." She gave us a brief encouraging smile and disappeared inside.

We waited as patiently as we could. Voices echoed faintly at the top of the tower, but the words were indistinct. Shortly we heard a bubble of laughter, which might be cruel or might not be. It was hard to tell.

When the woman returned, I could see by her face that the news was bad.

"I am so sorry," she said. "Apparently it was an accident that happened some time ago. There's nothing we can do now."

She shook her head sadly. Even the feathers on her bonnet drooped.

Kitty crossed herself. "God rest his soul," she murmured.

"Thank you for your help, Missus. May God bless you for your generous heart." I meant the words as I said them to this sad, small English lady.

"Are you both local girls?" she asked. As if we could be anyone.

"Yes, Missus. My name is Margaret Meehan, and my friend is Kitty Dooley. We live in Kilvarna."

"Why, I live not far from there myself," she said. "I am Mrs. Edward Speke."

Kitty and I crossed ourselves and were away before she could close the tower door.

CHAPTER 3

TOM RIORDAN AND THE OTHERS told themselves that the Whiteboy raid on Major Harris's finest grazing pasture was to avenge the damage to young Conor Maloney's fiddling arm, but the raid was intended to express more than personal injury. Each week the evictions increased across the west of Ireland, where the land was good for cattle. Scores of acres were sown with new grass, as hundreds of families were put out of their homes onto the roads. Something had to be done to halt the process, which would scour Clare of her own people and replace them with white-faced cows.

Tom had first joined in Whiteboy actions when he was barely sixteen, and at twenty he was the leader of the group around Kilvarna. His contacts with other likeminded men ranged far and wide, and he was known for his close mouth and steady nerve. Men like Tom were the pride of Erin.

They gathered in the moonlight, the young protestors, armed with shovels and hefty picks. They gathered at the edge of the grazing meadow that used to be home to a score of families. All gone now, vanished into the slums of Ennis and Limerick. Their potato patches turned to pasture, their cottages tumbled down.

"We'll have to work fast, boys," Tom said. "Do as much damage as you can, spread yourselves wide to cover the ground. It's a bright night, and Speke's men may not be long in coming."

They had decided to do the deed on a moonlit night, despite the risks of discovery. They had a plan to scatter over the surrounding fields if they were found out—there were too many to be chased by one man, or two. They hadn't taken the trouble to disguise themselves in the white shirts or women's nightdresses that gave their comrades the Whiteboy name. It was dirty work tonight.

Nine young men set off across the meadow. Each stopped and began frantically to dig, turning over the clods of grass as fast as he could. Within a few minutes great swaths were cut across the grazing land, the acreage swiftly ruined for cattle raising, the earth scarred with a great anger. The men worked silently, methodically stripping the value from the landlord's unfortunate decision to plant grass where cabbages had grown.

By the time most of the new meadow was turned up, the men were soaked through with sweat. Their faces were black with the flying dirt.

"This is enough now, isn't it, Tommy?" asked Martin Griffin. "It will be weeks before there's a decent growth for grazing here again." He sounded weary and even a little sad.

Tom surveyed the damage.

"The message is clear. That's what we want. But there's one more thing to do."

On a knoll in the midst of the ruined pasture, Tom molded the raw earth into the form of a grave. He stood over it with his long-handled spade.

"Let them know that we mean to stop them."

"They can't shoot us like rabbits and starve us off the land," said Michael Dooley.

"When Mr. Speke takes his morning stroll," said Hugh Sweeney, "he'll be rubbing his eyes in disbelief."

"Next time we'll burn it," said Tom.

CHAPTER 4

THE CORPSE WAS STRETCHED OUT on a board set between two stools. Even by the weak lickings of the peat fire you could see the wasted yellowing of the flesh, a man like a bag of old dry leather.

"And him just twenty-three years old," said Michael's mother in a bitter voice.

"The fever doesn't care," said Kitty. She knelt on the dirt floor near the open hearth, at her brother's feet. Beside her, I could feel the anger and grief coming off her, almost like a vapor from her skin.

"Recall that Our Savior died at thirty-three," offered Father Martin. As if that mattered to Michael, lying there dead in his own house after a week of the bloody bowel pain.

"Not every man is granted the comforts of a long life," the priest continued.

"And some are not granted a comfort or a life at all." Tom's voice dark with anger sliced through the priest's words.

I turned from Kitty to find his face in the crowd. How dare he use the wake of Michael Dooley for a political harangue. After he just spent the past few days at Michael's side, begging him to live?

"The babies are dying of hunger, the old of weakness. A strong man like Michael Dooley is sent to the devil before his time, and you call that a lack of comfort?"

"O surely not to the devil," cried out old Mrs. Griffin, crossing herself. "Never say such a thing, Tom."

"Working on the road with nothing to eat but the stones around him killed Michael," said Kitty. She pulled her black shawl closer over her face, harder now than it was.

I put my arm around her and glared at Tom. I watched him force himself to swallow the harsh words that ached to pour out of his throat. The death of Michael Dooley was a terrible blow. One of Tom's own invincible band had fallen, murdered by the oppressor as surely as if he'd been shot.

"Who's going to take Michael's place on the relief works?" a voice asked in the unexpected silence.

"I will," said Kitty. "Mam can't lift the hammer. And now it's just the two mouths to feed. I'll go out in the morning to see Mr. Speke."

"Bad business when young girls have to break their backs hauling stones like a man," said an uncle of Michael Dooley. His jacket hung on his frame with room to spare, a man who was broad until a year ago.

"If we can just keep on 'til the harvest, we'll be right again," said John Sweeney. "Only two more months until the first digging. Not a speck of the rot on the leaves this year."

Father Martin grabbed his chance.

"Then let us kneel and thank God in His Highest Glory for our blessings, while we pray for the soul of poor Michael. May others be spared the torment of fever that took him."

He pulled a rosary of thick beads from his belt, and the people in the small house knelt, facing the body. The chanting began, familiar words in a foreign tongue sent up to heaven, begging for mercy on the souls of a dead man and his friends.

At the end of the *Ave Marias*, when the mourners rose to their feet again, I left my post next to Kitty and joined the keener Nuala Lynch near the body. It was time to begin the keen for Michael

Dooley. Another woman, a Dooley aunt, came forward as well. We began to sway, just a barely perceptible movement of our hips and shoulders. Tears began their silent courses down our faces shrouded by dark shawls. Like black crows spreading our wings, we gathered close around the corpse.

"Ah Michael, acushla, how could you leave me alone?" cried out Bridie Dooley, beginning the grief.

Hastily the priest blessed the house and pushed the few steps to the door. I knew he wanted no part of what came next.

The light from the small fire was uneven but enough for me to see the small jug of poteen passing from hand to hand among the men. Precious fluid, the last drop in the house. Gone were the waking feasts of other years.

In smoke and in sorrow, the keening began.

The sound started low, in our hungry bellies. In the earth beneath our feet. Drawing the deep raw energy from the depths and then soaring on a scream to the black sky. Wailing, keening, rending the air with our grief.

Changing the very essence around us, we opened a space with our voices, where men could die and rise again, where babies starved for mothers' milk could suck sweet teats never empty, where women howled and screamed and tore the clothes and nearly the hearts from their breasts. And we rested and began again.

Weaving in and out, up and down, in a ribbon of overwhelming sound, the mourning for Michael Dooley pitched ever higher. Responding to our cry, men and women in the room backed away from the plank on which the corpse rested. A space between the boundaries of life and death came into being.

In the smoky firelight, the men clumped together nearest the door. As many times as they had heard the keening wail, it still raised the hackles on the backs of their necks. Just wait until Nuala Lynch got started, with the voice on her that could turn a butterfly to ash.

As I watched the men pass the poteen from hand to hand, I knew they had moved into the firmament of the living, beyond the border of shadow and death. Only we four keening women remained in that nebulous land, held there by the power of our voices and the need to express a grief for all. As I joined my voice in an ear-splitting howl of loss and pain, I felt the rage surge underneath. Michael should not be dead of fever carried from the workhouses by skeletons wandering the roads of Clare. He should be working in the green fields, sowing the wheat and living long enough to bring in the harvest. Instead the crops were being shipped off to feed the English, and Michael was cold dead.

My voice changed as my anger grew. I became a banshee and flew to the shores of England to open my shrieking mouth wide over the fields of men and oxen, over the villages where babies toddled and mothers stood in the sun.

"You are stealing our food," I cried to them. "Your whiskey is made of our life's blood."

The men and the oxen did not hear me.

"We crawl past wagons of grain marked for your bellies, with no strength of our own left to stand. Hunger is everywhere."

I flew with my great black shadow to the manor house of the landlord and breathed my horrible death stench into his open windows.

"Your greed is killing Ireland," I howled. "On your land we're dying every hour."

I spread my rusty black rags wide over the landlord's roof and put the fear of his own death into him.

Whether he heard me or not, I did not know. I returned to my own place and my own voice, quieting now into unity with the others.

I was not small, young Margaret when I soared into the shadow space. I was something bigger, more powerful. The cords in my throat strained to sing the fury, the injustice, the grief. Nuala

Lynch was teaching me the old ways, the poetry of the best keens
that had ever been sung. And the way to sing the truth in words
that some can hear—and some will not.

It was Nuala's turn now, as the main keener at the wake. As
she drew herself up to begin, we calmed our wild chanting. Even
Michael's mother wanted to hear every word of the lament, the
song that Nuala had composed in his honor.

"O Michael, my darling, why did you leave us?" Nuala
echoed the mother's wail, sending shivers down my arms.

> The skeletons on the road are your companions now.
> Surely you don't find their bony friendship
> a greater comfort than your own warm hearth?
> You could be sitting with your pipe alight,
> a small jug by your side.
> You could be dancing with your great strong legs
> a step that never was equaled in Clare,
> and clasping to your own broad breast
> a woman who could make you laugh.

Nuala's voice sobbed for the future that never would be.

> Michael, you lived with your mother and sister
> And that you did with honor and grace:
> the kindness of your heart was noticed by all.
> But what of the lover you might have been?
> What of the sons who would have been your pride?
> They lie dead unborn. The famine fever
> stole your beautiful manhood from you.
> Michael, come back from that dark place!
> Swim through the Cauldron like Cú Chulainn's warriors
> Who, dead, arose to fight another day . . .

Bridie Dooley gasped a great sobbing sound as Nuala's wail intensified, demanding that the man who had been robbed of his life return. Uneasily the mourners around the room glanced toward the rough plank bier. I could see the uncertainty in their faces. Surely the old woman did not have the power to raise the dead, though her moans might curdle your blood.

Nuala howled her anger at the wasted life. We joined our voices until the pitch began to change and Nuala continued on alone, bargaining.

> We'll make a marriage bed of softest straw,
> and you shall have a bride with full white breasts,
> not any of the starving girls whose dugs are flat and empty.
> Her belly will swell with babes instead of hunger.
> Will she not tempt you to rise, mavourneen?
> Ah no, the promise is too little and too late—
> A handful of raw cornmeal that sours and scours your innards.

But bargaining did not change the finality of death. Even a keener had to admit that at the end.

> Go, Michael, to the place where your spirit can rest.
> Leave this poor shell here to rot
> like the foul black mess of the pratie fields
> and go to where hunger is a stranger.
> You'll find your brothers and sisters there,
> soon yet your friends and neighbors.
> Have a look about for priests and Englishmen,
> who may be absent indeed.

In other years, at other wakes, we would have picked up a chorus and added a line or two to Nuala's lament. She could have continued for the whole night, slaking her thirst with whiskey when she was dry, slinging a clever word arrow at a mourner who deserved it. Thirty years of keening had sharpened Nuala's ability to move the people in the crowd from sorrow to anger to joy at their own continued living. But these days people were hungry and not far enough away from death to dance with him. The old ways were diminishing before our eyes.

I could see that she was tired. She bent toward me and asked me to continue the wail, softer now, a sad farewell. Nuala made her way to the stone seat near the hearth. After a bit, the notes of a pipe began to twirl around my voice, and Pat Maloney's fiddle set in. The people of Kilvarna quieted hunger with music for a few hours.

I sat vigil with the body for the night so Kitty and her mother could get some rest. The cottage was quiet after the neighbors left. Only embers remained of the turf fire. Sitting on a stool with my back against the stone wall, I could barely see the two slight figures, mother and daughter, huddled in a toss of straw in the corner. They were sleeping deeply. In the morning Michael Dooley would be buried, and then Kitty would walk three miles out to the road-building project to take his place. I wished her a dreamless night's rest. I was tired and hungry, but the six hours of darkness would pass quickly. It was my gift to my friend. I yawned and shivered and tried to recreate the heated energy of the keening inside me. When that failed to warm me, I turned my thoughts instead to Tom Riordan. Maybe that was a sin, while sitting up with the body of his best friend, but I was only sixteen and in love.

The funeral was brief, a few Latin murmurs over the scrap wood box containing the earthly remains of Michael Dooley. He was luckier than many who died in the workhouses or fever hospitals. Their bodies were tossed into common graves, the earth shoveled into their open mouths by strangers.

Tom dropped back beside me as we walked from the cemetery. His eyes were dark with sorrow, and my heart ached.

I longed to smooth the sadness from his face.

"When we were boys, Michael and I used to go out in the boat together. He taught me to net the herring without tumbling over the side myself."

"It was hard for Michael to give up fishing. He loved the sea."

"You can't fish when your tackle is sold to buy potatoes."

Ahead of us, Kitty protectively tucked her mother's arm beneath her own. Six Dooley children and a husband gone, and none left now but the two of them.

"I wonder if Kitty will get the job on the relief works. Speke gives places first to men who owe him money," I said.

"That's English charity for you," Tom said. "They'd just as soon see the lot of us dead."

"We'll get back on our feet after the harvest, Tom. Didn't you hear Mr. Sweeney last night? He says he's never seen such healthy plants."

Tom brushed his fingertips across the thin planes of my face, where last year I'd had rosy curves.

"For someone who keens for death as you do, you are a marvel at ignoring the truth of its coming."

"I can't see borrowing trouble, as you want to." Sometimes he pushed me to the edge of my patience. Why did everything bad always land at the doorstep of the English?

"There's been another food riot in Ennis," he said. "Now there're armed guards taking the grain to the harbor. It won't be long before Speke throws us all out into the road. And takes his pleasure in it."

"No man with a conscience would take the job of landlord's agent." I thought back to the kindness of Mrs. Speke and wondered again at their pairing.

"There's some say he'll get what's coming to him. One way or the other."

"Tom, have a care what you say!" I had a sudden horrifying flash of Tom's fair hair tangled in a hangman's noose.

"I'm not going to stand by and watch my friends and family starve to death, Margaret, not without a fight."

"Just keep yourself safe. Leave Edward Speke to go to hell in his own good time."

We had reached the lane of the clachan, where the cottages huddled together, a dung heap outside each one. I stopped at my father's house.

"I'm going to walk out later and meet Kitty."

"Right. Maybe I'll see you both, then."

For a moment Tom's hazel eyes held me in a shared memory of happier times. Before the hunger came to Kilvarna.

I watched as Tom continued down the lane toward the Riordans' place. There was a violence in him that never was there before. The hunger affected people in different ways.

My mother, for instance, had gone limp. Wilted like a dying plant at the end of that terrible harvest last year. Most days she sat by the cold hearth, her hands folded in her lap, waiting for something to happen. Or not. The black mess of the potatoes in the field had somehow found its way into her soul and rotted it too.

The cottage was dark after the bright June sun.

"Michael's funeral was over in no time at all, Mammy. You could have come. Mrs. Dooley would have been comforted to see you."

"All the way to the churchyard? I'd be dead myself before I walked halfway there."

"The air would do you good." She had wasted away to nothing. She closed her eyes. I tried to stir her.

"I sat up with the body last night, to give Kitty a rest. Nuala Lynch did a beautiful job with the keen—I wished she could have gone on forever." I couldn't tell whether Mammy was listening. I continued anyway, as if she were really there.

"Did Jimmy and Da have anything to eat before they left this morning?"

They worked on a relief job to the north, building a bridge of stone in a field that went to nowhere.

"Two oat cakes held over from yesterday. There's another, for you. It's little enough."

"I'll share it with Kitty. She's gone out to take Michael's place on the relief works. I don't think they have any money for food at all."

Mammy's eyes were still closed. "Last Friday I sent Jimmy over with three boiled potatoes. It was all I could do."

"I'm sure it did them good," I said, patting my mother's hand. "You always were generous."

I remember the occasional beggar—an old man or a woman with a child on her back—coming to the door of the cottage with a bag, when I was a child. They never carried it away empty. Now beggars walked the roads by the score.

I ate half the oatcake, a few dry crumbs of comfort. I could have gobbled the other half in a minute but I wrapped the piece carefully and put it away. When the new potatoes were harvested, life would go back to normal. I was encouraged by the thought of Mammy sending food to Mrs. Dooley.

The sun was still bright as I walked through the fields to meet Kitty, though the air held the coolness of evening on the way. As I hopped over the stone wall onto the road, I saw Paddy Foley and his cousin Sean trudging toward me. Though still in their twenties, they each had half a dozen children to feed. The relief wage must barely keep them.

"Did you see Kitty Dooley on her way behind you?" I called out.

Paddy looked at Sean and away again, reluctant to answer.

"She's just leaving now, I expect," Sean said. "She was delayed."

"Delayed?" I narrowed my eyes at them. Paddy broke first.

"There was a terrible row," he said. "Awful to witness."

Sean nodded. "Kitty Dooley has claws like a wild beast."

"Kitty! What happened? Is she hurt?" I was ready to run.

"She got into a fight with that fellow Speke, about the money owed her brother Michael. First Speke told her she couldn't take Michael's place on the works because he was off the list, being dead. Then he let her work the half day if she could swing the hammer, which she did—"

"Like a man," said Paddy.

"But at the end of the day, Speke told the paymaster to give her a penny for the half day's work and tell her not to return. 'What about Michael Dooley's money?' she says. 'We don't pay dead men,' says Speke. 'He wasn't dead when he worked for it,' yells Kitty. Speke turns away and tells the girl to go home—"

"I wouldn't have turned my back on her, indeed," said Paddy.

"And she's got a murderous rage in her heart. She throws the hammer at him like it was a goose feather, and lucky for Speke it missed. She goes at him with her fingers flying and he turns around and wallops her across the mouth. I won't repeat what he said, out of decency—he's a bastard through and through."

"But is she all right?" I gave them a taste of my keener's wail.

Paddy put his hands up in front of him and backed away from me. Coward.

Sean answered. "Three fellows grabbed Speke and threw him down, and Kitty got her wits back in time. The civil engineer hauled Speke up and dusted him off so he was good as new."

"Kitty was sitting on the wall crying her eyes out when we left," said Paddy. "I don't think Speke will be adding her name to the relief list anytime soon."

I wanted to spit nails. The English made rules and broke them when they felt like it, as if they owned the world. Not a word of sympathy for the loss of Kitty's brother, which drove her to the madness—just a half day's work breaking stone for which she would never be paid. And the Foleys enjoying the sight like spectators at a cockfight. I left them at a run, without a word of good-bye.

When I reached Kitty on the road, I put my arms around her and stroked her hair. "My poor darling—you're not hurt, are you?"

Kitty smiled through swollen lips. "I've gone and killed my mother now, I truly have—I have no money and no way to get any. We'll have to leave Kilvarna . . ."

". . . *and go to the workhouse*" were the words Kitty couldn't say. I heard them too clearly in my head.

A touch of mad anger ignited Kitty again. She swung her arms wide, whirling away from me, her shawl flying. "Do you know what that filthy old Speke had the nerve to do? He rode up to me after and whispered that he could put something better than his fist in my mouth. As if I would ever be that desperate—no piece of shite like him could pay me enough! Even if I was a whore, like he said."

"Disgusting," I said. "You should have picked up the hammer again and gone straight for his—"

"He was up too high on the saddle for me to reach them," said Kitty. "I would have had to kill the horse."

A choking, sobbing laugh escaped, enough to put a distance between Kitty and the rage.

"Let's go home," I said. "And we'll try to come up with a plan to get money. I couldn't bear living in Kilvarna without you."

I handed her the oatcake, but she was too exhausted and grieved to eat more than a bite. She put it away for her mother. I felt like a pig for having eaten the other half myself.

The only practical plan we came up with was for Kitty to find a husband straight away. A man to earn the relief money and take over the lease of the patch.

"I don't know if I can, Margaret. I don't have a dowry or even a pig. Who would want to take on the care of my mother, too?"

"Someone who wants to get away from his own mother," I said. "Into a place of his own with a girl to keep his bed warm at night. Maybe you don't fancy old Mr. Speke—but there are lads here that wouldn't be so bad. They follow you around at the dances."

"And you always want to dance with Tommy Riordan. If I have to get married, why don't you do it too?"

"It's not the right time for me yet. I can feel it in my bones. I want to spend more time with Nuala Lynch, learning the keen. How could I do that with a baby hanging from my breast?"

"Babies come with marriage, there's no way round it," said Kitty. "I guess I could be someone's mammy, if I had to. I guess I'm ready."

"So who shall we go for?"

Kitty giggled. "This would be funny if I wasn't so desperate."

"A man is the only answer." I thought for a moment, mentally sorting through the available targets and eliminating them one by one. Too old. Too smelly. Front teeth black stumps. "What about the Shaughnessy with the thin legs? He comes down from the Burren to Mass on Sunday, and surely he'd want to swap his rocky field for your half-acre."

"He wouldn't be too bad, I suppose. His legs aren't crooked, just skinny." We contemplated her future.

"You could bump up against him at Mass this week, on the way out the door," I said. "No, better to bump him on the way in, so he has time to think about it during the Blessed Sacrifice."

"Bump him?" Her voice rose. I guess Kitty's nerves couldn't take in the idea of bumping a man so soon after she had just tried to kill one with a hammer.

"Just moan and almost faint a bit on the way in, when you're next to him. He's the one with the curly hair, isn't he?"

"Jackie. His name is Jackie. He was two years ahead of us at the school."

"Jackie it is, then. And before you can count to six, you'll be Mrs. Jackie Shaughnessy, thank you, and planting cabbages in Kilvarna." I hoped I sounded more confident than I felt. Marriage was forever, until death and maybe beyond.

"It seems so hard, so calculating, to be looking for a man when poor Michael is only just buried," said Kitty, wavering.

"If poor Michael hadn't died, you wouldn't have to do this so quick. But do you think he would have fed you for the rest of your life, if you had a chance of marrying?"

"I'll bump Jackie Shaughnessy on Sunday, then. If I lose my courage, give me a shove."

"You know it's the only thing, Kitty. You know it, truly."

"I do, Margaret."

Around the last bend in the lane coming into Kilvarna, I saw Tom Riordan waiting. From the black look on his face, I guessed he had met the Foley cousins.

Tom jumped off the wall.

"I'll kill the son of a bitch."

"You will not," I said. "Kitty's not going back to the relief works. And if you don't leave off your threats of murder and mayhem, Tommy, you'll get yourself in real trouble."

He looked hard into my eyes, and I think he saw the fear underlying my harsh words.

"Are you hurt, Kitty?" His tone was gentle.

"Nothing more than a belt in the mouth," she said. "I've had worse from my da."

"Violence never makes a woman happy," I said. I didn't like the preachy way I sounded but I couldn't help myself.

"Sometimes violence is the only way, Margaret," Tom said. "Sometimes there's the need for war and such." His face was in shadow and I couldn't see his expression. "The British hate us. And after hundreds of years, now they see a way to get shut of us. My friends have told me things that never were taught in school."

"These friends of yours will lose their leases if they keep up that kind of talk," I said.

"We're not going to wait until half of Clare is dead, Margaret. There's food on its way to the harbors. Food that Irishmen grew and Irishmen need. It's criminal to keep it from us in these times."

I knew I couldn't continue an argument standing on the wrong side. I surrendered. "I'm just desperate with worry about you, Tommy."

"I'll be all right," he said.

I held out my hand to Kitty, who was sitting on a wall out of the line of fire, and we walked the rest of the way home. I was troubled by the thought of Tom's new friends, men from outside Kilvarna. Men in touch with Limerick and with Dublin. Tommy had always wanted to be a hero.

My father told us that a wagon owned by a farmer outside Ennistymon was attacked on its way home from the market fair, in broad daylight. A group of lads disguised in women's clothing, with one pistol among them, stopped the farmer in the middle of the road and demanded the food in the wagon. The farmer protested, but Da said that the cold feel of the pistol barrel against his forehead persuaded him that two barrels of flour, some turnips, and four small pigs were not worth the investment. The Whiteboys didn't steal his money, but they let him know that selling his crops for export would bring him no joy in this hungry year. The food and the squealing pigs were carried away over the hedges, and the fellow holding the pistol leaped from the wagon, gave the horse a good thwack on his rump, and ran away.

Kitty said that her mother found a few pounds of oat flour and six turnips at the back of the house one morning. *Who got the pigs?* I wondered.

CHAPTER 5

ON A THURSDAY IN LATE July I walked with Nuala Lynch through a field of stinging nettles. The hem of my red flannel skirt was too short to shield my bare legs from the stinging hairs of the plant, and I'd been stung once already, which was enough. The welt was red and painful.

Nuala wanted to pick the top leaves of the nettles while they were tender. Boiled, they made a nourishing soup, and the liquid was good for the swelling in her legs. In the past month or so I'd seen the years come down upon her, bringing spells of breathlessness. I found the time to bring fresh water and clods of turf for her little fire every day. Her sons were gone and she had no daughters. Not everyone wanted to be a companion to the singer of death, I discovered.

It was a hot, humid day like so many others in this unusual summer. The rain threatened to pour down at any moment. We had climbed up a hill outside Kilvarna, to a meadow that was part of Major Harris's grazing lands. From the hill I could see across the broad farmlands, striped with greens and golds and the blue-brown of the river. I could see the clachan and beyond it the outlying cabins of mud and stone spread out across the fields like sheep in a pasture. It was hard to believe that families were starving in a land as rich as Ireland. Yet I knew from my own empty belly that it was true.

"Mrs. Lynch!" I called across the field. "Have you all you need?" I saw the old woman's black figure picking its way down the bank to the Lisdoonvarna road.

Nuala Lynch did not turn. She sat her backside on the stone wall at the edge of the field and swung over it to the road, disappearing from sight.

Keeping my feet clear of the stinging nettles, I followed. When I reached the wall I saw why Nuala had gone.

A family huddled on the road. Four children sat in the dirt, each one scrawnier than the next. Among them they didn't own a full set of clothes, and the smallest was naked altogether. The mother had another baby tied on her back in a shawl. The father, pale under his thin beard, sat with a sixth child on his knees, cradled against his chest. The little girl's eyes were sunken shut in her gray face, and her body dangled in the loose-jointed way of the several-days' dead. The stiffness had already passed.

Nuala Lynch approached them first. "God bless all here," she said. "I see you have troubles on you."

The father raised his head. "We've been on the road these past three days, without a morsel of food. By the grace of God, would you have anything for the children?"

We looked at their sad faces. "I have nothing but uncooked nettles, and you're welcome to them. Better still, if you come along to the house I'll cook them for you with a bit of meal. Only just down the hill." I saw her momentary hesitation. She too was wondering how to approach the matter of the dead child.

I knelt on the road in front of the man. "Oh, poor babe." I murmured as I touched the girl's waxy dead cheek with the back of my hand. The mother's eyes were dark and stared into another world.

"That would be a mercy," said the man. "We're making our way to the workhouse."

I saw the woman flinch.

Glancing toward his wife, the man continued, "There's no

other choice now—the roof was pulled down around us and we've nowhere to go. A year behind on the rent and Speke evicted us." The man lowered his gaze to his dead daughter but not before I saw the powerless, stopped-up anger. "This little one was sick already when we struck out for Ennistymon. You can get a coffin there, they say."

Ennistymon was another day's walk for this weak band. The child wouldn't last that long unburied. I could already smell the scent of decay, sweet and unmistakable. I tried to keep my face from showing the distress in my heart.

"Perhaps it would be best to let your daughter rest in the churchyard in Kilvarna," Nuala Lynch suggested, her voice as calm as my face.

The mother shook her head stiffly at her husband. "We're staying together, Dennis Quinn, you promised."

The man looked very ill himself. His coat flapped on him like a scarecrow's garment. Likely in the workhouse his wife would become his widow.

"We'll thank you for your kind offer of a meal," he said. He ignored his wife's words and with difficulty rose to his feet, shifting the burden of the corpse in his arms.

"Come along now," he said. The woman followed him like a wraith, and the children rushed to cling to her skirt.

Nuala Lynch led the procession down the hill. I lifted the smallest straggler to ride on my hip, as I used to carry my youngest sister before she died. It was a long trudge to Nuala's cottage. By the time we reached it, the sky had opened again with drenching rain.

Inside the cottage was bare except for the pot on the open hearth, a four-legged stool, and a rough bed of straw. What luxuries Nuala had accumulated over the years—her clay tobacco pipe, a dresser and table, and a woolen blanket to keep off the chill—had been sold last winter. She had nothing to offer these strangers but the dirt floor and the sharing of a nettle soup.

Dennis Quinn hung back at the door with his terrible burden.

"Come in, come in," said Nuala Lynch. "Rest the poor child on the straw. Death has been here often enough to know his way around."

At the man's alarmed look, I spoke up. "You're in the house of Nuala Lynch. The keener Nuala Lynch."

Both Dennis and his wife crossed themselves automatically. "We're honored, Mrs. Lynch. Your name is known well in our parish," he said, and he ducked his head to come in through the small door. He placed his daughter on the bed of straw and smoothed her ragged shift to cover her legs.

I went to fetch water for the nettles. In an hour we could give these poor people something to eat and then, perhaps, help them let go of the dead.

Mary Quinn's infant awoke and began to wail thinly. The woman put her knuckle into the baby's mouth for suck.

The children looked around the cottage. "Are we going to stay here, Mam?" asked the biggest boy.

"For a night only, love," she said. "Now sit quietly and wait for your soup."

He followed me and took up a post at the door of the cottage. When I came up the path with the water bucket, he ran to lift it for me. The sooner the soup, the better.

When a handful of meal had been added to the nettle broth, I left the stirring to Nuala Lynch and walked home. It was a great relief to get out into the air, away from the crowded room that reeked of death and sorrow. My heart rose with every step down the road. I was glad to be young, a girl with a life ahead of her. Perhaps the Quinns' suffering was the last of it before the August digging of new potatoes.

Tom Riordan sat talking with my father inside the house. Compared to the pallor and sadness of the beaten-down Quinns, Tom looked very much alive. My heart thumped, and I ran my hands through the dark mass of curls clinging to my neck and fluffed them before he noticed me.

"Destroying the very houses they live in. Knocking the walls down before their eyes, and the wives and children looking on—" When he saw me Tom broke off.

So it wasn't any good news that made his color high and his eyes bright. "You're talking about the evictions."

My father nodded. "Tom says that Major Harris ordered a great parcel of his land cleared away to the north, and Speke sent the constabulary to pull down the houses of those that hadn't paid the rents."

"The fellow I spoke to said there's families living on the road itself, turned from workers to beggars in the space of an hour," said Tom.

"I know," I said.

"If it could happen there, it could happen here." Da's voice was shaky. We had pawned everything we had for the rent last autumn.

Tom stared at me. "I only just heard this news today. How is it that you've beat me out?"

I would have laughed at his surprise if my heart weren't aching.

"Nuala Lynch and I met one of the families on the Lisdoonvarna road today. One of their children has died and they're hoping for a coffin at the workhouse." I couldn't compress the Quinns' suffering any further.

"Not much chance of that," said Tom. "Government work-houses, British rules. The already dead are not admitted."

"Is the family out in the rain, then?" asked my mother softly. I hadn't realized she was paying attention. So often she was off in another silent world.

"No, Mam, Mrs. Lynch brought them to her house for the night. Quinn, their name is. Four children and a baby besides." I didn't want to upset her so I kept my voice steady.

"Mrs. Lynch is going to try to get the child buried here at

Kilvarna." I saw the small sunken face before me, a child for whom no keen was sung. "But the mother doesn't want to be parted from her."

"A decent burial in holy ground might help." My father looked around the empty cottage. "Tom, have you a scrap of wood to make a box?"

"She's such a little thing, it wouldn't take much," I said. I realized I didn't know the child's name.

Tom hesitated. I knew he would much prefer to fire a volley over the head of a landlord's agent than to build a coffin for a dead child.

"If you don't have a piece of wood—"

"I can do it," he said. "I'll bring it tomorrow early."

"Good man, Tom," said my father.

I rested my hand on Tom's shoulder. "Will you come back with me over there?" If I knew Tom, he'd jump at the chance to get the cruel details of the evictions firsthand. But I'd send him home in time to make the coffin.

An unwholesome fog lay in wisps over the fields the next morning, rising in thickness on the higher hills. The rain had stopped during the night, but our clothes were still damp from yesterday's soaking. We shivered, standing in the mud of the churchyard. Tom had delivered the coffin as promised. Nuala Lynch had spoken earnestly with the mother and at last called upon Father Martin to lend a hand. The priest's authority had broken through the poor woman's resistance.

The coffin of Alice Quinn was lowered into the hastily dug hole, Father Martin murmuring prayers for the repose of her young soul and merciful forgiveness for her sins. I'm sure I couldn't imagine what sins they might be. After the last shovel of earth was flung, Dennis Quinn thanked us and started off with his family down the road to Ennistymon.

Tom and I walked away from the churchyard in the other direction. We held hands tightly, protecting the hope of our future between us. I wished for Kilvarna to return to the life we had expected, to the dream of a cottage of our own, a warm fire, milk and potatoes and butter and love.

As we made our way past the potato fields, we did not look closely at the green leaves. If we had, we would have seen the first patches of black rot on the underside of the leaves and stalks. The blight had returned for the new harvest.

CHAPTER 6

THE MORNING AFTER THE QUINN child's burial was misty and quiet, the sun still pale over the fields. When I opened the door to take the night pot out to the dung heap, I was surprised by the sight of Longnose Callahan running down the lane like a wildman. He waved his arms above his head, the long tails of his old coat streaming.

"We're all going to die! We're going to die!" he shouted. Callahan's cry contained an urgency that brought us all out into the lane. Longnose had earned his nickname not for the length of his nose but for his habit of sticking it into other people's business. What news did he have?

Callahan was a big man, despite this past year's meager dinners. His reddish hair bristled in sideburns and eyebrows, and his feet were the size of fresh hams. Not the man you would expect to see staggering through the middle of the clachan, unless he were the worse for drink.

"For God's sake, what's the matter, Callahan?" demanded old Rose Mackey from the door of her house. Her scrawny little body seemed hardly enough to support the weight of her skull. She ran after Callahan and pulled at his coat to stop him, David to his Goliath.

If he didn't stop, I thought, Rose might hurl a stone to bring him down. But Callahan turned, and I could see the tears coursing down his face.

"There's no hope for us now," he said. "We'll all starve." He seemed not to notice he was crying.

"Come to your senses, man," said Rose sharply. "What's got into you?"

"It's the blight," he said. "The blight. I was up in Griffin's patch to see how his crop was coming, and I saw it. The spots on the leaves, same as last year. I ran to my own patch and it's turning black on the stalks. The blight's returned." He put his massive hands over his face.

By this time a knot of men had gathered near Callahan. "Maybe it's only up north," said Jack McGrath, who rented the acre furthest south.

"Shut your damn mouth, Callahan. Those seed potatoes we put in were good," said Michael O'Hare, whose patch was on the other side of Griffin's. He looked as if he ached to apply his fist to Callahan's jawbone.

"We're dead," Callahan moaned. He folded his great thick legs under him and collapsed.

"Get up and quit your sniveling," said Rose. "There's none of us here would let you starve if we had potatoes ourselves, and you know it."

"You're doomed too, Rose Mackey. None in Kilvarna can save themselves now."

I saw in his face the black look of hopelessness.

My father spoke up. "Best go out and check the fields. At least we'll know." He turned to walk out behind our cottage, to his green field of potato plants. Other men followed their own paths to the fields, leaving Longnose Callahan to his misery.

I ran to catch up with Da as he jumped over the stone wall surrounding the patch.

"Do you think it's true, Da?"

"Longnose Callahan is a meddlesome old fart of a man but he isn't a liar. And he would recognize the black rot if anyone would." The Callahan family had already lost two children to the hunger.

My father bent to examine the lush foliage of the potato plant, turning its leaves over tenderly to look for the white hairy fuzz on the underside that was an early sign of the blight. I peered over his shoulder as he knelt in the dirt. No fuzz found on that plant or on any others he touched—nor the patchy brown spots that quickly turned the leaves to wilted black. I remembered too well what last year's blight looked like. Using his broad fingers as a spade, Da dug under a plant to check the growing tubers. They gleamed white in the soil, clumps of perfect lumper potatoes not yet large enough to pull.

Carefully he patted the soil around the base of the plant. "No rot here," he said. Three small words to express a world of emotion.

He rose from his knees. "Longnose planted a few spoiled potatoes, and that's all there is to it." He started back across the field whistling. My father never whistled when things were bad.

In the cottage my mother sat in the usual place, wrapped in her black shawl. Mam hadn't gone out to see the commotion. She barely moved from her seat during the long summer days, and the flesh was melting off her. When I boiled greens or Indian meal, Mam ate only a spoonful. "I'm old and don't need it," she would say. "Save it for your brother." I didn't know how old my mother was, but surely she wasn't above forty. Kitty's mother, who was the same age, could run rings around Mam any day.

"Did you hear Longnose Callahan in the lane, Mam?" I asked.

"I did. Has he lost another of his children?"

"No," I said. "He's found the blight on his field."

"God help us," said Mam.

"It's only up in the north patches. Da says not to worry."

My mother set her lips together and would say no more.

◎   ◎   ◎

Nuala Lynch told me that in the time of the high kings of Ireland the first of August was the celebration of the first harvest. In the Year of Our Lord 1846, it was the day of Kitty Dooley's marriage. She had no wedding dress, no dowry but the rent owed on a small cottage and a patch of potatoes. The bridegroom, Jackie Shaughnessy, seemed more than willing to leave the crowded stone-roofed hut where he lived with his five brothers and two sisters—thrilled, even, by Kitty's obvious interest in him. The two of us joked that Jackie had never before realized what a fine figure of a man he was.

My brother Jimmy and I stood up for them at the brief ceremony during Sunday Mass at the old stone chapel. Kitty looked beautiful, her hair shining copper under a shawl pinned with roses. Jackie held himself straight and proud as they knelt in front of the altar and whispered their nuptial vows. For once, Father Martin did not spend his sermon preaching on the responsibilities of marriage and family. I think myself that he was glad to see a wage earner enter the Dooley situation before Kitty and her mother starved to death.

After Mass we escorted the bridal couple down the lane to the Dooley cottage, a misty rain falling. No wedding feast awaited us at the house. The Sunday best clothes of the guests had been sold the winter before, and the garments of the bride and groom were as worn and threadbare as any. The crowd who would have celebrated a Dooley marriage in past years had diminished to a few friends, most of whom had recently attended the wake of Michael Dooley.

Tom Riordan and Hugh Sweeney disappeared behind the cottage as the rest of us went inside. Where had the two of them gone? Even though a wedding without food and drink was something sadly new, the least they could do was honor the family by staying for an hour or two. My romantic thoughts of Tom as my groom were rapidly turning to irritation.

A moment later they reappeared with a flat basket covered

with leaves. Tom winked at me as they entered the house.

"We've brought you a wedding present, Kitty," said Tom.

Kitty looked surprised. No one expected a thing, not in these times.

"Jackie will need the strength to carry out his duties," said Hugh, "and it's not the crushing of stone on the roads that I'm referring to." He grinned at skinny Jackie.

"So we helped ourselves to a few trout from the generous Major Harris's stream, and here they are, clean as a whistle," continued Tom. He presented the basket to Kitty. The silvery scales of four large trout glistened under the leaves flecked with red blood.

"Tom, you could be hung for poaching," said Rose Mackey. She shook her head. The landlord's streams and lakes were patrolled by guards more than willing to shoot Irish poachers.

"And are you going to report me?" he asked, giving the old woman his most winning smile.

"No, boyo, you'll most likely hang for something else," she replied.

Kitty smiled and Jackie clapped Hugh on the shoulder. "A mouthful of trout will make all the difference," he said with a serious nod.

Kitty blushed and ducked her head. I realized that until this very moment we had been more concerned with the matter of daily survival than with the details of Kitty's wedding night. Jackie wasn't too bad, though. He wore his humor in a quiet way, and the brown curls he had parted and slicked back for the wedding ceremony were springing to life every which way again.

The guests gathered to admire the fish. I leaned against Tom's shoulder, half proud of his daring and half angry at the chances he took. I wouldn't be the one to change him—that I already knew.

Mrs. Dooley sent the small boys out to gather what dry fuel they could find. The flavor of fresh trout would be such a welcome one. Two bites each would be more than any of us had had in a year—at least, those of us who didn't poach.

As Mrs. Dooley readied the fire, Pat Maloney broke out his fiddle and old John Sweeney his drum. The skin was stretched tight over the wooden rim, which had seen its first use as a seed sifter thirty years ago. Sweeney's thick fingers wielding the beater could bring forth a rhythm to make the dead dance. Soon the two were joined by the sweet piping of Simon Mackey, whose mother Rose had forbidden him to pawn his whistle, no matter how bad things got. And she was right. Sometimes in the night, she told me, Simon would play to ease the children into sleep, when the little ones were restless with the hunger.

The rain outside fell more steadily, a drop now and then sizzling on the fire. The aroma of the fish made two dozen mouths water, mine among them. Heaven must be where you could get all you wanted to eat, and more.

The surprise wedding dinner continued until every bone was sucked dry. Tom and Hugh were praised for their daring. Major Harris and his minion Speke were mightily damned. And the music played while the rain fell and the newlyweds cast quick glances at one another from the shelter of a circle of friends.

Midnight came at last. Bridie Dooley would be spending this night at our cottage. She put her arms around Kitty as we stood near the door ready to leave. Her voice was lowered but I could still hear every word.

"It was a grand wedding, acushla," she said, hugging her daughter close. "For the way it started out, with Michael dying, I think it's going well now. Jackie's a good boy and he'll take care of you."

"And you too, Mammy. He's thrilled to think he's the one man with two women to dote on him." Kitty's voice betrayed her nervousness. "You'll be fine at the Meehans tonight?"

"I will," said her mother. "And you'll be fine here. Just try to think the best of the man and make him happy. These things have a way of working out over time." She caressed Kitty's thin cheek with her hand. "I won't be popping in until later in the morning," she said. "There's no need to hurry. Get used to him a bit."

"Oh, Jackie's going to see the roadwork foreman first thing," Kitty replied. "He wants to get on the relief list right away. He's no slugabed." A small amount of wifely pride crept into her quick words to her mother and surprised me.

"That's why you married him," said Mrs. Dooley.

I held the door open for Kitty's mother, into the dark night.

In the light of morning, the potato fields surrounding Callahan's ruined half-acre were wilted and brown. By late afternoon the foliage was black. By the time the moon rose, all the potato fields in Kilvarna had been infected by the blight. Not one was spared. The first harvest rotted in the dirt.

Tom Riordan saw desolation around him wherever he looked. His father's rented acres were a graveyard of blackened plants, where yesterday green foliage had turned toward the sun. The Riordan family spread out across the fields, sacks in hand, digging the underdeveloped potatoes with their bare hands, hoping to lift them from the ground before the rot of the leaves and stems spread into the tubers. Everywhere in the fields of Kilvarna, the people were digging.

The small round lumps in Tom's bag were already spongy to the touch. Tom squeezed one between his thumb and forefinger and it broke easily, rottenly, into gray pulp. He flung the mess to the ground.

"It's no damn use," he called to his father across the patch. "What's lifted today won't be fit to eat tomorrow."

His father looked around the fields at his sons and daughters crouched in the scratched-up soil. "We have to try. It's all we can do."

"Maybe it's all you can do," replied Tom. "I have some other ideas."

For the family's sake he continued to dig until darkness fell. The fields were all but emptied and the heap barely filled the first root cellar. At a quarter of their harvesting size, the potatoes were a fragile lifeline to the next year.

His mother tried to put a bright face on it. She boiled a pot of the new potatoes and had them ready in a basket when the family came in.

"We'll have a little supper after a hard day's work," she said, hugging the two youngest boys, who nearly were asleep on their feet.

Those two wouldn't remember the new potatoes of other years, Tom thought. As big as a man's fist, satisfying to the stomach and the soul. And the harvest that continued for a month or more, digging as you needed and wanted.

Tom ate his share in silence, knowing as they all did after the first taste that the potatoes were off. It wasn't only the small size of them.

He sat in the darkness of the cottage crowded with sleepers and made his plans.

Our field was in no better shape than anyone else's. Jimmy and I did the best we could to lift the potatoes, and we lay down on the straw that night exhausted by the effort. Da had walked off into the hills in the darkness after the digging, without a word. He had taken to walking when Mam had taken to sitting speechless next to the hearth. Sometimes he returned in an hour, sometimes not.

In my sleep I dreamed I heard the wail of keening. I opened my eyes to the gray light in the cottage. A rainy day outside, and the wailing kept on. Howls of grief and hopelessness, human voices twisted into animal sounds. The dogs themselves joined in, not in understanding but in empathy.

Out in the lane the sound echoed from wall to wall. The people of Kilvarna were wailing in desperate grief, the sound carried down from the fields above the clachan, adding voice upon voice.

I saw Rose Mackey standing in the rain in front of her own door. The old woman's face was set and shut. Her hair hung loose down her back. She isn't right, I thought, and I ran toward her.

"What's happened, Mrs. Mackey?" I put my arm around the tiny old one, shielding her from the downpour. "You're getting soaked to the skin. Let's go in the house before—"

Rose Mackey stirred herself and looked up at me. "No. I'm trying to get up the courage to look in the potato bin. But I just can't bear to know. Those people up on the hills, they're keening for their own deaths, they are. The potatoes dug yesterday have all rotted to filth this morning. My son came down and told me."

I felt the fear of it seep into my bones. "The new potatoes? The new crop? Not all of them, surely?"

The old woman nodded. "Simon rose early this morning to check the bins at his place. There's a pool of rot, not the wee potatoes he put there yesterday."

"But what of the others? Maybe it's only—"

"Listen, Margaret the keener," said Rose. "Do you hear them keening all around you? Starvation walked into Kilvarna in the middle of the night. The Callahan man was right."

A shudder ran through me. "Go in from the rain, Mrs. Mackey, please. I'll check the bin for you. Go in."

From the O'Gorman cottage next in the lane we could hear wild sobbing. What use was the hope of a miracle, of potatoes firm and sound?

While Rose Mackey looked on, dripping, I stooped to move aside the hatch of the stone bin. The smell told the tale. Where yesterday Simon Mackey had filled his mother's bin with hastily dug potatoes, today he would find a sodden mess. The blight had affected the plants so that the rot penetrated to the core of the tubers, reducing their firmness to watery slime in the space of a day and a night, whether above ground or below.

A wave of bile burned in my throat. I swallowed and turned my face away from the open bin. The odor of rotting potatoes was not unfamiliar, but this had a fetid undertone that bespoke sickness and death.

Rose Mackey lowered herself to her old knees in front of the bin. In the teeming rain she reached into the viscous heap, pawing through the corruption in search of a whole potato. One by one, she found her treasures—tiny misshapen lumps, grayish, patched with black. She laid them carefully in a row beside her. Tears streamed down her cheeks, mixing with the rain.

Unable to watch, unable to fix it, I fled to my own house, around to the back garden where the large root cellar held our hasty harvest. Jimmy stood at the pit, the digging fork in his hand. He thrust it down again and again into the cellar opening, bringing up a dripping load of blackened fibrous slime.

"There's not a one left." His voice cracked as it had when he was thirteen. He was a tall lad now, with hair as dark as mine and long arms sticking out of his sleeves. He threw the fork aside.

"Da's up in the field to lift what we might have missed yesterday. Not fucking likely he'll find anything." Jimmy spat as close to the opening of the cellar as he dared. "And that howling. Can't they shut their goddamn gobs? I'd like to stuff a rag down their fucking throats." He looked at me, waiting for the older sister's reprimand.

I hadn't the heart. Let Jimmy curse like the devil himself if it gave him ease. I rubbed my palm on the tight place between his shoulder blades. "Something will turn up," I said. "We'll manage. We always have."

Jimmy shook my hand off. "I'm not giving up. The Meehans don't give up." He turned away and headed up toward the field.

I closed the lid over the root cellar. The rot cellar. I wanted to run to the Dooley house, but I stopped myself. Kitty was married now, and that changed everything.

◎ ◎ ◎

The blight spread more quickly and more thoroughly in its second coming. Some said it was due to the hot, wet summer. Some said it was punishment from God. But whether the punishment was meted out for being Irish or for being sinful was a matter of debate. In the end it didn't matter. The potatoes were rotten masses of pulp before the first digging.

Twice as many men as before lined up for the public roadwork, and the relief committee, headed by Edward Speke, held an emergency meeting. Too little money was available, too many impoverished laborers asked for employment. It was finally decided—in a vote not at all unanimous—to rigorously enforce the British rules for qualification of each worker as deserving of relief. That would shave a considerable number of loafers and liars from the rolls, indeed, stated Mr. Speke.

◎ ◎ ◎

The Whiteboys in Kilvarna did not organize themselves as a structured unit or even call themselves by the name, no longer hiding their identities in women's clothing. The group led by Tom Riordan met in the long twilight under a particular oak tree at the back of John Sweeney's half-acre. The old man himself was not a part of it. His son Hugh carried on the family tradition of rebellion.

The stench from the putrefying potatoes in the field caught each man in the back of the throat and strengthened his resolve. They were young men, hungry and angry, gathered together in a desperate attempt to keep food available to their families and neighbors. They had no theories of social revolution. Only Tom

Riordan saw the broader picture.

Martin Griffin spoke quietly, nervously. The information he had to offer was sure to provoke an action, more dangerous now that there were firearms at hand. But he plunged on. "Farmer Kenny takes his grain in two wagons down to Limerick next Tuesday. He's selling the lot to the merchant trader, and it's going down the Shannon to England."

"That's the third trip the man has made," said Hugh.

"Three trips too many, I'd say," said Michael Rourke in his slow steady voice. "It should be a crime to sell our food away."

Not likely to change, they all knew. The laws were made by the very same men who profited from the trade. Ships continued to leave Irish harbors laden with wheat and whiskey and livestock. A few tons of Indian meal sent in were poor replacement.

"Kenny should be discouraged from making any more bad bargains," Hugh agreed. "And he can serve as a lesson to others."

"He's been warned before," said Tom. "He's lamentably persistent."

"Shall we meet him going or coming, do you think?" asked Martin.

"He's already had the profits twice. Let's meet him on the long road going." Michael Rourke's words held a meaning that they all understood.

CHAPTER 7

EDWARD SPEKE'S CAMPAIGN TO REDUCE the number of laborers supported by the public relief works got underway immediately. He first struck off any worker who lived in a household where someone was already receiving benefit. Jimmy Meehan was sent away home, his fists clenched in powerless rage. Other younger sons and brothers were banished as well.

Then Speke strolled past the laborers, smoking his tobacco pipe and watching them at their backbreaking work. Now and then he would nod to a favored man, a tenant whose rent Speke would not want to miss. Those men never lacked for work, although they stood around as supervisors more often than they picked up a hammer. Some still held the lease of three or four acres, which they in turn rented by the half acre to others, collecting the rent due to them before the largest part went to Speke. They might even be called farmers themselves rather than destitute laborers, were it not that their fields lay in black ruins just the same.

Of the eighty-odd workers clearing the bed for the new road, seven were women. Filthy hags, in Speke's opinion, with stringy hair and sagging skin, women past their useful purpose and not worth the looking. He couldn't turn them off the rolls because they qualified as the sole support of their households—middens of Irish brats with gaping mouths. He'd been to their cottages too often. His own wife and young daughter lived like gentry in this polluted land, behind locked gates and proper gardens.

His review of the roadworks nearly completed, Speke caught sight of an unfamiliar figure, a skinny scarecrow of a boy. Hadn't seen him before. Speke hated the idea of a pauper evicted from some other godforsaken parish sneaking into his own relief works. Bad enough the paupers they already had.

"You! Laddie! Get your arse over here and identify yourself!" he hollered.

The young man looked up in surprise. He set down the stone he was lifting and walked toward the relief works' chairman.

"My name is Jackie Shaughnessy, sir," he said.

"Shaughnessy." Speke spat on the ground near Jackie's bare foot, yellow spittle. "And what holding might you have that would entitle you to a place on this works?"

"The Dooley acre, your honor, sir. Last week I took Kitty Dooley as my wife, and the foreman added me to the list in place of her brother Michael that died."

Speke's face flushed purple. "Will I never hear the end of the dead Michael Dooley?" he shouted.

Down the line some men stopped their work to listen.

"Who gave you the lease on that land, boyo? The lease is in the name of the cursed Michael Dooley, not your own! Do you think by sticking your prick in that wild girl's hole you'll get the lease of the land as well? She's a demon bitch and she'll cost you this job—" Speke took a breath to continue the tirade and then realized what he had said. The Dooley whore had bewitched him again.

The lad stood before him, his mouth gaping open in shock.

"Flynn!" Speke bellowed for his foreman.

"Begging your pardon, Mr. Speke—" began Jackie, in an attempt to preserve the future.

"The only begging you'll be doing is on the roads," said Speke.

Flynn appeared, reluctance in his slow steps. He held the foreman's job because he was the brother of the blacksmith who worked for Speke, but it did not suit him well.

"Flynn, get this Shaughnessy intruder off the rolls. You were a bloody idiot to take him on in the first place. And throw off any other Shaughnessys—and any Dooleys left alive as well! Jesus be damned, you're a scurvy lot with your plotting and stealing from your betters."

Speke turned away without bothering to wait for Flynn's nod. His throat was hot. He spat on the ground again as he walked the few paces to his horse, a chestnut stallion more attractive than the man.

"Tell your bride she can beg for it herself when she wants it," Speke said in a soft vicious voice to Jackie, leaning down from his saddle. Then something in the look on the boy's face made him wish he hadn't gone so far. He dug his heels into the flanks of his horse with more force than necessary to depart.

"Go on, son, you heard the man," said Flynn, giving Jackie a push on the shoulder. "Sure you're not the only one to be let go—he's cutting the list every day, the bastard."

Jackie didn't look around as he left. He trudged the three miles to his new home, where his bride and her mother awaited a small sum of money that would never come from the relief works in Edward Speke's vicinity. There had been no food yesterday and there would be none today. Regarding tomorrow he couldn't say.

Kitty and I spent the morning foraging for wild greens in the meadow south of Kilvarna. The situation was growing desperate. If we didn't gather enough today, then tomorrow we planned to walk the dozen or so miles to the sea, to join the crowds scouring the coast for seaweed and mussels. I counted on bringing something back for

Nuala Lynch as well. The old woman didn't complain, but the keening that had supported her all these years had fallen off almost entirely. None but the largest farmers had anything to spare now—and they weren't calling for keeners.

Our shawls each held a bunch of sorrel, picked a little past its prime. The bitter flavor and acid bite made it hard to swallow, but its nourishment was worth the struggle. We were bringing it home to boil into a little soup.

I pushed my arms through the scratchy bushes ringing the meadow, looking for a few berries that the birds and the earlier gatherers might have missed. The stems were stripped clean of fruit. I ached for the days when our stomachs used to be full of sweet berries and our fingers purple with juice.

Around noon Kitty spotted a dense mat of green fleshy leaves hugging a flat rock in the field. Red stems curled over the stone, spreading in abundance.

"How did anyone miss this? Look, Margaret, it's a grand heap of purslane." Kitty tore off a handful of the succulent plant and stuffed it into her mouth. The Shaughnessy household had already consumed the oats that Jackie's wage had bought two days ago.

I didn't mind the taste of purslane. It was moist and easy to chew, and there was a great lot of it. I sat down in the grass beside Kitty and picked and ate. A handful in my shawl, a handful in my mouth. I looked over at Kitty.

"Kitty, you look like a cow with a cud!" Green saliva flecked the corner of Kitty's mouth, where a stem of purslane hung loose.

Kitty stuck her tongue out and licked the plant in. Her tongue was green.

"I don't care. If I could chew grass I would, sometimes, I get so hungry. And then I could squirt the milk out, fresh and creamy." She grabbed her breast as if it were a cow's teat. "Jackie would lap it up, I'm sure." She giggled.

"You're worse now that you're a married woman," I said. "I

thought marriage would improve you."

"It's not so different having Jackie around. He's quieter than my brother Michael but he's a man just the same, earning the wage and waiting for the dinner. Of course a husband likes to poke and suck a bit. It's not so bad, Margaret. You should try it with Tom." She looked at me slyly. "Or maybe you already have."

"I have not. Tom is a serious man, and he's more interested in politics than in poking." I didn't like the righteous tone in my voice. I worried more about Tom's politics than I let anyone know. I leaned over and gave Kitty a quick hug. "I'm happy it's going well for you, Kitty dear. Jackie seems to think the world of you already."

"I don't think he knows the temper I've got," replied Kitty. "I try not to show it to him. Of course he hasn't provoked me yet."

"A week gone by? He must be a saint."

"He's a good man. I think we'll get on together all right."

In the hot sun of midday I felt the wisp of a chill shadow. I shook myself and stood up. Kitty wiped the green juice from her lips and patted her stomach. "Now that was a feast."

"Seaweed tomorrow?"

"It would be a delight," said Kitty.

CHAPTER 8

JIMMY MEEHAN TOOK THE LONG way home from the works, over the hills and up toward the stony meadows where occasionally you might have a chance at clubbing a hare, if you were quick enough with the big stick. His sister walked up here collecting wildflowers, she and the keener Nuala Lynch. Margaret was an odd one, always hanging about the old woman, listening to stories that happened hundreds of years ago. Jimmy enjoyed the poems and songs as much as any man of a dark night, but his main focus was on the here-and-now. He rustled the fragrant brush with his stick, hoping to flush out his long-eared quarry.

In the flat rocks, indentations had been formed by centuries of rainwater, and in those puddles lived grand snails. If he couldn't go home with a hare, then a pocketful of snails would be better than nothing. He leaped from rock to rock, looking for the brown-and-white whorled shells. When he was a child, Mammy used to fry them up in butter for him as a treat.

The air in this rocky place was sweet. The offensive odor of the rotting fields permeated every lane in Kilvarna below, and a beggar man passing through yesterday had said that there was nowhere any different in Ireland. The man had a cloth sack at his waist half-filled with grayish potatoes, which he offered to sell to anyone who had a coin. Some said the beggars had been living higher than the workingmen, buying tobacco with the money they got from selling food. But no one in the clachan had any shillings to buy potatoes from a beggar.

Jimmy looked out over the hills, which in July had been colored brilliant green. Shades of black and brown met his gaze on this August day, the shriveled potato patches of his neighbors. Farther afield were the green pasturelands of Major Harris's domain, dotted with cattle and sheep. Mr. Speke had lost so many of his livestock that he employed men to guard the pastures now. He brought them in from the villages, surly men who were of the Protestant background like Speke himself, and who wouldn't take pity on a starving countryman.

The hunt for snails was going slowly. Jimmy didn't want to walk into the house empty-handed and announce that he had lost his relief work too. He had standards that he tried to meet, even at the age of fifteen.

He had wandered off his usual path through the rocky meadow, veering up toward the higher ground in the north. The cottages were sparse here, the land suited to shallow-rooted meadow plants, not cabbages or potatoes. Already abandoned by their famished tenants, many cottages stood open and forlorn.

On the other side of a stone outcropping Jimmy saw a foot.

The bones of a small foot, held together with the remnants of a tendon.

"Sweet Christ," he said aloud. He clambered over the rock and on the other side saw a stone hut built into the side of the out-cropping. There were no windows, only an open doorway in which lay the remains of a child. The foot had been gnawed and dragged by whatever hungry creature—dog or crow—had first laid claim to it. Other creatures had nearly finished the rest.

As he forced himself to approach the hut, he noticed the smell. It was worse than putrefying potatoes and stronger than that wee child's corpse could have produced. Jimmy knew he would have to look into the door but he did not want to at all.

"Jesus, Mary, and Joseph, bless their souls," he prayed. "Have mercy on all within." He couldn't think of anything else to say. He crossed himself in protection.

When he looked inside, it was as bad as he feared. A family, lying together in death in the tiny dark space. He counted the mother, the father, and three children, decomposing into a single pile of rags and bones. Jimmy swallowed the lump in his throat and tried not to imagine that the last child had survived long enough to be left alone, desolate, in this pile of stone from which all life had fled.

He had heard from his father that there were instances such as this. Beggar families struck down by the fever, taking shelter in any place they found. Local families too proud to ask their neighbors for help, or too weak.

He backed away from the door, stepping carefully around the child. He wasn't sure exactly what would be the right thing to do, but Jimmy was pretty certain it should involve the priest.

Taking note of where the hut stood, Jimmy began his long walk down to Kilvarna. The two snails in his pocket were forgotten.

◎   ◎   ◎

"Ah no, what a tragedy indeed," murmured Father Martin. Jimmy Meehan had arrived at the priest's door in a sad state of mind, to relay a tale even worse.

"It would be best to tumble down the cabin around them, I think," he continued. "Like a cairn, it would be, up there in the hills. I'll bless the place and say the Requiem, so they can rest easy. Perhaps your father and Tim Griffin will go with us."

Father Martin had no idea who the family might be. Like the Quinns who had wandered through with their poor little girl, many people were on the road carrying a burden of sickness and death with them. He knew the roughly three hundred families in the area around Kilvarna. He even had a passing acquaintance with some who attended the Anglican church in the next village. But the traveling people were more numerous and more anonymous every week. He had all he could do to minister to the souls in his own little corner of the parish. What little support he had from the Church was barely enough to keep him alive and working. His prayers to the Holy Family were growing more desperate by the day.

"I didn't know whether to push the bones back inside the hut, Father, or to leave them out. I wanted to do the right thing," said Jimmy.

What a dilemma for a lad to face, thought the priest.

"Nothing you did or didn't do would make a difference to them now," he said kindly. "Their souls are with God in heaven. Their bodies are returning to the earth, as we all do." Some of us in a manner more wretched than others, he added silently.

Jimmy seemed satisfied with this response of the faithful. He brushed the tangled black hair off his forehead and stood up straighter. "I was cut from the relief work today, Father. Myself and a dozen others."

"I heard something of that," replied the priest. "It will be even harder now. Perhaps I might have a word with Ned Geary, to ask if he'll take on any men to finish his harvest all the quicker."

Farmer Geary raised a hundred acres of wheat. He had a reputation as a fair man who never let a beggar go in want from his door. Rumor said that he had given a hundred and fifty pounds of his own money to the relief committee for the purchase of Indian meal for the poor—ten times the amount sent by the landowner Major Harris from England.

Jimmy's face brightened. These days, any hope at all went a long way.

"Now go and wait for your father so we can take care of this sad trouble," Father Martin said. "We've enough time to walk up there and back tonight."

CHAPTER 9

Jimmy Meehan went home and told his mother what he had found up in the rocky hills. Not in detail, of course, but just as a piece of news. She sat on the stone next to the hearth in her usual place. Mere skin and bones she was now. Mam only looked at Jimmy and looked and looked, without a word.

Eventually Jimmy left her and trotted down the lane to find Jackie Shaughnessy. He wanted to give him the tip that Father Martin was going to talk to Ned Geary on their behalf. He was sure it would bring a smile to Jackie's face, and Kitty's too.

Mary Meehan had looked at her son Jimmy with eyes full of compassion for the terrible things he had seen, but her own heart was too tired to move her body.

She had swallowed a tiny sip of the foxglove potion, just the littlest bit to stop the fast beating in her chest. Like a bird, it had been, trying to get out. The bitter herb had slowed its wings, and now her heart sat nestled, waiting.

Mary had stewed the green leaves of the foxglove herself. After the blight had come again, stealing the life out of Kilvarna, she had climbed to the edge of the forest and searched out the plant, its tall spike of pinkish-purple bells easy to find. Her own mother had shown her how to strip the leaves—only the leaves— and brew the medicine for a weak heart. Never the flowers, she had said, nor the seeds, which are a deadly poison. Only the leaves. And Mary had taken only the leaves.

A tiny sip of foxglove to quell the pain in her heart, to stop the weakness that pervaded her body and her soul. She hadn't told the children. They did not need to know. Both Margaret and Jimmy were survivors. Of all the babies she had borne and lost, only those two had the strength of will to conquer the creeping hopelessness of poverty. She would not worry about them when she was gone.

The blight had taken everything else from her. The strength of her good husband, aged by hunger and want. The health of her own body, betraying her with its false beats. The joy of her friends, whom she shielded from her suffering, hiding herself away in this cottage. Her future, her wisdom, her grandchildren.

The story Jimmy told today could be their own, she thought. Starving together in the corner of the cottage, in the midst of the clachan, sick and weak and diseased and spent. Left for the dogs and the rats to find.

But Jimmy and Margaret would never let that happen to them. They had vitality, youth, optimism. The little bird in her chest flapped its wings again.

Surely they would be better off without her. What food there was could be shared by three. They wouldn't be dragged down by her sad face every morning and night. She had tried in the beginning, for their sakes, but now the best face she could put on was an impassive mask. It became harder every day to fight off the hopeless terrors.

She reached her hand down to the little clay bowl on the dirt floor beside her. Just another sip to stop the beating, to kill the fear.

The bird in her chest buried her beak in Mary's heart, a sharp sudden pain from such a tiny creature. Mary drained the last of the medicine from the bowl.

In a while the bird was quieted. She fluttered her wings only faintly, and less often.

Will my daughter keen for me? asked Mary Meehan at the last. The bird flew away without reply.

Other men went with Father Martin to tumble the stones down over the family in the hills. Dan Meehan had his hands full with his dead wife, his daughter weeping without cease, and his son so grief-stricken he couldn't speak.

Rose Mackey, Bridie Dooley, and Kitty were washing the body in preparation for the laying-out. It hadn't been so long since they had done the same for Michael. They fussed with Mary Meehan's hair, trying to hide the bare patches on her scalp, not knowing whether the hair had fallen out or been pulled. They covered her ragged dress with a shawl, and they washed her feet so tenderly.

Rose was relieved when Nuala Lynch came to take Margaret away, up into the fields where she could open her cries to the sky. Wordless keens, motherless keens. Rose wouldn't want to hear them.

On her way down the lane she was accosted by her neighbor Mary O'Gorman. They had lived next to one another for thirty years or more, sniffing the same dung piles and listening to the wails and laughter of their children. But they were not friends.

"Good evening, Mrs. Mackey," said Mrs. O'Gorman in a silky voice that belied the viciousness in her heart. "I'm distraught to hear the news of Mary Meehan."

"Terrible, terrible day, Mrs. O'Gorman," replied Rose Mackey. "Such a heedless accident."

"I never heard that Mrs. Meehan had the weak heart, did you? Foxglove poisoning, of all things. And her own mother an expert in the healing herbs. So strange," murmured Mrs. O'Gorman.

Rose took a step backward, away from this plague of a woman.

"She hasn't been well for a year or more. Perhaps it was her heart all along," Rose said.

"She never came out of the house, you recall. How it must have hurt the Dooleys to miss her company at Michael's wake and Kitty's wedding." Mrs. O'Gorman looked as pained as if it were her own wake.

"The Dooleys are in the house now preparing her body," replied Rose. "They've remained closest friends to the end." She would give her no satisfaction, at all.

Mrs. O'Gorman's lower lip protruded in a hideous parody of a pout.

"I don't know if you've heard the sly rumor going 'round, Mrs. Mackey, but people are saying that Mary Meehan killed herself deliberately. That she brewed and drank the foxglove without suffering from a weak heart at all." The woman licked her lips, an ugly habit. "Suicides cannot be buried in hallowed ground. They've committed mortal sin."

"It's a malicious creature you are, Mary O'Gorman," said Rose. "You're committing a greater sin by carrying rumors and lies than did any poor soul that misjudged a dose of medicine. They're evil words out of your mouth and it's no surprise."

Mrs. O'Gorman thrust her face forward. "It's been called to the attention of Father Martin. Someone other than myself, of course, came to the same conclusion. I merely wondered if you'd heard, since you are a bosom friend to the family."

Rose was certain the creature was lying. How much worse it would be on the Meehans if an inquest were called. The government would send a man from Ennistymon. They might conduct an autopsy, a violation that Rose knew would have horrified her friend. Mary Meehan had been a modest, loving woman before she had gone downhill.

"Tell Father Martin he can talk to me, Mrs. O'Gorman," Rose said. "I will testify in a court of law that Mrs. Meehan had been taking the foxglove for a year or more, so she was. The weak hearts ran in her mother's family." She glared at her adversary.

"It's up to Father Martin to pursue it," said Mrs. O'Gorman, as she turned to go into her own cottage. "If I were you, I wouldn't count on following the cart to the cemetery."

"Great pleasure it would give me to follow yours," muttered Rose, loud enough that Mrs. O'Gorman might possibly have heard.

The moon had risen high in the dark sky by the time Father Martin presented himself at the door of the Meehan cottage. The tumbling of the stone hut into a cairn up in the hills had been undertaken with as much respect and decency as the men could employ, but the task had shaken every one of them.

Mrs. Dooley let him in. The room was crowded with friends. Kitty and Jackie Shaughnessy sat in a corner with Margaret, whose eyes were swollen with weeping. Tom Riordan held her close against his chest, an unusual display of open affection. Rose Mackey stood like a rooster near the door, bright eyes focused on the priest. Nuala Lynch was a dark presence in the background. Dan Meehan and his son hunched near the open hearth, where the body of Mary Meehan lay arranged in front of the stone seat where she had spent her last year. A gathering of wildflowers was spread over the stone.

"God bless all here," said Father Martin as he entered. He made the Sign of the Cross over the people and went first to the body, where he knelt in prayer for a long minute. He had performed the sacrament of Last Rites earlier today, after poor Jimmy had found his mam lying dead.

He wanted to speak to Dan Meehan alone concerning this matter of the accidental poisoning. The Church had a strict view against the taking of a person's own life, and if the comments of Mrs. O'Gorman had any factual basis, he would be forced to deny Mary Meehan a resting place in sacred ground. It was a cruel thing, to be cast forever into the darkness without hope of redemption. If Mrs. Meehan had deliberately brewed and swallowed the foxglove to end her life, then she had committed a mortal sin that would doom her to hell in the hereafter.

Father Martin rose to his feet and went to shake the hands of the bereaved men. The shock was apparent in their faces. He opened his mouth to ask Dan to step outside when he became aware of two women moving in close beside him, one on either side. Rose Mackey and Nuala Lynch. He had an uncomfortable sensation of being flanked by harpies, withered creatures of talon and beak. He could feel the eyes of everyone upon him.

It was so much simpler to determine the sin if a man had hung himself.

"Your wife will be much mourned, Mr. Meehan," he began.

"She will," agreed Rose Mackey, slipping in before the priest could go on. "Sure we knew she was suffering from the weak heart, like her mother before her, but we never dreamed it would take her so quick."

Jimmy was roused from grief by his surprise at Mrs. Mackey's words. "She never told us," he said.

"Mothers don't tell their children everything. Nor their husbands, either," replied Rose with a firmness of purpose.

Dan Meehan looked at the floor. "She just faded away. We didn't know what to do. The daughter tried everything."

Father Martin forced himself to try a different tack. "Did she seem overly troubled, Mr. Meehan? Without hope? Without solace in her faith?"

When Dan did not appear able to answer, Rose Mackey stepped in.

"She had a Rosary in her hand every day," she lied.

The priest cleared his throat uncomfortably. "I should have stopped by more often. I could have prayed with her."

"It was the heart ailment that took her, Father." Nuala Lynch's tone showed her determination to put an end to this painful conversation. "I myself brewed her the foxglove potion last year, when she told me of her trouble. She took the drop of it whenever she needed. Today she might have taken a second dose, not remembering that she had taken the first. If anyone is responsible for poor Mary's death, I suppose you could say it was me."

"An accidental overdose is no one's fault," said the priest with relief. "You must be more careful, Mrs. Lynch, in instructing your neighbors about the dangerous nature of herbs." Unless you're drumming up business for yourself, indeed.

Then Father Martin spoke loudly, so that all present could hear. "Be comforted that Mary's earthly troubles are over and she rests in the peace of the Lord," he said, and he blessed the neighbors again as he left, escorted to the door by the harpies.

That Mrs. O'Gorman was a certain troublemaker, he thought, as he passed her cottage down the lane. He also hoped it was true that even a mortal sinner could be forgiven if the Last Rites were performed before the body was cold, and the soul lingered. Mary Meehan had still been warm when Jimmy found her.

The keening that night was Nuala Lynch's alone. My broken heart had broken my voice as well. The sounds that came from my throat echoed the keener's words in painful sorrow but could not rise to the poetry demanded by death. My mam was gone. I could not get beyond that simple thought, that awful truth.

We buried her on Saturday in the churchyard at Kilvarna, where the smell of rot from the potato fields drifted in the soft air. Two starved children were laid to rest at the same time, brought in from a cottage beyond Speke's pastures. Their father dragged the bodies behind him, wrapped in rags and lashed to a door. The Sweeneys lent him a spade and then finished the digging for him when they saw how weak he was. After the service the man turned around and walked home, without asking even a drink of water for his journey.

◎ ◎ ◎

Tuesday morning was clear and bright, a good day for harvesting. The farmer William Kenny nearly changed his mind about driving the two loads of grain down to Limerick, it was such a fine day to spend in the fields. However, given the unsettled state of the country, he thought it prudent to sell off his crop as quickly as possible. There were rumors that the harbors might be closed and exports banned.

The two heavy wagons made good progress down the long road. They passed through Kilfenora with no trouble, although Kenny had to swing his whip a few times to drive off the beggars. Their faces were hollow and their arms like sticks. They reached for the sacks of grain with bony hands, their cries for assistance pitiful. Still, they fell back at the flourish of the whip. They hadn't the strength for an organized attack.

Farmer Kenny drove on, confident that he had done his part to help the starving peasants by subscribing forty pounds of his own money to the relief committee. He had dismissed all but two of his laborers, to conserve his available cash, and he had gone back to working in the fields himself. Hard times called for hard measures. Other small farmers he knew were selling out and going to America.

He was thinking about the opportunities offered across the

ocean when he rounded the curve of the road heading down into Corofin.

Four men appeared at the wagon, the first grabbing the reins from his hands, two more hauling him off the seat. Before he could cry out a warning, another band of men had tossed his eldest son from the wagon following. The lad was thirteen but no match for them. Kenny could hear him struggling in the dirt. He himself lay face down with a foot on his back.

"Let the lad go," he shouted as best he could with a mouthful of dust.

"You'll go together," replied one of the men. That was not a comfort.

"You've been warned, Kenny, against selling the grain to the English." The man with his foot on Kenny's back pressed a bit harder when he said the hated word.

"We've told you that robbing Ireland of her food is a crime. But you're still driving your loads of corn to the sea." The calmness of the man's voice frightened Kenny more than a roaring shout.

"When will you stop, traitor?"

The speaker answered his own question.

"Now," he said.

Four bullets were discharged simultaneously by the men on the road. There was the sound of a horse's scream, cut short.

"Jesus," cried out a voice. "That's hard."

"Shut your mouth and finish the job," said another. Another explosion echoed.

Kenny's son began to cry, sobs of fear. The farmer recognized the sound and prayed.

The four horses lay fallen in their traces, shot at close range through the foreheads. The last one had been thrashing but now was still. Blood slowly seeped onto the road.

"You can leave your wagons here and walk home," said Tom Riordan. "Your horses won't be much use to you now."

Hugh Sweeney wavered next to the body of the gray horse, clearly a man in pain at the sight of slaughter. Tom gestured to Martin Griffin to grab Hugh and disappear into the stand of trees nearby. The others silently retreated to their hiding places. Michael Rourke kept his hands on the shoulders of the sobbing boy.

"Take this lesson to heart, farmer, and tell your friends what happens to men who send their corn to British markets. Tell them that we begin with the horses. Tell them they can end it there," said Tom.

He withdrew the pressure of his foot from Kenny's back. "Count aloud to fifty before you and the lad get up," said Tom. "And think very carefully before you report the loss of the horses to the constables. You could lose more than livestock."

Tom and Michael ran for the woods with the mumbled counting in their ears. The eight young men returned to Kilvarna singly, through fields and hedges. Some were more shaken by this first violent action than others. All mourned the waste of four good horses.

The wagons loaded with grain would be empty by nightfall. When Farmer Kenny returned the next day with borrowed horses and armed companions to retrieve his property, he would find nothing left of his teams but hides, hooves, and heads.

CHAPTER 10

LUCKILY BOTH JIMMY AND JACKIE were taken on by Ned Geary for the harvest, along with three other fellows. Jimmy got six shillings a day, and even beyond that Farmer Geary treated the workers to a dinner of turnips and oat porridge at noon. That was the best part, my brother said.

A hundred acres of wheat and barley was a big crop to harvest. And after each field was gathered in, Geary opened it for a day to women and children for gleaning. Like crows we scattered over the field, on hands and knees scouring the earth for overlooked kernels to grind into flour, for oats that horses would never miss. None of us went away with an empty shawl, and for a week or so we had something to eat every day.

When a man was as generous as Ned Geary, it was hard to hold it against him that he sold his corn at market for a profit. He had to pay his rent to Speke, same as we did.

Yet as the month of August wore on and we realized with a blackness in the pit of our stomachs that the second blight was worse than the first, we resented the export of food all the more.

Scores of horses were shot to death on the roads, as warnings to the farmers. Foremen on the relief projects were attacked by desperate men who needed work. Cattle and sheep on the land-lords' estates were crudely butchered in the dead of night. Mr.

Speke threatened to close down the roadworks altogether if the violence continued.

The weather began to chill in September. A harsh winter was on its way, said the old ones who followed the signs of nature. And when I looked around the clachan, I could see the hungry summer reflected back at me in the wan faces and protruding bellies of the children. There had long been poverty in Clare—some people said since the terrible rape of the country by the Englishman Cromwell—but it was eased by the sharing of those who had a little more. Now we had nothing to share. Even the music was dying. People who hadn't eaten in days did not walk over the fields at night to a neighbor's house for dancing or storytelling.

I spent more of my days with Nuala Lynch, learning the old laments, listening beneath the words, hoping to find in the ambivalence between life and death some answer to the grief in my own life.

Kitty complained that she never saw me anymore. "You're sticking to the side of Nuala Lynch like a snail," Kitty said. "She's old. I don't see how you could be more interested in spending time with her than with Tom. Or with me."

"Maybe I like her company," I said. "Maybe I don't care that she's old. Maybe someday we'll be old too, Kitty. Did you ever trouble yourself to think of that?"

Kitty shook her head. "I'll never be old," she vowed. "It's against my principles."

Edward Speke evicted every one of the families whose cottages lined the southwest corner of his sheep pasture, for arrears in the rent. The next night Tom Riordan called a meeting of the Whiteboys at Hugh Sweeney's place. They stood outside in the fading light, full of the rage of men in the first grip of starvation.

The campaign to stop the food going to the harbors had frightened farmers and given wide employment to strangers with guns. Perhaps the plunder had kept a few families alive. But now the people were being turned out onto the road, their cottages reduced to rubble.

Most of the men put the blame squarely on the brutal Speke. If he continued with the evictions, none of them would have a roof over their heads by Christmas. Anyone who even gave shelter to an evicted family was subject to eviction himself. Speke's policy would be the ruin of Kilvarna, if no action were taken.

Tom Riordan's face had lost its boyish look and become angular. His expression was serious as he spoke. "I'll be going down to Ennistymon on fair day to see some lads from the south and get the news. I could bring up the subject of Speke, if we're decided on it."

Sean Foley shook his head. "Let it go for now, Tommy. Taking a man's life is a terrible responsibility. Some might consider it murder."

"War, Sean, not murder," said Tom. "The British invaders have been killing us by the thousands for centuries. Now they're rushing the process. Speke is an agent of the enemy."

"Just the same, it's a man's life, Tom. It would be a warning to the agents and landlords, but isn't there some other way? I myself don't fancy hanging for the death of a miserable bastard like Speke." Sean Foley had a wife and small children.

Tom's face was set. "I'm telling you, lads, that we don't do the shooting ourselves. They send someone in from the outside, a stranger who will do the job quick and get out. And in return we might have to take one of theirs, down in Tipperary or Limerick. It's all Ireland that's in this fight."

"I'm not ready to declare a death sentence on Speke," said quiet Martin Griffin. "The only work we've got is the public relief—and bad as Speke is, he's got his hands on the money."

"It's a death sentence he's declared on you, Martin, as sure as you're standing here. How long can you go on hammering stone twelve hours a day with nothing in your belly?" Tom could not bring himself to mention the loss of Michael Dooley, but he didn't need to, in this band of men.

"The government is sure to send aid to us soon," Martin insisted.

"And how many millions of starving Irish are going to be standing with their hands out for the fistful of meal from a dozen ships? Are you going to be one of the lucky ones, Martin? One fistful at a time?" Tom picked up a stone and hurled it over the dead fields.

"Speke relishes his power," said Hugh Sweeney. "I hold that against him."

"Did you know he went himself to oversee the wrecking of those cottages yesterday? The constabulary did the dirty work but he enjoyed the view." Michael Rourke's tone was bitter. "I'm with Tom here. Speke is the devil himself. Even if the landlord posted a new agent, he couldn't be half as bad."

"I can't bring myself to this decision," said Sean Foley. "I see what you're saying, and the risk to us is low, but I can't get over thinking it's not the right thing to do."

Martin nodded his head in agreement. "Let's wait a bit, Tom. There's no going back once we've done it."

"We could give him a written warning." Tom's younger brother Danny spoke up. "Demand that the evictions stop. Show him up for the fucking bastard he is, and tell him he's being held accountable."

"Put up a notice, do you mean?" Martin nodded in the direction of the clachan.

"Right. Tom's Margaret is good with English, she could write it for us."

"Nevertheless I'm going to the fair day with a purpose," said Tom.

CHAPTER 11

COPIES OF THE NOTICE WERE posted at a crossroads on the Lisdoonvarna road, on the wall of Pat Maloney's cottage where men gathered, on the door of the chapel in Kilvarna, and on the post of the main gate into Major Harris's estate.

I was proud of my efforts, although I couldn't tell anyone what I had done. I used the best English that I had learned at school, and in grand big words I accused Edward Speke of moral corruption, avarice, greed, heartless disregard for the poor, and deliberate intentions of removing the population from the land. I warned him that such harsh actions as he had recently taken would not be further tolerated. I ended with a plea for his charity and assistance to the starving tenants in their dire distress—until Tom insisted that I change it to a threat of retribution if the situation under Speke's control did not improve.

Speke's reaction to the notice was not long in coming.

My arms prickled with a load of fresh straw that I had gathered for Nuala Lynch's bedding. The old woman's legs were so swollen now that she moved around with difficulty, so I took it upon myself to clear out the moldy straw that filled the corner of her cottage. I was carrying the new straw inside when I heard the thud of horses' hooves on the road.

A moment later I saw Mr. Speke ride past the cottage on his huge chestnut stallion. Following behind in a horse-drawn trap were the bailiff and three constables. They stopped at the group of three cottages belonging to Nuala's neighbors, the Morgans.

After them came a ragged group of men. At first I thought they were beggars, until I saw the crowbars in their fists. I darted back into the cottage.

"Speke's come with his housewreckers!"

Nuala's lined face showed no surprise. "I couldn't pay the yearly rent on gale day," she said. "The bailiff served notice yesterday."

"But they didn't stop here. It's the Morgans they're after."

"First the Morgans. They tumble down ten in a day."

"Why didn't you tell me?" I knew it was absurd to feel hurt, as if Nuala didn't trust me enough, but the feeling arose anyway.

"What would it do to worry you, my dear? You've been so good. And there's no preventing, if Speke has in mind to do it. He's a malevolent creature."

I heard shouts and wails from down the road. They hammered my heart like blows.

"Can't I do anything?"

Nuala shook her head and I ran outside. I stood out of sight behind the stone wall that separated the Morgans' land from Nuala Lynch's, and watched as the bailiff handed a paper to the agent. The unpleasant bark of English commands shattered the air. The three constables entered the first cottage. The Morgans massed near the road, crying and wailing.

A woman ran out of the cottage holding a small child by one hand. With the other hand she dragged a wooden cradle. An iron kettle sailed through the door past her, tossed out by a constable clearing the house. A flurry of blankets followed, which she snatched up as soon as she put her children down by the roadside.

I watched as the housewreckers set to work. They were horrifying in their efficiency. Two men climbed up on the roof and tied a thick rope around the center beam. They pushed the rope down through a hole in the thatch, and a man on the ground ran into the cottage and brought the rope out the door. The roof men used a saw to weaken the roof beams and broke the supports on each side with crowbars. Then they jumped down to the ground, and the whole crew began to tug on the rope. I heard the terrible whoosh as the beams collapsed into the cottage, tumbling the thatch into the interior and breaking the stone walls as they fell. Coughing and spitting in the dust, the men leaped to finish the job with their crowbars. They hacked and smashed away until the ruins were pulverized. It took less than half an hour.

Speke stood in the road, surveying the destruction. The housewreckers began on the second cottage, and three Morgan women threw themselves at Speke's feet. They cried for mercy, they begged and groveled until I flushed red from the humiliation of watching. They stretched their white arms upward in supplication to the agent, and he looked at them in disgust.

"Away!" He kicked at the closest woman with the toe of his boot, to clear the space to mount his horse. She rolled from his kick and rose to her knees, her weeping transformed to fury.

"Kick us like dogs, Mr. Speke? May you rot in hell for eternity!" she screamed, pointing her long finger at him. "Cursed be the day you were spawned! And cursed be your children! May every roof they live under fall upon them with a crash. You're deserving of a knife in your throat, and there's many here that would put it there for you, you filthy piece of dung." She drew her breath to curse anew.

Speke called to the bailiff. "Get these savages off my land before nightfall. They're not to hang about crying and mewling over their losses. On their way to the workhouse before dark."

The woman spit at his back as he rode off alone.

The second cottage fell inward and the wailing began again. Curses turned against the housewreckers, Irishmen who betrayed their own neighbors for a few shillings' wage. Sickened, I turned back to Nuala's cottage, praying that the old woman would be spared this outrage.

Nuala Lynch had already tied up her few belongings in her shawl.

I had a desperate idea. "I'll go and find Tom. He might be able to keep them off for a time."

"No use to that," Nuala said. "The magistrate signed the eviction order, and it will be carried out."

"How can you be so calm about this?" I was shaking with anger and fear.

"I have in mind where to go," Nuala said. "And it's not the workhouse."

"Won't you come to us?" Our hospitality consisted of a roof and an empty hearth. But while Jimmy had the place at Geary's and Da was at the roadworks, we weren't destitute entirely.

"No," she replied. "I'm going to spend the last time I have in the company of kings."

Had the distress broken Nuala's mind? "Oh, come with me," I said, putting my arm around her shoulder.

"No, Margaret. I know where I'm going. You can walk with me if you like. That would be a help."

Another great crash shook the air outside. The cursing wove itself around the wailing in a counterpoint of tragedy.

Together we walked out the door of the cottage where Nuala Lynch had spent forty years of her life. Two constables were on their way toward us.

"Stay, old woman," invited the younger constable. "We'll give you a shilling if you'll knock your own house down. Save us the trouble of doing the work."

"Close your trap, you bloody idiot," hissed the other officer. "Don't you know that's Mrs. Lynch, the keener? Her that makes the awful howl at funerals. Don't get that old witch riled up, mate."

We passed the men in black silence and began our journey toward the broad green hills in the distance. By the time Nuala's stone cottage was tumbled down, we were too far away to hear it.

CHAPTER 12

THE PACE OF EVICTIONS INCREASED as the weather grew colder. Snow fell, unusual for the west of Clare. The October wind cut through the rags of the poor and through the thick wool clothing of the townsfolk in Ennistymon.

Tom Riordan knew he was in the vicinity of the Ennistymon workhouse before he saw the long gray buildings. He knew when he saw the crowds of beggars, stick figures with flapping clothes barely covering their skin. Men, women, and children in the last stages of deprivation clamored to be let into the workhouse where there was a promise of food and shelter. But the workhouse was full to bursting, and no new residents were taken in, by order of the guardians.

He walked past the iron gates, giving a wide berth to the huddled sick and dying. He had nothing to give them but his struggle to free the people from oppression, and for that he needed his strength. Famine fever would take them all down.

On the side street past the grain store Tom met his man from the south. He was younger than Tom expected, a lad with fuzz on his cheeks. But the lad listened carefully to Tom's description of Edward Speke and his chestnut stallion, and he repeated back to Tom the route that Speke was expected to ride without a flaw. Tomorrow evening the land agent planned to attend a conference of local relief committees held at the town hall in Kilfenora. The young man from Limerick would make certain Speke never arrived.

High on a hillside overlooking the grand sweep of the land was a meadow. A man who stood on its grassy height could feel like a chief of Munster, surveying the tribes who owed him loyalty. Because of this, Nuala Lynch told me, the meadow was the burial place of kings. Mounds of overgrown brush covered ancient tombs, eight that Nuala had counted. But one in particular had always been her favorite. Constructed of standing stones, each four feet high and six feet long, the tomb was shaped like a wedge, or a coffin. A massive flat stone served as a roof and two upright slabs as a door. Long ago the tomb had been looted of its fine gold ornaments, and the bones within had crumbled to dust. For a small old woman such as Nuala, the tomb was a livable shelter.

A path led down the hillside near the tomb, and every day I brought her water and a bit of whatever food we had. It was a shock, at first, to think of Nuala Lynch living in a tomb. It was dark inside, having only the light from between the two door slabs, and the floor was a rubble of stones. I had smoothed the floor for Nuala's feet, and I had made a bed of dry grasses along the side wall. I brought turf and sticks for a small fire, which warmed the ancient stones inside and cast flickering shadows even in the daylight.

Still, it was a tomb.

The landlord's order to tumble an old woman's house had led to her living in a house of the dead.

I continued to plead with Nuala to come down to our cottage.

"I need to stay here," Nuala would answer. "I am keening for Ireland."

Practicality was no argument. "I would find it easier not to climb up this hill every day," I would say.

"A keener's life is full of challenges," Nuala would reply drily. "It's meant for me to spend my remaining days here. My voice will echo over the hills to the sea."

The lad from Limerick had picked a spot where the road to Kilfenora turned abruptly to the south. There was no clear view ahead or behind, and a mass of gorse bushes provided cover, brown and dry as they were. He knew nothing about the man he was to shoot, except that he was an Englishman who served the interests of an absentee landlord with a frightening taste for evictions. It was enough for him. The hatred of the English oppressor had been bred into his bones, for his grandfather had been hung in Westmeath in the Rising of 1798.

He established his position in the late afternoon, more than an hour before the target was expected. His borrowed horse was tethered in an adjacent field. His heavy pistol was loaded and ready, and he did not expect to need more than one shot.

Ned Geary had done the best he could to keep the extra laborers busy with the harvest and the threshing. Knowing that the wage he paid them was all that kept them from destitution, he pushed off the time when he would have to let the men go, until finally there was no choice. His own financial situation was less than stable in these hard times, and he had seen more than one neighboring farmer turn his lease back to the landlord and set off for America. William Kenny had been the most recent emigrant, his whole family boarding a ship bound for Canada on the winter seas.

Tomorrow he would have to tell the men that the work was done. But he had come up with a plan for the building of a new bridge over the Kilshanny that he thought might be approved for a relief project, which would provide more work for the men. It seemed as if the projects were almost deliberate in constructing useless roads going nowhere, in Geary's opinion. He was eager to present a plan to employ the needy and add a new river crossing at the same time. To that end he was attending the local relief committees meeting tonight in Kilfenora.

Ned Geary ate his farmer's meal of boiled cabbage and bacon, sopping the liquid in his bowl with brown bread the wife had baked that day. It would be a cold ride to Kilfenora, crossing a track through the rocky Burren in the twilight, but he was a man with a purpose. He could make better time if he traveled on horseback rather than take the two-wheeled trap. And if he arrived at the town hall a bit early, the committee might give him a listen at the start of the meeting. With luck he could be home in his warm bed before ten.

Only Hugh Sweeney shared Tom's knowledge that the plan was to be executed this night. The two young men sat edgily near the fire in the Sweeneys' cottage as the sky darkened in the twilight. The days were long when there was no work to be had. Around them the people of Kilvarna waited for deliverance, for the aid from the British government that most were sure was coming any day now. "The Queen won't let the country starve," the people reassured one another. "She'll help us in our time of need."

Ned Geary's copper gelding trotted at a brisk pace along the road to Kilvarna. In some places great high hedges arched nearly across the road, like dark tunnels, and in other places the land was flat and open. The farmer could see faint glows from the tenants' hearth fires twinkling like faery lights over the fields. So many souls, so many mouths to feed. How the poorest of them managed to hang on at all, he didn't know. He did the best he could with his own resources, but with the evictions increasing every day, it was like a tidal wave sweeping the people from the land and tossing them upon the bare roads. Ned shook his head in dismay.

As he rounded the next curve something skittered across the road in front of him. His horse reared up, startled by the sudden movement. A stone, perhaps. Ned tightened his grip on the reins and brought the horse under control.

A movement to the side of the road caught his eye. A man stood there, in the dusk. Did he need help? Ned opened his lips to call out to him but the words never reached the air.

The young man from Limerick fired a single shot at close range into the man on horseback riding toward Kilfenora in the twilight. The ball tore through Ned Geary's chest and pulled him from his saddle. As he tumbled to the ground in a bloody heap, his assassin calmly returned the warm pistol to his pocket.

"Retribution for your crimes," said the lad. "May the devil greet you with open arms, Mr. Speke."

A gurgling swishing sound came from the farmer's punctured lung as he tried to breathe. It lasted no longer than the time it took for the young man to find his own horse and be off across the fields.

Ned Geary's horse stepped off the road, away from the smell of blood. He found a patch of grass among the stones and busied himself with grazing as the evening grew darker.

An hour later another horse pounded his hooves on the road to Kilvarna, urged to speed by the riding crop of his master. Edward Speke had gotten off to a late start, due to an unseemly argument with his wife. Defying his expressed wishes, Eliza had been giving food from their table to beggars at the gate. Not for the first time, he had locked her in her room and threatened the servants with dismissal if they opened the door. He would mete out her proper punishment tonight when he got home.

Speke's chestnut stallion caught the scent of blood and death as he flew around the curve where Geary's body lay. He shied to the right and stumbled. Speke glanced down as he applied the crop to the horse's flank to straighten him out. Another peasant dead in a ditch. The countryside was turning into a goddamn charnel house.

The gelding belonging to Ned Geary found his way home about midnight, riderless. The two men who worked on the Geary farm set off at once in the cart, lanterns swinging on each side. The mare in the harness stepped slowly and carefully over the rough road, keeping pace with the men who searched on foot. Alongside them ran Geary's favorite hound.

They feared the worst. The attacks on landlords and agents had not yet extended to the farmers themselves, although there had been many fine horses shot. It would seem so terribly unjust for a good man like Ned Geary to be punished for crimes of greed and exploitation done by others.

An hour of searching had not found a trace of the man. They were more than halfway to Kilfenora when the dog stiffened and growled. He leaped ahead of them into the darkness, and then they heard a howling that rivaled the banshee wail. The two men looked at one another and shook their heads in sorrow.

They brought the body of Ned Geary back to his home on the cart, the hound crouched beside his master all the way.

At the inquest the next day, both farmhands testified that there had been no sign of a scuffle, no footprints in the dirt of the road. Whoever had shot Ned Geary had done so in cold blood, standing in the field beside the road, waiting in the twilight.

Edward Speke did not come forward, if he even realized he had ridden past the murder scene.

◎   ◎   ◎

"Accidents happen in war," said Tom Riordan. His face was pale and his light hair stood up in tufts on his head, where he had grabbed it in frustration.

"An accidental murder," replied Hugh Sweeney.

"How could we have known that Mr. Geary would be riding the same road at the very same time?" asked Tom again, of no one. "That's the trouble with leaving the job to strangers. One man on a brown horse looks much like another." He shoved both hands into his mop of hair again, holding his head as if in pain. "If you want something done right, you have to do it yourself."

"No, Tom, you're not thinking of going after Speke again, are you?" Hugh looked at his friend with horror.

"Not now, not now. But he's even more deserving than before. A good man has died in his stead."

"I can no longer see the reasoning for Speke's death," said Hugh in a low voice. "The thought has been knocked clear out of me." When they had heard the news of Ned Geary's shooting that morning, Hugh had turned color and rushed off to retch violently on an empty stomach.

"Speke is waging a campaign of evictions in the county, with no mercy, and he's corrupting the relief works. He's a devil on horseback and an agent of the enemy." Tom made his voice cold and hard. "I regret the death of Ned Geary but not half so much as I regret that it was not Speke."

Hugh shoved his hands in his jacket pockets to avoid wringing them together. "Do you think they'll trace it to us, Tom?"

"I don't think so," Tom said. "And it's not us, it's me. I'm the one who made the arrangement." His mouth twisted and he spit in the dirt. "Next time I'll be more specific about the color of his eyes."

Hugh Sweeney took a deep breath. "That's it for me, Tommy," he said. "I can't do this. I'm going away."

Tom drew away in surprise. "Away? What, because of a small mistake? No one but the two of us knows it."

"No, it's all of it. The hunger, the suffering. The blight. All the clachan is dying. I'm going to leave before I'm dead too. I don't want to starve and I don't want to swing."

"Can't I change your mind, then? You know I'll carry all the blame for this. I'll swear it was myself alone, in service to Ireland."

Hugh looked at the ground and shook his head. "I've got to go. I'll get a ship to America. New York, maybe, or Boston." He paused. "You could come with me, Tom."

"I can't," he said. "I'm needed here. And then there's Margaret."

"Margaret won't be happy standing at the foot of a gallows," Hugh said.

"I learn from my mistakes," said Tom.

They stood in silence for a few moments.

"It will look bad if you run away directly after a shooting," Tom finally said.

"Right. I'll stick for a few days then, and tell my family I'm planning to leave. I was hoping to avoid the weeping good-byes."

"There will be more than enough weeping at Geary's wake tomorrow night," said Tom. "They'll have run out of tears by the time you leave."

CHAPTER 13

THE WAKE FOR NED GEARY was held in the comfortable farmhouse where the Gearys had lived for generations. Ned's blasted body was laid out on the bed in the back room, covered with a sheet of finest linen. The room was lit by the glow of a dozen candles.

Most of the mourners gathered in the main room of the house. They were not the same crowd of laborers and tenants who had come together at the passing of Michael Dooley, not by any means. These guests were dressed in clean respectable clothing. Their hands did not claw at the platters of brown bread and butter set out on the sideboard, since all of them had eaten a reasonable dinner that day. They spoke in quiet tones, some with the speech of Scotland and Britain, none in the Irish language of the land. Ned Geary had been a well-to-do farmer, and his friends came from the same class. Inside the farmhouse they ate and drank and socialized, but underneath the talk ran a thread of fear. If Ned Geary could be assassinated in the twilight of an evening, what safety was there for any of them?

Outside the farmhouse a group of laborers stood awkwardly on either side of the door. They had come to pay respects to the dead man, who was generous and kind and would be sorely missed. Jackie Shaughnessy and Jimmy Meehan had lost their work with his death, as did three other men. The bullet that pierced Ned Geary's breast would bring hardship on more than his own family.

Hugh Sweeney stood miserably in the midst of the crowd with his father and brothers, his face pale in the dim twilight. Tom Riordan stood with him, desperately reminding himself that Ned Geary was a casualty of war. Tom felt sick inside, having been the indirect cause of this death. When the man had been Edward Speke, it was easier. A man who made himself into an inhuman devil encouraged inhumanity to be reflected back upon him. Tom wasn't sure how he was going to force himself to go inside the house and gaze upon the dead face of an innocent victim.

I waited with Kitty at the edge of the group from the clachan, wondering if we would be invited inside the farmhouse. I'd never been in such a place, and my stomach was butterflies at the thought of keening for Ned Geary, without Nuala Lynch at my side. Nuala had sent me from the wedge tomb today with encouraging words, but I wasn't sure that a keen was even welcome here. I looked again for Tom's face in the crowd, to give me courage. If he could stand up to do the hard things he had to do, then so could I. But Tom's eyes were turned away from me, only the blond back of his head visible behind Hugh Sweeney's shoulders.

The Widow Geary's face was puffy with weeping when she emerged from the house at last. Father Martin held the door open and then took her arm in support.

"I thank you all for your prayers," she said. Her voice was shaky and my own eyes filled with tears. "Mr. Geary would have been pleased to see you here. He tried to do the best he could for you as long as he could. What a wicked heart must have plotted his death." She steadied herself with a long breath. "If you come back to the gate in the morning, we'll have some bread for you to take."

We had not come for food.

I forced myself to step forward, embarrassed by my shabby dress but wanting to offer what I could.

"Mrs. Geary, if you wish a keener to—"

Father Martin shook his head. "The Gearys have done without that shrieking for a generation," he said firmly.

"Thank you for your offer," said Mrs. Geary. "We've some English friends inside who would find the practice disturbing. But please give Mrs. Lynch my regards."

I flushed. I wasn't offering my keening for pay, as was the custom in times past. I would have done a powerful keen for Ned Geary on my own. But it wasn't wanted any longer.

The widow withdrew into the house, and the priest cast a blessing to dismiss our ragged group before he followed her.

The people slowly walked through the farmhouse gate and dispersed across the fields. Kitty and Jackie went off together.

Tom waited for me at the gate. I was surprised to see the grieving lines on his face, the way his forehead creased and his eyebrows drew together. Something more than the wake of a farmer was bothering him.

He reached for my hand and squeezed my small fingers in his own, until I put my other hand on top of his to stop the pressure. "You don't know your own strength," I said.

He released my fingers instantly. "Come and walk with me, Margaret. I need to shake off these feelings I don't like having."

We walked through the growing darkness, arm in arm. I could almost feel the tension in Tom's body, a rigidity as he held himself in check, fighting whatever demon was possessing him. At first I wondered if it had to do with me, if I had in some way displeased him, maybe with my offer to keen for Ned Geary. But as we trudged along the rocky road, Tom put his arm around my shoulders and held me closer, so I knew it wasn't myself that was the cause of his unease.

I wished we had a place of our own to go to, where I could

rub his shoulders and ease the stiffness of his back, where I could listen to his wild talk and bring him to quiet with my kisses. Perhaps Kitty's marriage was having an effect on me, after all.

The night was warm for October, a wind from the sea bringing softness instead of the driving sleet of last week. We walked in silence for a while, Tom's steps gradually slowing as we left the Geary farmhouse farther behind. At last I ventured a word.

"Is it so very bad?" I asked softly.

I had heard Tom sigh perhaps only twice before in his life. The weight of pain was in the sigh, pain and disappointment and regret.

"There's nothing at all I can do to right something that went wrong," he said. "Terribly wrong."

I stopped to face him and saw the naked truth of his hurt. Betrayal was the worst of the sins for Tom, and in some way I saw that he had betrayed himself. The man inside the hardened shell of his political agenda was bleeding.

I put both arms around him and held him tight against me. "It can't be as bad as you're seeing it, love."

"It is that bad," he replied. "It is that bad and worse." He freed himself from my embrace and turned away.

"Come and sit with me, Tommy," I said. "Away under those yew trees. Maybe you can unburden yourself."

A grove of yews, with their soft green needles and red berries, was the most comfortable place available in this rocky place. I led Tom by the hand, and somewhat reluctantly he folded his long body down to rest his back against a trunk. He seemed ready to bolt at any moment. I settled myself close beside him on the needle-covered ground.

"I cannot tell you what happened." Tom's tone was close to belligerent, a soldier self.

"I'm not asking you to tell me. I just want to help you get over the pain you're showing."

"What has to be done will be done," said Tom. "It's not for

myself that I'm fighting." He dropped his head between his knees.

God in heaven, was it Tom who shot Ned Geary? The dreadful thought came to me unbidden. I heard my own heartbeat as I tried to stop myself from asking him.

"Look at me, Tom," I said calmly. "Would it be best for you to talk to Father Martin? Could you confess to him and pray for absolution, for whatever it is that happened?"

He shook his head. "I've done nothing to confess. What happened was an accident. I wasn't even there, but I cannot get it out of my mind."

He didn't do it. I breathed in relief. I wondered if he realized we were talking about Geary's death, in not so many words.

He did. He held out his arms to me, and I nestled against his chest. "I've never been so alone before, Margaret. So accountable. The games are over and the real war begins, and Hugh's pushing off for America. I have no other to stand with me."

"You have me," I said, and I covered his mouth with my own to take away the hurt and the loneliness. He returned my kiss in a way that he had never done before, a powerful need rising in him, the resilience of youth overcoming the blackness of death.

He buried his lips in the soft skin of my throat and pushed aside the shawl that covered my threadbare dress. His mouth found my breasts, his hands cupping their whiteness gently, his lips urgent.

I arched toward him, responding with an aching pain in my most secret place that I had never felt with any of his kisses before. There was a desperation in his seeking comfort in me that I matched in my own way, surprised. For one clear moment I thought about asking him to stop, telling him that I wasn't ready for this forward step into the future. His hands were moving down my body, stroking me, pulling my hips toward him in a way that felt so right, so natural.

"Margaret, Margaret, my love, my darling girl," he breathed.

"I'll never hurt you, you're my own sweet love."

Underneath me I could feel the strength of the earth, the sunlight and beauty stored in the dark roots of the yews to spring forth in greenness, in youth again. For an instant the dead face of Michael Dooley floated in my mind, a young man cheated of the sweetness of loving and being loved. I could not bear that Tommy might miss that too. I brought his lips up to mine again.

I guided his hand to the moistness between my legs, the first time that he had been invited. I hadn't expected the touch of his fingers to set me on fire but they did. Without further thought I opened myself to my lover, the healing bond between us forged in the blood of my body. I held Tom as he quivered and went still, a sigh escaping his lips again. He withdrew his body from mine but not his soul.

"O Margaret," he whispered. "Will you ever forgive me?"

"There's nothing to forgive, Tommy dear," I whispered back. "I love you. It was meant to be tonight, I think." I kissed him tenderly. His body was spent, his muscles relaxed. He was no longer alone.

I pulled the tattered dark wool of my skirt down over my thighs. Then I laughed, a sound that came from some deep well of joy within me. "Now we'll both have to go to confession," I said.

"We've nothing to confess. You are my wife, my own," he replied, and he kissed me again.

CHAPTER 14

STARVATION HAD COME TO KILVARNA with the winter snows. The skeletal women who foraged for nettles and greens to feed their children could find no sustenance in the frozen earth, covered as it was by an unaccustomed blanket of snow. In the night men with knives would make their way silently, in broken boots, through dark pastures in search of livestock from which to draw a pint of life-giving blood. They carried the blood home in pails, an occasional red blotch in the snow leaving a record of their mission to feed their children. Soon the horses and cattle were all brought into the farmyards at night, lest they be drained to death.

A quiet had settled over the clachan, indeed over the whole county of Clare. No dog was left alive to bark. Roosters and hens were long since gone. Children cried with the hunger in their bellies, and mothers wept at ever-increasing deaths, but those sounds grew fainter as the winter wore on.

Money from the relief works was getting even harder to come by. The committee had petitioned for another loan from the British Treasury, which was turned down as a matter of course. Collect the rate taxes from the people who owe them, they were told. That's how your poor relief should be funded. It's not the responsibility of the government to support a nation of lazy Irish beggars at the expense of hardworking Englishmen.

More families died, and paymasters across Clare were threatened by masses of starving men who held shovels and picks to work on the roads.

It was common now for us to go without food for two days at a time. Jimmy had lost his job in October when Ned Geary died, and though he had gone to see about work on another road project, he was one of hundreds clamoring for the few places on the list. He came home discouraged and bitter. Da earned eight pence a day on the relief works, but it was hard to buy enough to feed the three of us, what with the scant supply and the rising prices. Still, we were better off than many. Two days' hunger could be borne. Five or six days without a scrap could mean death to people already weakened and sick.

Down the lane the cottages were emptying. The O'Gormans had left for parts unknown, to take their chances begging. It was rumored that in the south of Ireland the farmers were able to give a handful of oats or a turnip to those who knocked at the gates, that it wasn't so bad there as in the west. Truthfully, no one in Kilvarna was sorry to see the back of Mrs. O'Gorman when she went.

As I walked past the O'Gormans' deserted cottage on my way to see Rose Mackey, the tiniest voice whispered in my mind. "A place for you and Tommy," it said. "So close to your father but alone for the two of you."

I let the precious idea swirl into my everyday organized thoughts, a sweetness in it like honey.

I stopped for a moment, peering in the doorway. The dirty straw of the O'Gormans could be swept out, the rats chased off with a stick. An old iron kettle stood on three legs over the charred hearth, surprisingly not taken away to be sold. I looked up at the thatch above and thought it seemed sturdy enough. We would have all we needed. Even if we stayed just for the winter, until the land was ready to plant again. Tom could work his father's patch, and I could help with my father and Jimmy. It would be a life together.

I held my shawl close against the chill wind. A center core of happiness warmed my heart at the thought of making a home for Tom, a place where he could be at ease with himself and with me. A place where we could make love to each other in the sacredness of marriage.

When I entered old Mrs. Mackey's cottage, my heart dropped like a stone. Rose Mackey was wrapping her bowl and spoon in a bit of rag to pack into her cooking pot. Just like Nuala Lynch had done when the housewreckers were on their way to tear down her house.

"Mrs. Mackey, are you being evicted?" I cried out. "Are the housewreckers coming here too?" The vision of myself and Tommy snug in the cottage next door was ripped away.

"No, it's not the housewreckers, curse their bones," replied Rose Mackey. "Simon's wife and the baby have died, so I'm going up there for the other wee ones." She sighed, an old woman who had seen too many babies come into the world and go right out again.

I crossed myself. "God rest their souls. I'm so sorry. Was it the fever?"

"The hunger took them," Rose said. "Carrying a baby is hard when you've nothing to eat. Poor thing was barely the size of a minute when it was born, but it had taken the strength of the mother by then."

Rose looked at me with her old, wise eyes. "Your friend Kitty Shaughnessy needs watching over," she said. "Her mother's not going to last long enough to be of help."

"Kitty! Having a baby? How do you know? She never told me."

"I can see it in her face," said Rose. "Even so thin, the look is there. And she'll need more help than she can get from that Shaughnessy lad. He's done enough already."

"Why wouldn't she tell me?" I felt left out and stupid.

"Maybe she doesn't know herself. Some of the women have stopped their monthlies from hunger," said Rose. "But Kitty herself is four months' gone, I'd say." She shook her head. "It's a struggle bringing new life into such a harsh world."

Rose Mackey had told me something else I hadn't known. "Do you think Mrs. Dooley is slipping away, then?"

"I do, poor dear. She can hardly rise from her bed, and her legs are swollen with the famine dropsy. She won't be with us for long." Rose pressed her lips shut in the futility of protest.

"What shall I do about Kitty?" I still missed my own mother.

"What can any of us do to help the other?" sighed Rose Mackey. "Do as you are able—and with God's grace the spring will come."

The old woman put her hand on my arm. "Shouldn't you be thinking of getting married yourself?" she asked. "You'll be having a warmer winter with Tom Riordan inside the house than out."

I blushed to my toes. Did the whole of Kilvarna gossip about Tom and me?

"We haven't talked to Father Martin yet," I said.

"It will not come as a surprise," Rose said with a smile. "Would it be a surprise to Tom himself?"

My face got hot. "He's happy to marry me, without a dowry at all. But where we would live is a trouble."

"The pair of you can live here, if it suits," offered Rose. "At least until Speke knocks it down."

"In your own cottage? Oh, no, we couldn't impose on you." I declined the offer, as I knew I must. Mam had brought me up to be polite.

"There's nothing left here but the bare dirt floor," Rose replied. "Sure you're welcome to it."

"We couldn't take such advantage of your hospitality," I said again formally. I wondered if she could see the longing in my eyes, the wish to create a life of some happiness.

Rose laughed. "The rent hasn't been paid this year, has it? The place is no more mine than yours at present. A beggar from the road has as much right to it."

I let a grin spread over my face. "I'd much prefer to start my married life here than in that rat-ridden cottage next door. Here I'll have the memories of you close by."

"And I'll not feel so saddened at leaving the place behind, my dear. Should Mr. Speke come to collect the rent, your great strong lad can toss him into the dung heap." She picked up her bundle and looked around her little house one last time.

"Tell Nuala Lynch where I've gone, won't you? She's another I'll never lay eyes on again."

"She doesn't leave the tomb at all. I visit every day, but her strength is going fast. Each day I fear what I'll find."

"A keener fearing the dead? Now that's a queer thing," said Mrs. Mackey, her affectionate tone softening the words.

"I love her," I explained. "And I still have so much to learn. I wish she could live forever."

"Not any of us will do that," replied Rose, as she stepped through her door for the last time. "But take what joy you can. It's hard enough to come by."

As soon as Rose Mackey left, I tore over to Kitty's cottage. The door was shut against the cold, and I didn't pull it open as I would have in earlier days. It was a house of life and a house of death now.

"Kitty!" I called out. "Kitty, are you inside?"

The weathered wood door cracked open and Kitty's drawn face peered out. Her red-brown hair was lank and tangled, but her eyes brightened at the sight of me.

"Oh, Margaret, come in, come in. Mam has been bad, and I haven't been over to see you for ages."

A sour sick odor met my nose. I looked around the cottage and saw nothing in it but two pallets of straw and a pail. The wooden stools and the table were gone, burned for firewood or sold for food. Mrs. Dooley lay curled in her shawl on one of the pallets, her exposed legs swollen to twice their normal size. The darkened skin looked as if it would burst.

"She doesn't even hear us anymore," said Kitty quietly. "She said she was going away to join Michael and that's the last we heard from her lips." Kitty's own lip trembled but she bit it hard to stop.

"This is so hard," I whispered to her, putting my arm around her waist and laying my cheek against her hair. Poor comfort, when what was needed was money and food. Those were not in my power to give.

Kitty held my palm against the slight swell of her belly. "Have I told you my news?" she asked. "There's a Shaughnessy on the way."

"Is it true, then? Mrs. Mackey thought that might be the case."

Kitty smiled. "Jackie will be a proud man when I tell him."

"Jackie doesn't know, either?" I felt much better. When we were girls we shared every secret, and it was hard to give Kitty over to a husband.

"He's looking for work and until he finds it, I won't tell him there's another mouth to feed. Truth be told, I don't know how we're going to get through another week this way." Kitty's smile was replaced by a pinched fearfulness. She looked over toward where her own mother was starving before her eyes and cupped her palm over her belly, as if the unborn child could see.

"If only Jackie could get on the relief list. I don't know what made Mr. Speke take against me so bad that he won't even give him a chance."

I stared at Kitty. "I'm thinking it might have something to do with a certain hammer."

"People are attacking the foremen and stewards every day," Kitty replied. "Why should he grudge me for so long?"

"Grudges live longer than men."

"Oh, you sound as old as Nuala Lynch," said Kitty. "Surely Speke will forgive and forget if I tell him how sorry I am that it happened, such a long time ago when I was crazed with grief for my brother."

"I don't think—"

Mrs. Dooley gave a low groan from the floor where she lay. She struggled to raise herself up and fell back again in weakness. Kitty went to kneel beside her, stroking her forehead tenderly. "Don't cry, Mam," she whispered. "Everything will be all right again, soon it will."

I could see the shiny skin on Bridie Dooley's legs split in a dozen small tears, oozing liquid from the waterlogged flesh. Surely it must be painful. I felt a sudden urgency to put my hands on Nuala Lynch, to assure myself that the old keener was still alive. I had no food to bring her, or to give to Kitty either, but at least I could keep her company.

"I'll come by tomorrow again," I said. "And your mam will have my prayers. Now Nuala Lynch is waiting for me up the hill."

Kitty nodded absently, her attention distracted. Maybe she was trying to think of some way to keep her mother and her unborn baby alive. I wished I could be of more use.

Kitty lost the battle for her mother. Two days later Bridie Dooley was dead. No wake was held, no keen was sung. Jackie borrowed a wheelbarrow to carry his mother-in-law's body to the cemetery, her shawl around her as a winding-sheet. Father Martin conducted a funeral service in the snow for seven souls from Kilvarna, all dead together and laid gently into a single large grave. I stood there shivering and wondering how Mrs. Dooley would feel about her bones mixing with the McGraths and the O'Hares. But no one had strength to dig seven separate holes in the frozen earth. As the hungry weeks wore on, dignity and personal pride became concerns of the past.

◎ ◎ ◎

Tom and I stood in the doorway of Rose Mackey's empty cottage, the cold hearth awaiting new turf and a new family. Tom had been pleased by Mrs. Mackey's kind offer. But I could sense there was something else on his mind.

He ran his fingers through his hair, as he did when he was agitated.

"I've got to make one thing clear, Margaret," he said. "Married life cannot be allowed to interfere with my political work." He sounded out the words as if he had rehearsed them.

"I'm not trying to trap you, Tom, or tie you to my apron strings," I said. "Haven't I always supported your activities? Didn't I make the warning notice for Edward Speke myself?"

Tom looked uncomfortable. With great attention he bent over to brush the dirt off the knees of his trousers.

"Marriage would be a fine thing, Margaret," he said. "No one is dearer to my heart than you are. But I'm not as reliable as I would wish to be, owing to the state of things in the country. I need to be free to go where and when I'm called."

"That's understood," I replied. When had it been any different?

"I cannot promise you a tenant cottage of our own, not even a potato patch in these times."

"I know that," I said. "No one can promise anything for the future. I'm not expecting it." I made an attempt to keep my tone light. "But I love you, and I thought that you loved me." An uncontrollable quiver found its way into my voice. What had come over him?

Tom turned his face to me. "Are you thinking that I don't love you? How could you come to such a daft idea? The sun rises and sets on you, in my eyes."

I looked at the ground. "You don't want to marry me," I whispered.

Tom enveloped me in his arms, crushing me against his old jacket. "I do, I do," he said. "These aren't normal times, is all I meant."

"I have no dowry. And I have to look out for my brother and my da, even when I'm your wife," I said, needing his acceptance of my least desirable features.

"I thought you had a dowry of twenty cows to bring with you! The deal's off then," said Tom.

The world was bright again. "If I did have twenty cows, you don't have the grass to keep them. I'd have to look for someone else myself."

"You won't," said Tom as he leaned down to kiss me. "You won't." Then he released me for a moment so I could breathe. "Sunday next will be the day? I suppose I'd best see Father Martin myself. It's been a long month of Sundays since I've been to Mass."

"Nothing will change, Tommy," I said, my brow creasing with worry again. "You'll still be free. But we'll be together—"

"And stronger together than ourselves alone," Tom replied.

He began to cover my face with tender kisses, nibbling at my ear, gently pushing me up against the far wall of Mrs. Mackey's cottage, away from view of the single window. I returned his caresses with passion, dizzy with wanting him, the desire of my body and my soul.

CHAPTER 15

THE MAIN ROADS TO ENNISTYMON and Kilfenora were crowded with the dispossessed, chalk-faced stick figures with nothing but the clothes half-falling from their wasted frames. They walked and stumbled along the icy ways, calling out for food and help to any passerby. The children were silent as they trudged alongside their elders, small beings with oversized heads and deep-sunk eyes. Like a race of aliens they covered the countryside, resting in ditches and under bridges, every step bringing them closer to the day when they could not get up again.

Bodies along the roadside were savaged by rats, which grew plump on human flesh. Stories were told of poor unfortunates who were attacked in their cottages by the vicious creatures, their limbs devoured as they lay ill and dying. It made it all the harder to eat the white meat of the rat when we were able to trap one. Wild dogs too were surviving on the dead. An outsider had remarked to Father Martin that the stray animals in Clare looked healthier than the people. Gently, he said, he had explained the reason—the eaters of carrion were thriving in a land of plenty.

◎　◎　◎

Kitty Shaughnessy averted her eyes from the ditches as she walked the two miles to Edward Speke's office inside the main gate of the landlord's estate. She had made an effort to tidy herself, running wet fingers through her tangle of hair, splashing the frigid water on her face and neck until she shivered. She was requesting a meeting with Mr. Speke on the subject of work for Jackie, without which they would surely starve.

The agent's office was the room off the side of the stone barn. Kitty knocked on the door, wishing in her heart that she did not stand there. Begging from that devil Speke was the last thing she wanted to do.

"Enter!" called out a man's voice.

She barely had the strength to pull the heavy door open. She slipped inside and pressed her back against the door, momentarily dizzy from the warmth of the room. Speke had a fine turf fire in the hearth, with oak chairs drawn up in front of it for comfort. He sat behind a long table covered with papers and bound books, and when he glanced up at her, his face went from white to red.

"What are you doing here?" His voice was not the screaming rage that Kitty had last heard. Indeed it was absent any inflection at all.

"Beg pardon, Mr. Speke," Kitty began. "I've come about a job on the roadworks—"

He cut her off with a gesture. "Certainly we've had this discussion before, and with poor results. Your brother is still dead, I presume?"

Kitty flushed hot and controlled herself with effort. "I am sorry, sir, about that day, I am truly sorry. I was mad with grief—"

"And today you would ask me for a job? When I've got two hundred men who are lolling about on the works, drawing a week's relief for ten minutes of labor a day?"

Kitty shook her head and approached the table. The warmth from the fire was seductive. It had been so long since she had been warm.

"Not for myself, for my husband," she said. "Jackie Shaughnessy, from up the Burren. We have no food, and no work since Mr. Geary's death. My mother has died of the hunger." She drew a breath and decided to ask outright. "I was hoping your honor could find a place for Jackie."

"We have no places," replied Speke. He looked at the young woman standing before him, her demeanor of supplication and weakness. She was a comely bitch, thin as she was. He wondered how far she was willing to go to stave off her hunger. He could feel the hunger of another kind rising in his blood.

"Why don't you take a seat by the fire, and we'll discuss the matter between us," he invited, in a softer voice.

Kitty was drawn to the chair by his offer. So near the hearth that her toes tingled from the heat.

"We have no place for a man," Speke continued. "But you and I could come to a different arrangement, I think."

It took a moment for Kitty to grasp his meaning. She started to rise from her chair.

"A bag of oats and another of cornmeal," Speke said quickly. "That should hold you for a while." His breathing was audible in the small room.

Kitty slowly sat down again. Enough food to have kept her mother from starving, to keep her and Jackie and the baby in her womb alive until Jackie could find work elsewhere.

"It's no more than other women have done," he whispered. "And none so beautiful as you, my Irish witch."

Kitty swallowed the lump in her throat and forced herself to sit still.

"My husband would kill you if he found out," she said.

"You'll never tell him, will you? A wild kitty like you needs a real man once in a while, a man with something worth the trouble."

Speke was becoming surer of his bargain now. He leaned over to put his hand on her knee.

Kitty instinctively pulled away from his touch. Speke said nothing, moved not a whisker. He had seen this struggle before. After a long minute, deliberately, the girl leaned back in the chair and turned in his direction. "Each bag to hold a full stone's weight," she said firmly. It was all she could carry.

"I'll bring them now," replied Speke, trying to hide his eagerness. They always wanted to see the money first. He rose and went out the door to fetch the sacks from the barn.

Kitty leaped up from the chair, ready to bolt. It was one thing to agree to a bargain, another to complete it. She felt sick and overheated and famished with hunger, and not a little afraid. Jackie really would kill Speke if he discovered her sinful transgression. But Jackie and the wee one in her belly would die with her if she didn't find some food.

A quick poke from Speke and no one would ever know, she promised herself. She could tell Jackie that she had walked to Ennistymon and begged at the market fair. He wouldn't have wanted her to do that either, but he would be glad of the food.

Her heart was beating fast when Speke shoved two meal bags in the door ahead of him. She wondered how long the act would take. With Jackie it was over in a few minutes, before she felt much of anything.

Speke turned around and let down the heavy crossbar to latch the door.

"I've dreamed of this day," he whispered in a strange soft voice.

Apprehensive, Kitty clenched her teeth together. Was this the Speke she had attacked with a hammer, whose eyes she had tried to scratch out with her fingers? He approached her like a wolf circling its prey, his eyes gleaming and a bulge growing in the front of his riding breeches. She backed away slightly.

"You bitch, you dirty little bitch," he muttered. He reached out with both hands and grabbed her breasts through her blouse, surprised at the fullness of them for such a slim creature. He opened her blouse and stroked the white skin, dark chunky nipples inviting his mouth to bite. Holding her to him with a broad hand strong against her shoulder blades, he squeezed her breasts together until Kitty cried out for him to stop. In reply he bit her, hard, on her left breast. "Don't whine at me," he said. "Do exactly what I say, or you'll go home empty-handed." Kitty flushed with fear and shame.

"Get down on your knees," he ordered. "On all fours, you filthy papish whore." Kitty obeyed, her mind unable to absorb the vicious abuse he hissed into her ears. She tried to focus her mind on the reason for this violation of her body—the food. She tried to imagine herself anywhere else but in this room, with the man Speke kneeling behind her.

Speke unbuttoned his breeches. He leaned down and tossed her skirt up over her head, exposing her naked buttocks. Kitty began to shake, on her hands and knees, her hair streaming over her face.

"Not as dirty as I thought you would be," he said. "But still filthy." He caressed the curve of her bottom with his hand, spreading her legs wider, and then slapped her, hard. Kitty's tears ran down her face silently and dripped onto the floor.

In a low hissing voice Speke cursed her for a bewitching temptress, for leading him into this necessary sin, this God-fearing punishment of her excesses. He entered her from behind, like a dog, and with every thrust he filled her ears with abuse, words she had never known existed. For a time that seemed like forever he pounded into her, grinding her hips against him, in a fury of rage and loathing and desire.

When he withdrew, Kitty started to draw a shaky breath, in relief that it was over. Then her breath twisted into a shriek of pain as Speke drove himself into her other opening, tearing into her shameful hole where no man should be. Two thrusts and she felt him explode inside her, holding her tight so she wouldn't collapse on the floor.

"Fucking bitch," he said. "Your virgin arse is bleeding like a stuck pig."

When he released her she fell forward, bumping her chin on the hard floor. She lay immobile, unable to get up. The lower half of her body throbbed with pain. She couldn't even cover her nakedness.

Speke gave a deep and satisfied sigh. The girl had been worth it and more. He'd expected her to put up more of a struggle, but perhaps she was saving that for next time. Two stone of meal wouldn't last a month, and then his wild kitty would come crawling back for more.

He tucked himself back together. "Get up now," he said. "Take your pay and get out."

Kitty pulled herself upright by hanging on to the oak chair. She closed her blouse and wrapped herself in her shawl. She didn't look at Speke but kept her eyes on the door, where two cloth bags of meal awaited her exit.

The landlord's agent lifted the crossbar and kicked the door open.

Moving awkwardly, Kitty picked up a bag in each hand and staggered out. Slowly, excruciatingly, she made her way over the cold fields to her home.

CHAPTER 16

ON SATURDAY JACKIE CAME TO tell me that Kitty was too unwell to come to the wedding tomorrow. She had sent a bridal gift, a cup of oatmeal, which Jackie said she got by begging at the fair.

"It took too much out of her," Jackie said, shaking his head. "She does nothing now but lie on the straw. She misses her mam, I'm thinking."

"Would it do her any good to see me, do you think? I could sit with her for a while." I wondered why she hadn't told me she was going begging. Maybe she was ashamed.

"She doesn't want to see anyone. Even you, Margaret. That's not like our Kitty. But there it is."

After Jackie left, I tried not to feel disappointed that my own dearest friend would not celebrate with me at my wedding. But I knew the secret that she was carrying in her body, and I would not ask more of her for the world.

Tom Riordan and I stood up in front of Father Martin on that winter Sunday to be married in the eyes of the Church. In truth, I felt as if I were Tom's wife already. We had cemented the bond of our love in many ways throughout this difficult year. Our wedding was more of an outward gesture to the community in Kilvarna. With all my heart I wished that my mother and Nuala Lynch were there—but one was in the grave and the other in a tomb.

Dear old Rose Mackey had made the journey down from her son's hilltop cottage. Our marriage was an affirmation of hope for the future, she had told me, as she hugged me outside the church doors before Mass.

I didn't feel like a bride when I entered the church on this dark day of winter. The stone chapel was cold and damp, the congregation smaller than it had been a year ago. So many faces missing, so few children. The summer roses that had brightened Kitty's wedding did not by some miracle appear for mine.

But when I looked into Tom's eyes and promised to be his wife forever, I felt a rightness that transcended mortal connection. We were together, and we would never willingly part. His eyes shone back at me with a happiness that was all too rare in showing. I pledged him my life and my love forever.

After Mass our friends and family gathered around, wishing us all the health and prosperity that heaven could allow—and that Ireland could support. The weather was too bad to stand out in, so after a little while Tom and I walked hand in hand to Mrs. Mackey's cottage. Tom's mother had brought in a supply of turf for a fire and a woolen blanket that would warm our marriage bed.

I stirred Kitty's gift of oatmeal into a porridge—a wedding feast that the two of us ate from the pot, sitting close together in front of the hearth. Tom showed all the signs of launching into a serious discussion of the establishment of soup kitchens by Quakers who had come to the aid of the Irish people—until I put my finger to his lips.

"Hush, it's your wedding day," I whispered. "We'll not have another to spend like this. Leave the soup kitchens to boil on their own, for once."

Tom's protest died unspoken, I think, when he realized that his new bride was right.

◎ ◎ ◎

The following afternoon I carried fresh water and a bit of porridge up the hill to the wedge tomb, anxious as always for Nuala's health. The old woman was wasting away, her fingers so thin that the bones could be counted on each one. But still she gripped her life about her.

Nuala's face lit up when I crouched down to enter between the sheltering stones. "A visit from Mrs. Riordan, is it?" she asked with a dry chuckle.

"I don't know how I'll get used to the name." I crawled over to sit beside Nuala in the tiny space. "But I'm not finding the husband any trouble at all."

Nuala smiled. "An easier life than the present one is what I had wished for you, Margaret Meehan-that-was," she said. "The shadow of death hangs over the land."

As she gazed at me, her sight turned inward, to a place filled with ghostly shades. "I will not be here myself much longer," she said. I started to shake my head but Nuala stilled me with a look. "And I don't believe that you will, either, my dear. You'll not follow me but go your own way, far from the hills of Clare. To a place where keeners are silent and poetry comes not from the lips but from the brittle pages of books."

I disagreed. "Life will be green again here in the spring. Why would I leave, newly married and happy? I'll carry on the keening for Kilvarna, everything you've taught me. I'll never hold a candle to you but I'll try my best."

"Time will tell the truth better than I can."

She turned to the pallet behind her and pulled out a small bundle of cloth, a strip of fabric from an old petticoat, faded dusty red. "I have no treasures to give you, save my keens, and those are yours already. But I have one other thing, which has been with me most of my life, and it's time to pass it on to you." She unwrapped the bundle and held the object flat on her palm. A rough stone, no more than two inches in length, in some way reminiscent of a woman's shape.

"The keener Ann O'Brien—the one who was so kind to me when I was a girl—received this from a woman who knew the old stories, when Ann keened for her son. The stone is from the sacred well of Brigid, down in Liscannor near Kilnaboy. Ann said it was a statue of the ancient fire goddess, not the Catholic saint, and I wouldn't be one to argue with her." Nuala put the stone into my hand. It was like nothing I'd ever seen before.

"The well is quite a place for miracles," Nuala continued. "I used to walk down there myself in earlier years. Just a low hill with a spring running down the rocks, like a thousand other holy wells in Ireland. But inspiring to the mind and the soul. Brigid is the goddess of poetry and healing, you know, and she likes a good keen as much as any mortal person."

"*Saint* Brigid was what we were taught by the priests," I said, slightly uncomfortable with the crossing of boundaries into the pagan world of old Ireland. Maybe Nuala Lynch was affected by her time in the burial tomb of kings.

"Saint Brigid would do just as well," replied Nuala. "You never can tell who is listening to the prayers, on the other side."

The stone rested comfortably in my palm, a crude shape with a bit of rounding for a head. I wondered how old it was.

"Every so many years I've taken the stone down and dipped it in the water of the well, for luck and for vision," Nuala said. "I would ask you to do the same."

"I will," I promised, without a clear understanding of why, except that I loved and honored my teacher.

"Keep it safe on your journey."

Surely she meant the journey through life, I said to myself as I tucked the stone away.

It was the truth that Nuala Lynch was failing now. I could see the otherworldliness through her skin, could hear the urgency to communicate in her quieted voice.

I set Nuala's small cooking pot on the fire near the entrance of the tomb and brought out the handful of oatmeal.

"There's no need for food where I am going," Nuala said. "Take it back for yourself. I'll not be eating it."

"What nonsense you're talking." I continued to prepare the spare meal.

When the meal was cooked, Nuala sipped it with her spoon. She sighed, and I asked her why. "I would have liked a crusty baked potato." Her old face wrinkled as she licked her lips, remembering the earthy flavor. "But it's no matter."

"You needn't come up tomorrow," she said as I backed out of the tomb's entrance on my hands and knees. "I have everything I could want. Come up the day after, and bring your husband with you."

"He's not a great donkey that I can lead around by the nose," I said with a laugh. "But I'll ask."

The rap on the door sounded sharply in the dim light of the cottage. I was kneeling in the corner of the room, to one side of the hearth, fixing up a clean and pretty place to display Brigid's stone, on a bit of evergreen. I opened the door, surprised to see my brother Jimmy, his face creased with anxiety.

"It's Da," Jimmy said. "He's down with the fever, and I don't know what to do."

"I'll come," I replied. "How long has it been?" I gathered my shawl around me.

"He came home from the works tonight with the pain in his head so bad he could hardly see. He laid down and in a while started moaning. When I touched him, he was blazing hot. That's when I thought to get you."

I tried to keep my voice calm for my younger brother. "The black fever, most likely. There's little we can do but try to keep him comfortable," I said. "It runs its course."

My brother and I walked up the lane to the cottage that I had left as a bride only yesterday. Inside, I dropped down next to my father's pallet.

"Daughter," he whispered, rousing himself. "I didn't send Jimmy to disturb you."

"I'm happy to do what I can for you, Da. Lie still and let me put a cold cloth on your head 'til you cool down." I dipped a rag in the water bucket, wrung it out, and gently wiped my father's face. He smiled briefly at me and then closed his eyes from the pain in his head.

I kept on rinsing and wringing out the cloth until my father drifted into sleep.

"Have you had anything to eat?" I asked Jimmy, half asleep in the opposite corner.

"Not since yesterday, and probably not tomorrow," Jimmy replied. "Da's wage for today can be paid tomorrow evening, and I'll walk to Ennistymon to buy cornmeal next day."

I bit my lip. We had none of the wedding-gift oatmeal left.

"The government is going to set up a soup kitchen soon, Tom says."

"I'm not taking the charity of a soup kitchen, eating out in the open like pigs in a trough," said Jimmy.

"Would you rather starve?"

"I'd rather leave this blasted place behind me altogether," said Jimmy. "I could go to Dublin or Belfast and get a job in the city."

"I'm sure that people in Dublin are starving the same as we are," I said.

"Nothing's so bad as in Clare," said Jimmy.

"But nowhere is so beautiful as Clare, Jimmy."

"I'm just telling you. Now that you're married I'm free to go where I please."

It had never occurred to me that my younger brother felt so responsible for my welfare. I reached up and patted his cheek. "I can take care of myself, and Da too," I said. "Do what you need to do. God knows you've had more than your share of troubles in your young life."

"I'm not going yet. I'll help you take care of Da while he's sick."

"Pray that it will be a mild case," I said. "I'll be back in the morning to check on him. Try to keep him cool, and get some sleep yourself."

I watched out the single window of the cottage until I saw Jackie Shaughnessy on his way down the lane in the morning, presumably to gather with the other men of Kilvarna, who went off each morning in search of a penny's work. The day was cold but not windy, which was a blessing. Tom was making a trip into Kilfenora to see some fellows there, but I didn't ask the purpose of their meeting.

I stopped in at my father's house with some fresh water. Da was a long wrinkled heap on the straw pallet, his body bathed in sweat and fever. I laid the wet rags on his forehead again, but he barely stirred. Jimmy was already gone to wherever he spent the winter days. I wished I had a bone of chicken to make some nourishing broth, but I might as well wish for the moon. Promising to return in an hour or so, I went on to Kitty's down the lane.

My knock on the door got no answer. I took the liberty of pulling open the door. As Jackie had said, Kitty was lying on a mess of straw in the corner. Was there no one standing upright in Kilvarna these days?

"Kitty! Are you ill?" I crossed the small room to where she was lying.

"Oh, it's you, Margaret." Her voice was deadened of emotion.

"That's Mrs. Riordan, thank you very much." I imitated the accent of the gentry, trying to make her smile. "I'm the mistress of my own grand house now."

Kitty didn't give even a giggle. She turned her face to the wall.

I put my hand on her shoulder. "What is it, Kitty? What's wrong? Is it the babe? Or did Jackie beat you?"

Kitty shook her head minimally. "Go on, now, Margaret. I don't want to talk to anybody." Like my mother, Kitty closed her eyes to shut out the world.

"I am not leaving until you tell me what's ailing you," I said. "There's nothing you can tell me that I haven't heard before."

But there was. And eventually Kitty told me, in a choking whisper, as I stroked her hair where she lay.

I gathered my friend up into my arms and rocked her, like a babe. Kitty's thin frame was awkward in my embrace, refusing to relax its physical vigilance even to one who loved her well. I struggled to keep a relaxed, comforting feel to my body when inside I was torn apart with rage and loathing. My head felt as if it would explode. I understood the hunger that drove Kitty to her reckless bargain. I understood the powerlessness that left her open to Speke's brutal attack. But I could not get my mind around the damage that had been done to Kitty in her private self, the raping of her hope for the future. That was the one treasure that I would never give up. I would have killed Speke with my bare hands if he took it from me.

"Jackie doesn't know, does he?" I asked the question softly, already guessing the answer.

Kitty shook her head. "He thinks I'm grieving for Mam," she said. "I haven't told him about the baby. That's why I did it, Margaret. That's why. You know that. I'm not a whore—I'm not—what he said—" Kitty rolled away from me and curled herself into a ball, as if she wanted to disappear from the mortal world.

"You are the best girl there ever was, Kitty dearest," I said.

I got up to heat some water in the kettle. The cornmeal might be covered in innocent blood but the tragedy of it would be all for naught, if Kitty didn't eat.

Quietly, in the dim light, I stirred the coarse yellow mash until it softened. Kitty lay silent on the floor.

When the gruel was cooked, I brought a spoonful to Kitty, who looked at it and retched. "I can't swallow it," she whispered.

"You have to," I said. "You have to give food to the babe." I was embarrassed at the way my own mouth watered.

"Try, Kitty, please, for the sake of the babe. It's a mother's duty to keep herself alive as long as she can." I heard my own words, and pain shot through my heart. Two motherless children, Kitty and I were. But Kitty was in the greater danger.

I held the spoon to Kitty's lips and poured in a sip of the gruel. Kitty gagged but swallowed it. I fed her the rest, sip by sip.

"When Jackie comes home, you'd better tell him about the coming baby," I said as I prepared to leave. "There's meal in the pot for him, and he'll be happy. It will make it easier for you."

Kitty nodded. "But if he wants to touch me—" she shuddered.

I smiled sadly at my friend. "Tell him not until after the baby is born. Tell him it's usual to wait, he won't know. That will give you some time to heal." How much time Kitty would need, I couldn't guess.

That night I dreamed of Nuala Lynch. Close in Tom's arms, surrounded by his love and strength, I shook off the horror of Kitty's experience to slide into a dreamless sleep. Until Nuala appeared, her bony face radiant in the moonlight. She was wearing the age of centuries, wrinkled and creased, but about her there seemed an energy of youthfulness, a beginning rather than an end.

In my dream I watched Nuala Lynch sing a keen of the utmost beauty. The words floated in liquid silver from her mouth, spiraling, molten, melding into the moonlight that bathed her form. She sang of life in Kilvarna, of the long centuries where men fished the sea and worked the land, where women bore babies and milk flowed from their breasts. Then the words turned hot and angry, flashing bursts of fire, red flame, as the old keener sang of the invasion and oppression, of murder and injustice. Her voice lost its words as she sang of the coming of starvation and destruction, of disease and death. Black inky greasy coils of smoke lingered heavily in the air around her, smelling of sulphur and rot. Nuala's eyes and mouth opened into dark pits, her hair turning to streams of bloody hanks, the flesh falling from her old bones. Still she sang the keen, willing me in my dream to listen, and to remember. The gruesome vision cleared away as Nuala's voice softened and sweetened, restoring peace to her ravaged face and a brightness to her eyes that I hadn't seen in a long time. The sound of the keen was drawn from pure love, in remembrance and in regret, in anticipation and in hope. I awoke in the dark cottage surrounded by the power and grace and wisdom that had lived in Nuala Lynch. I was unsure how long the dream had lasted, but I knew that the old keener was dead.

In the morning Tom and I brought Nuala Lynch's frail body down to the cemetery for burial. I had wished to leave her in the ancient tomb on the hill of kings, but in my practical mind I realized it would be a grievous disrespect, not only to Father Martin and the Church but to Nuala's community as well. To be buried in hallowed ground meant that on the Last Day you would rise again in the midst of your loved ones and friends. Pieces of your restored body, sanctified in eternal life, would not be rolling around in ditches or floating up from the bottom of the sea.

Father Martin made obvious his hopes that I would let him finish the committal service at the grave without interrupting with my howls of grief. No wakes were held among the poor of Kilvarna any more, and every day's Mass was a requiem for the poor souls whose names the priest knew and in general for all those he didn't. Out of more than two thousand souls in Kilvarna nearly a quarter had perished already. Father Martin spent his time comforting the dying and consigning the dead to God.

I had not the energy to battle him for control of Nuala's leave-taking. I stood with my new husband in the empty churchyard, bereft of my teacher, my mother, and my best friend. Bereft of the community who would have opened their hearts in grief and celebration of the life and death of Nuala Lynch, moved by the keen that I had always imagined I would sing.

The cemetery was mounded with fresh graves, the community of the dead, who would not hear the wail of the keen or mark its absence. With silent tongue and heavy heart, I realized that I could not keen for all of Ireland.

CHAPTER 17

THE PEOPLE CALLED IT BLACK FEVER, *fiabhras dubh*. Typhus was the name the doctors used, but naming the disease did not provide a cause or a cure.

My father was in the final throes of his agony. For nearly two weeks I had bathed him and comforted him, had listened to his wild ravings, had seen the terrible tremors of chill and fever wrack his body. Now at last he had sunk into the stupor that marked the end, his skin a darkened purplish color, his breath raspy and slow. I found myself actually praying for his release.

Tom had offered to bring him to the fever hospital, but in his lucid moments Da begged us not to take him there. It was worse than dying at home, he said. And Tom said that was true. He had seen the trenches dug behind the hospital, in the new graveyard that adjoined the workhouse. Many sufferers entered by one door and left a few hours later by the other.

On the February day that my father died, Edward Speke closed the public relief works. No more jobs for workers, no more money for food. Instead, the government planned to set up outdoor soup kitchens, a bowl of broth each day for the destitute people who could drag their bones to the distribution point. One mouthful could tell you that the soup contained too little nourishment to support human life, but it was hotly denied by government officials in the newspapers. It was left to the starving Irish to prove the point.

◎　◎　◎

Edward Speke was accompanied by four constables when he made the announcement that the relief works were closed. They stood close around him, their clubs at the ready.

Two hundred emaciated men and a few scarecrow women stared at the land agent, scarcely able to grasp the sense of the English words. Starvation had slowed their thoughts, had taken the muscles from their legs and arms and hearts.

A group of younger men began to surge forward, led by Michael Rourke. The constables stepped in front of Speke.

"You cannot stop the works!" Michael shouted. "If we get no wages, we have no food. It's murder you're doing to us, Mr. Speke."

Other men took up the chant. "Murder! Murder! Murder!" The crowd moved restlessly.

Speke spoke coldly above the noise. "Outdoor relief in the form of soup will be provided to the destitute. Without your lifting so much as a finger. You can bring your tin cans—and your bitches and pups—to the kitchen at Kilvarna next week."

"How will we live until next week, I'm asking?" A panicky voice came from the crowd.

"On your savings, or on your beggings," replied Speke.

Michael reached the area in front of Speke, clasping his shovel at his side. He had not yet raised a hand when one of the blue-coated men shoved him in the chest, knocking him back against the men behind him. Sprawling, Michael took down a handful of surprised men with him. They struggled to rise from the frozen dirt. Others moved back out of the range of those swinging clubs, shaken by the sight of big Michael

Rourke taken down with one blow. A year ago he could have laid low all four of Speke's protectors with one fist tied behind him.

"Disperse, all of you!" ordered the constable. "Go on away, or more ribs will be broken. The works have been closed and that's it."

Fellows supported Michael Rourke as he turned away from Speke, humiliated. The men left the stones as they lay, in broken heaps along the sides of the unfinished road. Snow began to fall, and the coming of spring seemed very far away.

"Did Tom Riordan's plan for Edward Speke come to nothing?" muttered Martin Griffin to Michael Rourke as they limped homeward.

"You were dead set against it, as I recall," replied Michael.

"As were the Foley cousins," said Martin in defense. "But they're both gone now, and Hugh Sweeney off to America."

"Will you attack Speke with your soup can, then?" Michael grinned at Martin, ignoring the jab of pain in his chest. His ribs might be cracked, indeed.

"I wouldn't crawl to that soup kitchen, even if Speke himself was dipping the ladle."

"But what about your mother? Aren't you the support of your family, Martin?"

Martin looked uncomfortable. "She'll have to go and take the young ones with her," he said. "I'm not drinking soup from the hand of Edward Speke."

"Maybe we should stop in to talk to Tom," said Michael.

"We should, I think," agreed Martin. "It's been too long."

Tom Riordan was alone in the cold cottage when the two men banged on the door.

"I can't do it, boys," said Tom. "I can't risk the danger to Margaret. She's losing her father and her brother, too. I'm all she has left."

Michael Rourke shook his head. "We're not suggesting you

shoot him yourself, Tommy. Just play the go-between, as you were willing to do before."

"Things are different now," said Tom.

"Speke has closed the relief works today. He says the soup kitchen will open in a week but we're all to live as beggars until then." Martin grimaced.

"I'd like to know who we'd be begging the food from," he continued. "None that live in this part of the country, that's sure."

"Jackie Shaughnessy had a nice bag of meal in his house," said Michael. "He said his wife begged it somewhere in Ennistymon. He wasn't proud of it, mind you, but then he's eating and we aren't."

No longer was it expected that a family would share all they had with another. One man's good fortune was his alone.

"Kitty is an unlikely beggar," said Martin. "She must be thoroughly desperate."

"She's going to be a mother, and she needed the food," explained Tom.

"Jackie's a lucky man, with a wife like Kitty," said Michael. "I had hopes for her myself, not too long ago. Then she cast her net for Skinnylegs Shaughnessy, and I was abandoned—"

Tom laughed. "Jackie's skinny legs are not so remarkable now, are they? We're all giving him a run for his money."

A serious look returned to Michael's face. "We came to talk to you, Tom, about Speke. Hoping you could—"

"Contact your group of friends," finished Martin.

"The problem has gone way beyond Edward Speke, or any agent for that matter," said Tom slowly. "God knows, they're shooting landlords right and left but it's not making a damn bit of difference to the starving."

Michael and Martin glanced at one another. It was not the answer they had expected from Tom.

"But a man like Speke—" began Martin.

"I hate him as much as ever I did," said Tom. "But the death of one man is not going to cure the distress of the country. We need to take the rule of Ireland back from the English."

"Small steps, Tommy, small steps," said Michael. "We can do something about Speke. How can we take back Ireland?"

Tom was dead earnest. "Band together. Armed uprisings, across the country. It's been done before but not well enough."

Michael sighed. "We'll all be dead of the hunger and no use for carrying pikes," he said. "If you want my opinion, we'd be better off if we begged for seed potatoes and plowed up our fields as usual. The blight's surely gone by now."

"That's the point, Tom," said Martin. "With Speke evicting us or starving us off our plots, we're left with no patches to plant. Speke is the problem."

"You can't see beyond your own noses," said Tom. "It takes a visionary to change the way things are."

Martin's voice quavered. "You're not a rational man anymore, Tom. You badgered us to shoot Speke all last summer, and now that we've finally agreed it's the right course, you've changed your mind. What in the name of Christ happened?"

Tom did not tell his friends the truth. The truth was split in three and only a part peeled off for them. "I'm a married man now, and that's changed the way I see things. I'm looking more for a political solution. That seems rational to me." He didn't tell them about Ned Geary, though they might have guessed. Nor did he tell them about the secret meetings with John Mitchel, whose revolutionary plans for the Young Irelanders were so close to his heart.

"What can we do, then?" asked Martin.

"What Michael said—plow your field," Tom replied. "It's better work than the public relief. And beg some seed from a farmer who hasn't eaten it all."

"I'm going to ask Kitty where she goes to beg," said Michael, trying to ease the tension among the men. "She's got the golden touch, she does."

◎ ◎ ◎

The day after our father was buried, Jimmy left for Belfast. He was fifteen years old, a tall lad with a shock of hair as blue-black as the wings of a crow. In his determination to leave behind forever the rocky West, he turned his back on the soft breezes of Clare without a flinch. Only the parting from me gave him pause, I think.

"I'm not leaving the place altogether, Margaret," he said, although I knew he was. "I'm not shipping off to America."

"I'll never find you in a big city like Belfast. You might as well be across the ocean."

"There's work in the city, that's why I'm going," he said. "And if I find nothing there, I'll go to England. The people aren't perishing on the roads in England."

"I don't blame you for wanting a better life, Jimmy, but I'll miss you dearly." I reached up to hug him, feeling the sharpness of his shoulder blades through the thin coat. On his feet he wore the old boots that had been Da's. Cracked and worn, the leather would provide better protection on the roads than most of the gaunt wanderers had.

"You might visit me in the city sometime. When Tom is a star politician and gives a speech for the crowds. I'll find you and rec- ognize you even if you're fat and old and your hair as gray as an old donkey—"

"Bite your tongue! I'll be an elegant lady with a feather in my bonnet, that's who you'd better look for." I grinned. "A huge feather."

I hugged him again. "God bless you and keep you safe, Jimmy. We've had a hard time but things will be better now.

You'll do grand work in the city, I know you will."

Jimmy blinked the tears from his lashes. "Take care of yourself, Margaret. You know," he hesitated and then went on, "I always thought you were odd to go after being a keener, but if that's what you want, I wish you all success with it." He smiled. "Just don't be keening for me anytime soon."

"I'll always keep you in my heart, Jimmy," I said, swallowing back the wail of loss that threatened to tear from my throat. Somehow I found my older-sister voice. "A letter home once in a while would be welcome."

"Would you answer me back?"

"I'll tell you all the news of Kilvarna," I promised.

"Well, then," Jimmy said, and he put one foot in front of the other on the long road.

I watched until he disappeared around the bend in the road, another piece of my life stolen away by the hunger.

Jackie Shaughnessy's voice was raised to a pitch that carried through the walls of his cottage and escaped into the silent lane of the clachan. A wild raging quality to the sound, the words inaudible, but surely none that any wanted to hear for themselves.

I was on my way out the door of my own house when I heard him. I had been going to look for the first greens of spring, a bite of nourishment if not the sweetest. But I stopped dead still at the doorstep.

Oh God, Jackie has found out about Speke.

When Kitty started screaming and crying, I knew it was true. And before I could move, the Shaughnessys' door slammed open and a mad-eyed Jackie ran out, his face contorted with fury. I shrank against my own door, afraid to put myself in the path of such rage. Tom was away until tomorrow, not that he could have stepped in front of Jackie. The man was charging like a bull.

When he was gone, I ran to Kitty's door. Kitty was crouched in the corner of the room, rocking on the floor, hugging herself with skeletal arms. An incessant shrieking issued from her lips, out of control. I watched in horror as Kitty banged her head against the wall behind her, as if to smash all consciousness from her mind. When she did it again, I rushed to cradle her head.

Kitty was in another space altogether, not showing any sign of recognizing me. There was nothing in the cottage that showed a violent fight, only the scuffed dirt on the floor and an empty meal bag, ripped in two.

I held Kitty in my arms like a hurt child. "Shhh, shhh, quiet now, darling," I crooned. "It will be all right, everything will come right again, don't be afraid."

After what seemed like an eternity, Kitty quieted, trembling. I loosened my grasp and smoothed the hair away from Kitty's face. Jackie hadn't beaten her, at least. No blood or bruises were visible.

"He found out," Kitty whispered. "He found out where I got the food, and then he made me tell him what Speke did."

I opened my mouth to ask why in God's name Kitty hadn't lied—and then realized that would do no good at all. It was all past that point now.

"I thought he was going to kill me," Kitty said. "I've never seen a man so angry—even when my father was drunk—" She shuddered and could not go on.

"He didn't blame you for it—" I began.

"Oh, but he did, he did," Kitty said, and her voice rose again to a shriek. "I know he did blame me. He thinks I'm a whore, he thinks I enjoyed it, that I betrayed him with the devil—"

I placed my hand lightly across my friend's mouth, stifling the cries. "Did Jackie say those things?"

Kitty shook her head. "No, but I know what he was thinking. He'll never come back, he'll desert me and the babe, and we'll all die anyway! My life is ruined."

"Your life is not ruined. Jackie couldn't blame you for such a tragedy—he loves you. He'll come back, Kitty." I tried to reassure the hysterical woman beside me, with a hope that I didn't feel.

"He hates me now," she said. "But he hates Speke even more."

It hadn't occurred to me to wonder where Jackie was going when he tore by me in the lane. Now, sickeningly, I knew.

CHAPTER 18

JACKIE SHAUGHNESSY'S RAGE FILLED HIS vision with red mist and his heart with black hatred. That a man like Speke could do such unspeakable violence to Jackie's own young wife, the mother of his child, the most loving of hearts, passed his understanding. Jackie wanted to tear the throat from him, to stomp on his face until he was a bloody pulp. He wanted to cut the cock and balls off the monster and stuff them down his throat. He had never felt any emotion in his young life that equaled this need for retribution.

He had no thought for the future other than finding Speke. He had no plan, no weapon of punishment other than his bare fists. Perhaps if he had stopped to think, he would have called in his brothers to help him. Five of them together were a match for any fight, and more than sufficient for a single landlord's agent taken by surprise.

But Jackie ran on alone, panting and cursing, over the fields to the Harris manor, through the pastures, seeing nothing but Kitty's tear-streaked face and deadened eyes.

He caught up to Speke near a cluster of roofless cottages at the edge of the estate.

The agent's two-wheeled trap and pony stood by the side of the road. Speke himself emerged from behind the rubble of a cottage, where he had been checking to see that the evicted tenants were not sheltering in a makeshift shanty. He was alone.

Jackie saw the man silhouetted against the gray tumbled stone, a well-fed, well-dressed man with the hooves and horns of a devil. He charged at the image, flailing his fists as he ran, weaponless.

"Fucking bastard!" he screamed. "Fucking English bastard shithole!"

Speke, instantly alert, darted behind the rubble.

Jackie continued on, his bare feet propelling him toward the target of his rage.

He leaped over the wall in front of the ruined cottage, airborne for a fraction of a moment, his arms spread wide as if flying.

In that moment Speke aimed and fired his shotgun. One barrel, then the other.

Jackie flew a little further and then settled to the ground.

Speke left the shelter of the ruin cautiously, looking about for the madman's companions, cursing himself for venturing out alone, congratulating himself on an excellent shot.

The creature lay burbling on the ground, a great spray of blood around him.

"Kitty," Jackie Shaughnessy said. With the last of his sight he focused his hatred on the figure standing above him.

And when Edward Speke heard that single gush of a name, he knew exactly who the dying man was.

Leaving Jackie Shaughnessy where he lay, Speke vaulted over the stone wall and untied the reins of the frightened pony from the hedgerow. He turned the trap back toward the estate office. He would have to send a man to fetch the constables. It was a clear instance of self-defense. The attacker, some local lad, must have been crazed by fever or by drink. Speke would swear that he had no notion of why he was the target, aside from his position as a landlord's agent. These attacks were becoming all too frequent, he would say with outrage, showing no fear.

I paced back and forth down the lane, past my cottage, past Kitty's, past the old place where my father and mother had died and my brother no longer lived, waiting for Tom to return from his meetings. I expected him back before dark, and it was now late in the afternoon. I felt a physical need to set eyes on him, to see that he remained his own strong self, before I told him the news of Jackie Shaughnessy.

Father Martin had conducted the brief service in the cemetery this noon after Jackie's body was released from the authorities. I could see the pain in his face, grief for the sad losses that Kitty had experienced in the past months and the rough future ahead of her, and for the first time I heard the deep exhaustion in his voice. I realized that the priest must feel something like my own sense of being overwhelmed by the number of deaths in Kilvarna.

Walking eased my soul, as it had my father's. Movement was better than sitting still. When I spied Tom's familiar figure trudging up the lane, I felt a soul-deep relief that he had returned to me again. But the difficulty of telling him about Jackie filled the distance between us.

When Tom had almost reached the row of cottages, I stepped into the road to greet him. He smiled at my eagerness for his company, having only been gone for two days.

"It was a grand meeting, sweetheart," he said, clasping my outstretched hand in his own. "I have so much to tell you. Such dreams for Ireland as you can't imagine—"

"Tom." I interrupted him. "I have something I need to tell you. That's why I came out."

He faced me in the deepening shadows. "What is it?"

I swallowed. "Jackie," I said. "Jackie Shaughnessy's been shot."

"Dead?" Tom knew before I nodded.

"He attacked Speke—" As soon as the words were out of my mouth, I realized I had made a mistake. How would I explain Jackie's rage against Speke without revealing Kitty's terrible secret?

But Tom didn't ask me why.

"Tell me what happened." His voice was controlled and calm.

"Jackie went after Speke for—for some reason, and Speke shot him dead. Oh, Tom, Speke left poor Jackie bleeding to death on the ground! And the coroner's inquest ruled it was self-defense. Jackie had no gun—"

"Speke shot him as he stood?"

"He said Jackie was coming at him with a rock. Said he didn't even know who he was. Jackie just appeared out of nowhere."

"What about Kitty?"

"She's lost her senses," I said. "She bangs her head against the wall and cries. I don't know what to do for her."

"Maybe the Shaughnessys would take her in."

"They're all sick with the fever. None of the brothers came down for the inquest. Not a one to protest Jackie's death."

"It's bad for Kitty, poor girl. Speke had a hatred for her already."

I didn't want to tell him the rest of the story. I bit my lip and walked a little faster.

We reached the door of the cottage. Tom reached into his pocket and pulled out half a loaf of Indian meal bread, heavy and dark.

"Go on and eat without me," he said, handing it to me. "I'm off to the Rourkes' for a bit."

Surprised, I took the bread, which was more than welcome. Tom continued on down the road. Sometimes I didn't understand him at all.

❀ ❀ ❀

"It's myself alone I'm blaming," said Michael Rourke. He looked more miserable than Tom had ever seen him.

"I was just giving Jackie a bit of a rub about Kitty, how grand a beggar woman she was, bringing home the sacks of meal. I never thought that Speke was involved in any way—" Michael's voice dropped low but he continued.

"Jackie had heard gossip about women selling themselves to Speke for food, and he thought back to the cornmeal that Kitty had begged, and I could see it in his face when he began to suspect that it might be his wife. It was an awful look." Michael locked his eyes on Tom's. "He ran away home and the next thing I heard he was dead, shot by Speke with both barrels."

Tom stared at Michael Rourke. "Fucking Speke so they could eat?" he said, as if he couldn't believe such a thing.

"Now I don't know if it's true about Kitty," Michael hastened to say.

"It's no wonder she's banging her head against a wall," muttered Tom.

Michael said nothing.

"If it's not Kitty, then it would be some other poor woman," said Tom. "The bastard has our land and our crops and now he has our women, too. I'll see him in hell before this goes any further."

"Hell is where he belongs," agreed Michael Rourke.

Tom couldn't trust anyone but himself to do it. Past history regrettably proved that. He had walked back home from the Rourkes' heavy with the imagined corpse of Edward Speke, knowing that the man still lived and breathed, knowing that he would have to be the one to end that life. Tom accepted the responsibility as a true son of Ireland. He thought of all the thousands of Irish people slaughtered by the English over the centuries, seeing their murdered faces before him. He remembered the stories of priests hanged, drawn, and quartered and the songs of rebels put to the sword or dropped from a rope. He could look around and see his own friends and family in Kilvarna starving and dying of fever and want. Yet the fattened beef cattle were still being driven from the pastures of Ireland to the markets of England, as men like Edward Speke evicted the Irish from their land.

But few men were as monstrous as Speke.

When Tom asked me for the truth about what happened to Kitty, I tried to protect her as best I could, but I was no match for him. At last he had the worst out of me, followed by the lying testimony that Speke had given at the inquest.

I had expected an outburst of anger, although I hoped Tom wouldn't blame Kitty for trying to feed her husband and unborn baby. But Tom said nothing. He sat on the dirt floor, his back against the wall, his face carved in stone. Only his foot tapped a rhythmic heartbeat in the dirt. I didn't think he was aware of the movement, any more than a cat of waving her tail. Eventually I lay down alone to sleep.

In the morning Tom was gone.

Speke went nowhere without a bodyguard. The two were seated together on the high wagon bench, the reins in the agent's hands, as they drove a load of seed potatoes to one of the outlying tenant farms. Seed potatoes, each chunk containing an eye to sprout, were as rare as gold in this part of Clare. And each week that passed, the sacks were worth a little more.

Tom Riordan watched the wagon drawn by two horses pass along the road between two dead fields. He had hoped to meet Speke alone, to inform him of his crimes and exact the retribution. Tom was not willing to shoot an uninvolved bodyguard. Speke had been responsible for too many deaths already.

Quietly he followed the wagon, keeping to one side of the stone walls that divided the plots. The sun was warm on his back, and death seemed far away.

The wagon slowed as the team hauled its heavy load up a long hill. The bodyguard jumped down onto the road to lighten the load. An instant later, Tom was behind him, pressing the barrel of the gun into his back.

"Laddie, this is a good time for you to answer nature's call," whispered Tom in his ear. "Go on off into the brush to take a piss. And shake it good before you come out." He gave him a push with the barrel.

The man turned in surprise to look at Tom, recognized his lucky day, and sprinted toward the side of the road without a glance at Speke.

Speke, grasping the situation, touched his whip to the horses to urge them on. But an uphill pull was not going to provide his escape route. He stood on the board and swung the whip, handle first, in Tom's direction.

Tom felt the lethal handle whistle by his cheek.

Speke grabbed the shotgun from under the seat. The jouncing of the wagon skewed his first shot. As the horses slowed, Tom climbed up to pull the man down. With all his force Speke drove the gun butt toward Tom's skull, but he overbalanced and tumbled onto the dirt. The shotgun fired itself as it hit the ground.

Tom heard the blasts and thought of Jackie Shaughnessy, blown to shreds with that same gun, by that same man.

He picked up the spent weapon and before he knew it he had hurled it low at Speke, cracking him in the shins, bringing him down.

Speke rolled over and began to crawl under the wagon.

Tom hauled him out by the boots and kicked him onto his back. Speke twisted away, his two legs broken. Pain and fear and anger raged for control of the man.

"This is a face-up job," Tom said, bringing out the pistol from the waistband of his trousers. He looked Speke straight in the eyes. "For your crimes against the people of Clare, you deserve to suffer. For what you did to Kitty Shaughnessy, you deserve to burn in hell. But I'll leave that torment to God. May he have mercy on your black soul."

Edward Speke opened his mouth to cry out. Tom leaned forward and put a bullet into his forehead.

When the bodyguard came out of the brush, the smell of singed flesh and gunpowder still hung in the air. He had taken a very long time shaking the drops.

Tom headed immediately to Michael Rourke's cottage, through the fields and over the stream. None observed his passage. The land was silent, deserted.

Michael and his younger brother were listlessly working the soil at one side of their potato patch, breaking up the clots. Without seed to plant, the labor seemed pointless. When Tom appeared, Michael abandoned his spade and left his brother to it.

"Jesus, you look like you've seen a ghost," said Michael.

"I've created a ghost," said Tom. "God forgive me, but I had to do it."

"Speke?"

Tom nodded. "It's over. There was a bodyguard, but I don't think he'll cause any trouble."

"You didn't shoot him too?"

"No, I did not, Michael," replied Tom. "I'm not a bloody murderer." Tom's voice caught for a moment.

"If anyone asks, I need you to say I was here with you this morning. All morning."

"Of course you were," said Michael.

"What about Paddy, down there with the spade? Will he tell?"

"He won't. He's near dropping with the hunger as it is. One morning is the same as the next to him, poor boy."

"Give me a spade, and I'll work with him for a while," said Tom. "So he'll remember."

Tom and Michael and the twelve-year-old Paddy chopped at the dirt with their spades under the early spring sun, a familiar motion and comforting in its way. Tom wished he had been able to take one of the bags of seed potatoes from Speke's wagon to plant in this earth. But that crop would have sprouted as the marker of death.

CHAPTER 19

THE NEWS OF SPEKE'S KILLING spread quickly through Kilvarna and beyond. I went to see Kitty, who had not come out since Jackie was laid to rest. She sat on her straw pallet, her belly swollen with the child, her mind in another place entirely.

"Speke's dead, Kitty," I told her, trying to reach through the haze. "Someone shot him this morning. He won't be a danger to you any more."

"Dead?" muttered Kitty. "The devil doesn't die. He sits there in the corner and whispers to me."

I stared. "Did you hear what I said, Kitty? Edward Speke, the man, is dead. Shot dead."

Kitty dragged her gaze up to my face. "Michael's dead. Mammy's dead. Jackie's dead. The devil is not dead."

"Don't be so daft, Kitty!" I said. "Come back to yourself, for God's sake." I was frightened, not only by Kitty's odd response, but for Tom. He had left sometime early and wasn't back yet.

"Have you anything to eat, Margaret?" asked Kitty plaintively. "I've never been so hungry. It's the baby that takes all my food."

"No, I haven't a scrap. I'll go and see what I can find." For my friend, I tried to put kindness and calm into my voice.

"Don't go to Mr. Speke," advised Kitty. "He's been shot."

I left the cottage wanting to scream. In my heart I began a keen for Kitty, who so clearly was leaving this world behind.

◎   ◎   ◎

By late afternoon I was beside myself with worry over Tom. I dared not ask anyone if they had seen him, not wanting to draw attention to his whereabouts. Wherever that might be.

I wondered if he had fled to the south. But he wouldn't leave me without a word.

I worried that he had been taken by the constables. But Tom was too smart to be caught, if indeed it was he who shot Speke. Unless Speke had wounded him first. I couldn't bear to think of Tom lying hurt in the woods, or worse, in a government jail.

When I heard his step upon the path I leaped to the door and pushed it open.

Tom entered the house in silence, his feet coated with the dirt of the potato patch. Without saying a word he took a pistol from under his coat. My eyes opened wide. I hadn't seen Tom armed before. Then it was true.

"This can't be found here," said Tom.

"I'll take care of it. Give it to me." I spoke before I thought. But Tom was my husband and I loved him.

He handed me the gun. It was weightier than I had expected. Putting it down carefully on our bedding, I tore a square from the old blanket and wrapped the weapon.

"I'll be gone a moment." Hiding the package under my shawl, I walked up the lane to my father's deserted cottage, the home of my childhood. Around the back I shoved the wrapped gun deep into the thatch of the roof. Short of a fire or a house-wrecker, it could stay there without notice.

"I've been spading earth with the Rourkes all day," said Tom on my return.

"I can see by your feet where you've been," I replied carefully.

"The field would be ready to plant next month if there were any seed potatoes to be had."

"Shall we dig up the patch that was my father's lease?"

"What's the use of it?" asked Tom. "Speke dead or alive doesn't matter. We'll plant no crops this year. Just corpses."

I had no answer. But I would never sit there and starve while there was a breath in my body. I knew that.

Hundreds of people mobbed the soup kitchen when it opened in the middle of March. Two deep iron kettles, wider than you could get your arms around, were installed in an outbuilding near the Kilvarna chapel, across from the graveyard. The kitchen workers, protected by guards, prepared the almost-meatless soup from a recipe approved by the British government. It was meant to be nourishing and tasty, but it was neither. Still, it was all we had. Along with a quart of soup, each man received a small piece of rough bread. Women and children got less.

The sick stood in line with the starving, trampling over the muddy graves of those who had gone before them. Fever, dysentery, and hunger had laid waste, and, in the face of such suffering, horror had turned to apathy. Entire families were gone, and few had the energy to inquire after them. Mothers who had prided themselves on neatly swept cottages and healthy infants now waited for a cup of thin gruel to bring home to their dying children, whose louse-ridden, sore-encrusted bodies had not the clothes to cover them. Their cottages were ankle-deep in the filth produced by sickness, the air heavy with its stench.

I waited with the others, faint with hunger and anticipation. I had half-dragged Kitty out of her door. Only by coaxing her with the promise of a bowl of hot soup was I able to get her to move.

Kitty was a ghost girl, a shadow of her self, a stick figure with a round belly. She moved between reality and another place without seeming to notice the difference. I had seen starving people slip into a famine madness before they died. And I had seen the hallucinations brought on by the black fever. Kitty, however, had her own particular world that tormented her. I didn't know how to help. But when I had food, Kitty had food.

The crowd pressed around us and began to move forward to the feeding area, like cattle to the trough. The first group had finished their meal, gobbling the thin soup from spoons chained to the tables outside the kitchen. Men carried away the soup in tin cans, ashamed at their necessity, desperate to provide for their families.

For two hours Kitty and I waited our turn.

"I'm so hungry," Kitty would whisper, like a child herself. The crowd was strangely silent, dully patient. The fire of life had gone out of them. Children wailed and people coughed, but there was little conversation.

"Soon, soon," I would reply. I stroked Kitty's hair, trying to comfort her.

When at last our bowls were filled, we took our places at the table. Kitty tore into the dark bread, swallowing the chunk so quickly she almost choked. I watched a mother at the next table break off a small piece of her bread, chew it carefully, and then take it from her mouth. She fed the softened bread to the infant on her lap, like a mother bird. How hard it must be not to swallow it herself. What love there was in that spittle-moistened bread.

I drank the grayish soup, which would never have met my mother's standards for edible food. In the old days a soup like this would have been thrown to the pigs. It was hard to feel gratitude to the government for a broth flavored with resentment, hard to ignore the decisions that had brought us to this low point. For a moment I thought I might vomit, having filled a stomach so long empty. I took a deep breath and steadied myself. Hundreds of hungry people waited behind me, so I took Kitty by the arm and moved along. The kitchen workers were close at hand to wipe the bowls and spoons with soggy cloths, readying them for the next shift of eaters.

Day after day, I hauled Kitty to the soup kitchen. Still Kitty grew thinner, and her hair began to fall out. I braided it for her, trying to slow the loss, and was shocked at the flimsiness of the braid. Kitty had had such a beautiful tangle of auburn curls.

Tom refused to take charity from the government he despised. I didn't know what he ate or where. In my married life there was no communal meal of potatoes and buttermilk eaten around the hearth. Tom spent days at a time down in the town of Ennis, where the political men met. And where a small undercurrent of rebellion gathered momentum.

In the dark of our cottage at night, Tom shared the plans and dreams for Ireland with me, trusting me with his life. When his coat was covered in sticky black blood, I washed it in the stream, without asking whose blood it was. I held him in my arms to drive away the nightmares with my power.

"It's hard to rouse the men to action when they can't raise their own heads from the straw," explained the fellow from Miltown Malbay. The small room behind the pub in Ennis was dark and crowded with men. Tom Riordan knew many of them by sight, if not always by name.

"Surely not every Irishman is dying," said the man from Dublin. He had been sent across the country to Ennis to talk to the boys of the West about their support for a revolution. What he had seen in two days was appalling. Dublin was bad but Clare was hell.

"Those that aren't dying are emigrating," another man added. "It's not the wild geese flying—it's the sitting ducks sailing." Only a couple of short laughs applauded his crack.

The Dubliner turned to Tom. "Riordan, are you with us for the fight? Will your men rise if they're called?"

"We've less than half the number we had a year ago, but our hearts are twice as strong," replied Tom. "We're with you."

"Good man!" said the Dubliner. "John Mitchel himself told me that there were men in Clare and Limerick and Tipperary who will never rest until our nation is free. The sons and the grandsons of '98, the Young Irelanders of today! We need your brave souls, your guns at the ready, when the time comes for action." In this room of patriots his speech was not heard as political rhetoric but as sacred truth.

"We've had rumors that the French may join us," said Tom.

The recruiter slapped his hand down on the newspaper he had brought with him from Dublin. "It's written in the *Nation*, right here, by Mitchel's own hand. But Ireland can't depend on the help of others—the French have promised before. It's our own brave boys whose blood and courage will bring Ireland out of slavery—"

Whistles and cheers interrupted his speech. The men of the West felt connected again to the heartbeat of Mother Ireland.

The fever spread through the families of Clare at an even greater rate as the spring bloomed. When I heard that Tom's family was sick, I walked out to the Riordans' cabin to see if there was anything I could do. I had no food to bring with me but at least I could help in comforting the children.

My mother-in-law met me at the door of the house before I could even knock. Her shrunken figure filled the open half-door with a sad presence.

"I can't let you in, Margaret. You're not to cross the threshold."

"What have I done?" I asked, taken aback. "I was always welcome here before."

Mrs. Riordan managed a twist of a smile. "Tom made me promise. He said you're not to come in. We've got the fever and the looseness, and it's better for you to stay out."

"That's ridiculous. I could be of some help to you all." I moved forward to pull the door open. Tom was not going to dictate where I could go and where I could not.

"No, Margaret," repeated Tom's mother.

"But I nursed my own father and didn't get sick—"

"You're blessed indeed. There's not one of us spared." She turned to look over her shoulder into the fetid dimness of her house, where her family lay on the dirt floor spattered with diarrhea and clots of bloody mucus. The attacks were so frequent and violent that they had no time to run outside, even if they had the strength.

"Can I bring you some fresh water, or rinse out the clothes for you? What can I do to help?"

Mrs. Riordan shook her head. "We're praying for the mercy of the Lord. It's in His hands now."

I saw the wince of a spasm of pain on my mother-in-law's face. It would be cruel to keep her standing there in the doorway.

"Take care of my son," Mrs. Riordan said. "Tell him to stay away from here too."

"I'll pray for you all," I replied.

"Maybe you'll keen for us all," said my mother-in-law.

I wasn't sure whether it was a request or a comment. I walked back the way I had come, sad and frustrated and bitterly angry at the world that had brought us to this.

Within a week the Riordan family was gone. Only Danny survived the terrible contagion, for some reason known only to God. He appeared at the cottage door one morning, haggard and weak, the bearer of news that no one should have to hear.

Tom swallowed and went silent. He stood without moving.

I couldn't keep my voice to myself. "Oh no, tell me no, it's not true," I wailed. Hearing the grief, I clapped my hand over my mouth, gagging the sound, muffling the keen.

I wrapped my arms around Danny, so like his older brother but so wasted. "You'll stay with us," I said. "We'll be all right. We will." I would make them be all right.

The men looked at one another, brothers in loss and in pain. Danny straightened his frail body to match Tom's soldierly posture. "Thank you, Margaret," he said. "I'll cause you no trouble."

I thought the best I could do right now was to leave them alone to share their grief. They would not show it while I watched. I myself would walk up to the ancient tomb in the meadow, where the remembered voice of Nuala Lynch might join with mine in keening for one more Kilvarna family.

CHAPTER 20

ON A MILD DAY IN APRIL Kitty's baby was born. The little girl came into the world with a dead father and a seventeen-year-old mother crazed with hunger and sorrow.

When I held the tiny creature in my arms, wrinkled and streaked with blood, my heart eased a bit. For months I had been sick with fear that Kitty would not stay alive long enough to deliver the baby. Mrs. Sweeney, who had come to help with the birth, seemed less certain of success.

"Go and see if Father Martin is in his house, Margaret. This child needs baptizing today. If he's not there, I'll do it myself."

"Is she that weak?" Such a small one, so thin. More like a skinned rabbit than a baby.

"Better safe than sorry, I'd say." Mrs. Sweeney bent over Kitty to wipe her face with a wet rag. Kitty lay exhausted on the straw. The pain of childbirth seemed to have added itself to the great weight she held tight inside.

I took a few minutes to straighten the cottage before setting off to find the priest. As I carried in an armful of fresh straw to replace Kitty's soiled bedding, I felt a bubble of hope rise in my chest. Some day, when the hunger was over, life would return to normal again. Babies would be born to healthy mothers, and sons would follow their fathers to work in green fields. Only the old would die, and peacefully.

◎   ◎   ◎

Father Martin baptized the poor little thing with the name of Bridget, after her grandmother Bridie Dooley. She barely flinched when the cold water was poured over her head—which in my experience usually resulted in great howls of distress. Father Martin murmured a special prayer for new mothers over Kitty and blessed her where she lay. I held on to the infant for dear life. At least now her immortal soul was saved.

"I hear you had a letter from Hugh," Father said to Mrs. Sweeney. "How is he doing in the great land of America?"

Mrs. Sweeney smiled, but the missing of Hugh was in her face. "He's got a job in an ironworks in a place called Troy, in New York. Hard work, he says, but a pay packet each week. Hugh was a good son. I'll never get the chance to see my grand-children, in America."

"God willing, he'll make a fortune and send for you all."

"At least the younger ones. The girls would have a better chance out there."

"It's hard to see them go. Soon we'll have no souls left in Kilvarna, and I'll be out of a job myself." Father Martin made a small effort at humor.

"Oh, Father," said Mrs. Sweeney. "You could always go as a missionary to Africa. Give those Protestants a run for their money."

◎   ◎   ◎

I fretted constantly about the new baby Bridget. She was pale and sleepy, coming to life only occasionally to wail with hunger. Kitty let down very little milk, so I dipped a twist of cloth in water for the baby to suck. Kitty herself was feverish, unable to muster the strength to rise from her blanket, much less care for an infant alone. I tried to interest her in the baby, snuggling Bridget into her arms, telling her what a beautiful little girl she had delivered. But Kitty would cry out for her own mother, half-delirious from the fever that sometimes comes with childbirth. She cried for food, begging her mother to put the potatoes on to boil. "Just hurry the fire, Mammy," she pleaded. "The boys won't be home from the fields for hours, but I'm so hungry."

I thought my heart would break. The boys had been dead for years. Michael Dooley had been the last of them.

For three days I trudged to the soup kitchen, stood in line, and carried a tin of soup back to Kitty. Each time I left the baby wrapped in rags on the straw next to Kitty, I worried that the wee one would stop breathing while I was away. But the bundle was always in the same place, undisturbed, when I brought back the soup. I stopped first to touch Bridget's face with my finger, to see her open her eyes or move her limbs. Then I gently put my hand on Kitty's bony shoulder.

"Drink the soup, Kitty, and you'll have milk for the baby."

Kitty glanced at the sleeping baby. She seemed unconnected, a person looking at an object with only passing interest. But this was the life that Kitty had fought so hard to nourish, for whom she had given up her very self, before Jackie died. What terrible thing had distanced her from her own baby this way?

I didn't know how to fix it. I helped Kitty put the baby to her breast and watched sadly as Bridget listlessly sucked at a dry teat. Neither mother nor child seemed to have much of a stake in staying alive.

It was with a heavy heart that I went home to my own cottage up the lane, where Tom and his brother Danny often sat in dark silence, brooding over the past and the future. I could find no relief from suffering anywhere.

◎ ◎ ◎

"I cannot tell you how sorry I am about this thing, Tom. I'd kill the little bastard myself if he wasn't my own brother." Michael Rourke stood unhappily in front of our hearth, his cap in his hands.

"Jesus Christ Almighty, for a bowl of porridge, you say! I hope to God he got some buttermilk with it," said Tom.

I swallowed the words in my mouth and moved back against the wall, where I could support myself without shaking.

Michael Rourke's younger brother had betrayed Tom to the police. The constables investigating the death of Edward Speke had tracked Tom Riordan's whereabouts on the morning of the shooting, and for the promise of a full belly Paddy swore that Tom had come at noon to work the field at Rourkes'.

"I'll testify that you were with me all morning and make my brother into a liar," offered Michael. "But I think you would be better off avoiding a trial altogether."

"Are they coming to arrest him, Michael?" My voice sounded steadier than I felt.

"Tomorrow, most likely. I beat the shit out of Paddy to get him to tell me tonight."

"There's an informer in every village in Ireland, Michael. It's a national curse. I never would have suspected young Paddy, though." Tom's voice held the sadness of betrayal.

"I'll beat him again for you tomorrow. He's a disgrace to the Rourke name."

Hunger can turn a mind and bend a loyalty. Not everyone was strong enough to resist temptation.

"I'll need to be making my plans, then," Tom said. "It was good of you to come, Michael. Thank you."

"Keep well, Tom. You're a good man. Don't give up the fight."

I could feel Tom's energy, coiled like a spring until Michael Rourke had shut the door behind him.

"I don't have much time, Margaret," he said in a low, controlled voice. "I'll have to leave for Ennis right away. Danny can come with me and take a message back for you."

"A message?" I tried to keep from rising into a scream.

"To tell you where to meet me."

Tom put both hands on my shoulders, holding me firm, holding me strong.

"My friends will get us out of the country, on the next boat. That's always been the plan."

"Boat? To where?" I couldn't breathe. Three words were all I had.

"To America. I can continue the work there. And maybe someday we can come home."

He looked at me, a small blackbird caught in the tightening snare with him.

"Margaret, you will come with me, won't you? I don't want to leave you behind."

I closed my eyes for a moment, so I wouldn't have to look at him. I loved Tom beyond all measure, had always loved him. But he was asking so much.

"What will I do about Kitty? And the baby?"

"It's the rope if I stay, Margaret. I did what I had to do, and God knows it. Now I have to leave. Please come with me," he said.

"Away from Kilvarna," I said.

"Away to America," he said.

"How can I desert Kitty?"

Tom groaned. "I can't be traveling with a mother and baby. And I can't waste precious time arguing about it. You'll have to decide for yourself. Now could you go and fetch Danny for me? He'll be down at Maloneys' most likely."

I nodded. Action was better than standing still. I needed time to absorb the impact, to recover from feeling as if I had been punched in the stomach, breathless and sick.

"When you come back with Danny, we'll work it out," said Tom. His expression was resolute, but his eyes held the fear of abandonment.

◎ ◎ ◎

"You're sure they will pay for my passage?" I asked in a small voice.

"They will," replied Tom. "First class. Silver service at the captain's table."

I couldn't keep back the hoped-for smile.

Tom and his brother stood at the door, anxious to be on their way. But Tom wouldn't leave without an answer.

"And I could earn the money to bring Kitty and the baby over?"

"They'll always be welcome," Tom said.

"I hate to leave my home."

"You're not alone in that."

I reached up to kiss him good-bye. The kiss was sweet, just an ordinary kiss. It would not have to last the rest of our lives.

"I'll see you the day after tomorrow," I said.

"I love you," he replied.

◎ ◎ ◎

It would be a good day to go somewhere else, I decided, as I sat in the cottage alone, unable to sleep. If the constables came, they could rip the place to shreds and find nothing.

I looked around in the dim light, hardly believing that in a day's time I would leave this place. Despite the hunger and want, Rose Mackey's cottage had been a happy shelter, a place of our own, and a start on our life. There was nothing to carry away from it but the memory. And the stone from the well of Brigid. I must not forget that last gift from Nuala Lynch.

Was there to be keening in America, I wondered. Would I be able to pass along the old ways, or were they gone forever?

I had never given America much thought, even when Hugh Sweeney left, because I had always expected to live my life here in Kilvarna. A pang of loss bit sharply when I imagined my brother Jimmy, somewhere in Belfast by now. He would never know that I had gone to America, fleeing the shadow of the noose with my husband. And Kitty, how could I say farewell to Kitty?

I wiped away the tears that had begun welling in my eyes. What was the use of crying? It would be better to make myself useful.

I picked up the small stone from Brigid's well and tucked it away. Nuala had wanted me to visit the holy well. Today might be the last day in my life that I could do so. And if I brought back a cup of water from the well for Kitty and the baby, perhaps in some way it would heal the pain of our parting.

As soon as the first light allowed me to see the road, I set out for Liscannor. I walked toward the west and the south, toward the bay that gave shelter from the wild ocean. At Kilshanny I made my way through a crowd of gaunt strangers, their bodies as ravaged by hunger as those of the people in Kilvarna. They thronged the village street, hundreds of skeletons crying for food, some too weak to stand.

In America there would be no hunger, Tom had said. America had chased the British to their ships not once but twice, and the land was their own.

I ignored the hunger in my belly, as I had learned to do. But it was gnawing at me, the feeling of being eaten up from the inside.

The sun was bright when I reached the crossroads at Liscannor. The holy well of Brigid was in the center of a grassy knoll, the path to it worn by the feet of the devout. Alone at this hour of the morning, I stood at the foot of the knoll. I could see the fields spread wide in the distance. I could smell the salt sea in the air. It was a peaceful place for the heart.

I walked up the path on aching bare feet, eager for a sight of the holy shrine. I had expected something grander, a chapel even. What I saw was a dark wellspring in the earth, bounded by gray mossy rocks. The water trickled over the rocks from an invisible source, filled the well, and disappeared again under the soft sacred ground.

Yet I felt an energy in the water, a whisper of hope and healing. Scattered on the knoll around the well were the remnants of the prayers of those who had begged for Brigid's gifts. Spring flowers, lying withered in the grass. A lock of brown hair tied with a scrap of wool. Crosses woven of straw.

I hadn't brought anything to leave behind. I had only the piece of stone taken from the well, however many years ago. I peered at the stones circling the well, looking for a telltale gap or gouge, but the stones were worn smooth.

I knelt on the ancient hill, a quivering of hope in my heart. I felt a gratitude for being alive. I was young. I was still strong in my self. I carried all that was ancient and healing in Ireland with me, in the keens and in my heart. I was Brigid's daughter.

Gripping the small stone figure tightly, I dipped it into the water of the well. The water was cold, fresh. I had a sudden fear of the stone tumbling down into the eternal darkness of the well, lost forever. But I held on to it, moving the figure in a spiral through the water, making a pattern that seemed holy and pleasing. The prayer I said was a jumble of images, of Kitty and the baby and Tom and Nuala Lynch and an unknown ship that would sail to America.

I had brought a small cup to carry home the water from the well. As I dipped the cup, I heard the sound of horses' hooves on the road. A carriage approached, with two women passengers in the back and a pile of trunks. The women wore hats alive with feathers. My own clothes were so shabby that I was ashamed.

"One of the peasant pilgrimage sites," the driver said. "However, the water is clean and safe to drink, if you're thirsty."

"Oh no," I heard the distaste in the woman's tone. "We're nearly to the spa at Lahinch, I should imagine. I wouldn't risk the chance of disease."

And a holy well is not a drinking trough for English pigs, I said silently in return.

As the carriage continued on toward the resort spa on the bay, I began the long walk back to Kilvarna. I felt an optimism that had not been with me during that sleepless night.

◎　◎　◎

It was early afternoon when I reached the long hill leading down to Kilvarna. I was tired, but I wanted to fetch the tin can from the cottage and continue on to the soup kitchen. It would be easier to tell Kitty about my leaving if I softened the news with food.

I saw a woman leaning against the stone wall on the road. Kitty—who hadn't been outside her door since before the baby was born.

As soon as I came near, Kitty forced herself to her feet. Her face was chalky, her eyes ringed in dark circles.

"Thank God I've caught you," said Kitty. She put out a skeleton's arm to bar my path, as if I wouldn't have stopped for her.

"Kitty! What's wrong?"

An ominous haze of smoke drifted above the village.

"You can't go home," Kitty said. "It's all burned up."

She slumped back on the wall again, her strength spent.

I wanted to fly down the road but I stopped myself. For Kitty to come all the way out here, the danger must be real.

"My house?" I had learned not to startle Kitty with loud words or sharp questions.

Kitty nodded. "The constables came looking for Tom. They couldn't find him, and they couldn't find you, so they burned down Rose Mackey's where you were staying. Then they went to your da's place and burned that too. There's nothing but the walls left."

And they would find the gun in the ashes. I made an instant decision.

"Kitty, I have to go away, right now," I said. "With Tom.

You'll have to get better, to take care of yourself and the baby without me."

Kitty closed her eyes in exhaustion. "The baby's gone," she whispered.

"Oh no." Please don't say this to me, Kitty.

Kitty opened her eyes. "She was a witch made by Mr. Speke," she explained reasonably. "I threw her in the fire."

My insides recoiled. I leaned over and vomited bile into the dirt. For a moment I hoped that I was dreaming, that when I straightened up again Kitty would not be there. But Kitty was.

"Tell me the truth, Kitty," I said, grasping her arm. "What happened to the baby?"

But Kitty had gone off into that other world. She stared at me with fear.

"Did you burn up the baby in my house?" I screamed.

"There wasn't any baby," said pale Kitty, cringing. "Only a bag of oatmeal."

The loyalty of friendship crashed with the charred beams of my house. "Go to see Father Martin," I forced myself to say. "He'll help you, Kitty. God knows I cannot."

The county asylum was the only home for Kitty Shaughnessy now.

Unbidden, my keening voice rose, wailing my rage, my grief. I turned away from Kitty, away from Kilvarna.

I walked the road to Ennis, another weeping woman among many, my loss no worse than theirs. Other babies had died. Other homes had been wrecked. Other friends had gone mad. But when I got to Ennis I would have a husband on the run and a ticket to America. I would leave this starving homeland forever, bringing nothing with me but a piece of stone from Brigid's well.

CHAPTER 21

I HAD NEVER SEEN A CITY as large as Limerick. When Tom and I had arrived two days earlier, it seemed that the place held most of the people of Ireland. Shops and townhouses of gray stone lined muddy streets with high curbs. Wagons and carriages and donkey carts fought for space in the crowded streets around the quays. A dozen ships lay moored there, waiting for the tide so they could sail down the Shannon and head out the mouth of the river to the open sea. On a slight rise above the river was a huge stone castle, built for King John seven hundred years ago. English soldiers still manned its battlements.

On the first day Tom had secured our passage on the *Constance*, a three-masted ship sailing for New York. The ship looked smaller than many of the vessels tied up at the quays, but the ticket agent assured us it had survived half a dozen Atlantic crossings already, with an able captain and crew. One of its great attractions was the weekly ration of seven pounds of food, which was included in the ticket cost of three pounds, ten shillings each. Tom's friends had given him ten pounds to cover the expense of the voyage, which we used to purchase two blankets, a cooking pot, bowls and spoons, and some extra flour and tea. We hid the last two coins away as security for when we reached America.

The boarding of passengers had been going on since first light. The crew tossed bundles and boxes to the deck, followed speedily by their owners, landing every which way on the smooth wood. I had to scramble to collect our belongings as Tom bent to help an old man who had tumbled on his side and couldn't get up. The crew continued to haul people and packages over the side. A small hatchway opened to a ladder down to the steerage compartment in the hold of the ship, our home for the next few weeks. We'd be sailing on the next morning's tide.

Below decks, I stood stock still for a few moments as my eyes adjusted to the dim light. Rows of double wooden bunks lined both sides of the hold, divided into berths by narrow planks. Kegs, barrels, and crates crammed into the space fore and aft, lashed to the walls with thick rope. Already the passengers were claiming their spaces, stowing their belongings.

I looked up at Tom, whose cap nearly touched the beams that supported the deck above them.

"How are we all going to fit?" I asked.

"Like herring in a fry pan," he replied.

The bottom level of bunks had been taken first, so we slung our bundles onto a top berth. For a small person like me it wasn't too cramped, but Tom would barely have room to sit upright.

The stream of people and possessions continued to flow down the ladder. The noise level rose, the air grew stuffy, and suddenly I felt that I was making a dreadful mistake. How could I leave Kilvarna, my home? What had the death of Edward Speke done to me? The image of a small still baby tossed into the roaring flames burned behind my eyes, until tears welled up to wash it away. I swallowed my tears and tried to sniffle quietly. I couldn't go home.

Tom rested his hand on my hair. "I'm sorry, Margaret, I truly am sorry. But I couldn't bear to leave you behind."

"It will be all right," I said. "It will be all right in the end." I could never send for Kitty, though. It was too late.

"Why don't you go up on deck and take a last look at the city?" suggested Tom, trying to help.

"Will you come?"

"It's better if I stay out of sight," he said.

I wiped the tears from my cheeks and made my way through the crowded hold to the hatchway. The air smelled fresh after the closeness below deck. I found an out-of-the-way perch where I could overlook the quays, where the produce of Ireland was still being loaded onto English ships for export. The starving poor were being herded onto other ships.

It was better that Tom stayed below. The sights would just enrage him. Then I saw three policemen approaching the *Constance*. They signaled to the first mate, who joined them at street level. I couldn't hear what they were saying, but the man repeatedly checked his papers and shook his head in answer to their questions. At last the constables moved off, heading for the ship moored at the next quay.

The first mate grumbled aloud as he passed me. "Searching every ship indeed!" he said. "What's the fuss over a bloody land-lord's agent? One more or one less makes no difference."

My heart stopped. I looked at the dozen ships in the river and wondered how many had been searched already, and how long it would take the police to come back to the *Constance*. Did Tom know they were searching for him? On the road from Ennis to Limerick we had ridden in a cart, scarcely visible under its load of straw piled high. But I had thought that in the big city of Limerick he would be safe.

I hurried down to Tom, who had made friends with two of the small boys in the berth next to ours. He looked less tense than he had since we left Kilvarna, and I hated to bring that back upon him.

He smiled at me. "If it isn't Margaret Meehan herself. Fancy meeting you here."

At first I didn't notice his use of my family name. I had been a Meehan for seventeen years and a Riordan for less than one.

"Timmy and Matty Carroll are these two lads," he said cheerfully. "They're off to an adventure in New York, same as we are. Tip your caps to Mrs. Meehan." The boys grinned at me shyly. Their rags hung in shreds on their skinny legs and arms, and no caps were in sight. But their eyes were bright with the hope of the new world.

A few minutes later I whispered the news about the police search to Tom. His easy smile vanished. "I meant to tell you, Margaret. I bought the tickets under the name of Meehan. It's Tom Meehan and his wife that are traveling to America on this ship."

"Will I never be Mrs. Riordan again, then?" A sharp memory of Nuala Lynch's voice greeting me on the day after my marriage echoed in my mind. Was I losing everything that anchored me to Kilvarna?

"It will be safer when we reach New York," said Tom.

On the high tide the next morning, the *Constance* sailed. I lay cramped in our bunk next to Tom, my eyes open in the dimness, unable to sleep. From above I heard the shouts of the crew. Wood creaked and men swore, but their cursing had a note of excitement to it, at the start of a new voyage. With a lurch that I could actually feel, the ship left its berth and headed into the traffic on the river, to follow it to the sea.

I put my hand on Tom's shoulder, unsure from his breathing whether he was asleep or awake—although how he could be asleep in all the noise would be a mystery to me. His blond head was cradled on his arm, his knees bent to fit in the cramped berth.

"We're off," I whispered aloud. "Off and away, Tom." A small part of me dared to feel excitement at the new life we were starting together.

Tom heard my whisper and tried to turn to see my face. The berth was so small that he could not move. Instead he jumped down to the floor and climbed in again facing me. I smiled at him as I always had, his own girl. He eased his arms around me and held me close. For love of him I had left Ireland, and for love of Ireland he had been forced to leave. Now we were faced with five long weeks of confinement in the airless hold of a ship, our bodies intimately beside one another but untouchable in this public place.

Tom's consolation was that he would be reunited with Hugh Sweeney again. In a strange place called Troy, New York, they could work for the cause once more. I wasn't sure where my own life would be going.

Sixty-five men, thirty-three women, and twenty children were confined in a space smaller than the chapel in Kilvarna. During the first few days of the voyage, the realities of a long ocean crossing became clear. Seasickness kept many of the passengers in their bunks once we had passed through the mouth of the Shannon and reached the open sea. Their misery was unrelieved, and I was glad that neither Tom nor I suffered from the malady. But the sufferings of others were experienced nonetheless, as vomit cascaded from the bunks to the floor.

On the morning after we set sail, the second mate and the cabin boy came down to the hold with a sack of oatmeal and another of flour. The sacks contained more food than I had seen for months. Carefully the crewmen measured out the rations in pound or half-pound portions, for each man and woman and child. We eyed the dry foodstuffs suspiciously, not yet knowing where and how we would cook. But not a soul turned the food away when it was offered. The hardtack biscuits that were doled out were chewed and swallowed immediately by the famished passengers.

Water was portioned out likewise, from great casks in the hold. I took a sip from my bowl and my lips puckered. This was not the sweet clear water from the springs of Clare. It had a musty acid taste.

The second mate saw my face. "Better than sea water, young miss," he said. "You'll remember I said that, a month from now."

"Thank you, sir. I'm sure that I will."

The mate regarded me seriously. "It's no laughing matter if a ship runs out of fresh water," he said. "And the cargo down here won't be at the head of the receiving line."

He moved on to the next family of emigrants, eagerly thrusting their bucket forward. I hadn't meant any offense. It was going to be a long five weeks.

By midday on the second day out, the open brick hearths were fired and ready on deck for steerage passengers to cook their meals. The other women showed me how to stir the oatmeal, water, and flour into a thick pan batter that was cooked over the open fire until blackened on one side. It was still soupy in the middle. No one had enough time at the fire to cook anything properly. I stood in line with the women—and a few men—to wait my turn. If the weather turned bad and the sea was rough, there would be no cooking allowed that day. The danger of hot coals on a wooden ship was considerable.

Below, the noise was constant. I would lie awake in my hard bunk at night, unable to sleep, listening to the snores, the coughs, the creaks of the wooden ship, the murmured conversations, the quiet weeping of fear and homesickness. During the day Tom and I spent as much time as possible on the open deck, away from the stench of human waste and vomit that permeated the hold. All around us was the heaving empty ocean, not another ship in sight.

On the first Saturday night, a young man from Kerry pulled out his fiddle. The lantern swung its light in rhythm with the waves, and three other men found the breath to join in with their tin whistles. No drummer was found—an oversight on the part of the ticket agent—but the tapping of dancers' feet soon filled the space.

Tom and I sat on our bunk, soaking in the joy of the music and watching the young men and women struggle to keep their balance on the dipping boards. Timmy and Matty, the two boys in the next berth, stood in their bare feet to dance a hornpipe. We clapped for the love of their youth, for the carrying of tradition to a new land. Above our heads the lanterns cast long shadows and smoked the air. Aside from its rocking on the waves of the sea, the gathering could have been a *ceili* in Kilvarna, or Ennis, or Limerick, or Cork.

When the lights were extinguished that night and the last wanderer had climbed into his bunk, we slept more soundly, secure in the unity of our culture. All of us were cast upon the ocean, but we were children of the same motherland. Ripped from her loving arms by sad happenstance or by vicious plan, we cemented our memories in the year of our parting. In our hearts Ireland would forever remain as she was in May 1847.

The salt spray pelted my cheeks and chin as the wind picked up speed. I pulled my black shawl over my head and prayed that the storm would hold off until after our dinner was cooked. Huddled with two dozen other women on the deck, I watched with dismay as the rain began to turn the hearth fire into a steaming pile of ash.

The seaman in charge of supervising the cooking fire pushed through the crowd. "Gather your pots and pans and get below!" he shouted. A disappointed moan arose from the few who had yet to even warm their meals at the hearth. Uncooked flour and water was a paste that was nearly inedible. Nearly but not entirely, we had discovered.

The ocean swells began to tip the hot coals precariously near the wooden deck. "Out of the way, move out!" shouted the seaman. He sloshed a bucket of seawater over the hearth coals, regardless of any open pans not yet snatched up by their owners. "Get below and stay there!"

I awkwardly grabbed my pot and carried it down the ladder to the hold. As the last of the women descended, we heard the bolt of the hatch door slide home.

The Atlantic storm rocked the boat with a fury that made us all fear for our lives. People cried and screamed at the sound of the thunder, at the waves crashing against the hull of the boat. They were thrown from side to side as the *Constance* pitched in the swells. Slop buckets overturned and added their contents to the general mess of tumbled possessions and passengers.

We clung to the safety of our berth, our few possessions wedged behind us. Tom braced himself against the wood. We watched as the floor of the hold slid upward on a swell as if defying gravity, then swung back down into the trough with a jarring thump and rose up the other side again.

It was dark in the hold, the air and light closed off when the hatch was secured.

"Why have they locked us in, do you think, Tom? Do they imagine we'd climb on deck for a better view?"

"To keep the seawater out," he said. "If the water poured in here, we'd all drown, inside the boat."

With a smashing sound the only lantern flew from its hook and shattered. A quick tongue of fire flickered on the floor of the hold, until the man nearest stamped it out. "God bless you!" people shouted.

Plunged into total darkness, we endured the terrifying hours, some in prayer and supplication, some in wails and tears. Some kept a determined brave silence. Some clung for dear life to their loved ones. To have come so far just to sink like a stone would be hard indeed.

Gradually the rolling of the ship lessened, and the roar of the wind and the waves diminished. The whimpering of the children ceased as, exhausted, they dropped into sleep.

When the hatch was finally opened, the cleanness of a bright blue sky was a shock to our blinking eyes. How changeable was the ocean—and how little did she regard the poor exiles bobbing from one land mass to another across her surface.

The damage from the storm was soon repaired. We cleaned the floor as best we could with buckets of seawater, the lanterns were relit, and more people than usual crowded above on the small deck area to breathe in the fresh salt air. The only casualty was a little girl, whose wrist was injured when she was wrenched from her mother by the force of a pitch and thrown against a bulkhead. I wished I had been able to bring the healing herbs that I had gathered in Kilvarna—a poultice of comfrey would have eased her pain. But Tom and I had fled to the ship with nothing but the clothes on our backs.

The fever struck at the end of the second week out to sea. When the young fiddler from Kerry lay in his bunk writhing with pain and calling out for water, I recognized the dread signs. The lad was traveling alone and had no one to care for him. The woman in the berth above him had all she could do to take care of her three young children, who were restless and cranky.

I bent down to put my cool hand on his forehead, brushing away the thick dark hair that clung damply to his skin. He was burning with fever. He didn't respond when I asked his name.

Mrs. Garvey above answered my question. "His name is Patrick Coyne," she said. "His mam and sisters is left behind in Killarney, and he was supposed to bring them over by and by. Poor dear, he'll never reach America now."

"I'll do what I can for him," I volunteered. "I've known a lad of his age that survived the fever." Danny Riordan, Tom's brother. But I dare not mention the name, even here.

"God's mercy on you both," she said.

When the captain heard that a man was sick with fever, he sent down medicine and extra water. If you could catch the first cases, the mate said, then the disease might not spread through the hold—or worse, to the seamen. They were not yet halfway across the Atlantic, and there was no crew to spare.

I did my best to save young Patrick. I bathed his forehead with a wet cloth and held his hand in his brief periods of lucidity. I fed him sips of water as I watched the bruising swelling creep up his legs. I gave myself strength by snuggling into Tom's arms and resting there, as safe as I could be in the middle of the ocean, in the presence of patiently waiting death.

Patrick Coyne did not linger long. Though no one knew him well—or perhaps because of it—his burial at sea was well attended. The corpse was sewn up in an old sail and sent into the waves with prayers and lamentations. It was a terrible way to go, the mourners murmured, to be denied burial in your own land, to be eaten by sharks and have your bones drift down to the bottom of the sea. I kept my keening silent, fearing complaint from the English captain or the crew.

Six others died over the next three weeks, including the old man who had shared the wooden bunk with Patrick Coyne. Shrouds became merely flour sacks sewn together, and few people ventured up to the deck to watch the toss. Sharks trailed through the water behind the ship. I woke from nightmares of Tom's body being torn to shreds in their bloody jaws and worried constantly about Tom falling ill. I reassured myself by touching his skin in his sleep, which showed no sign of fever. And I prayed to Brigid, healer and saint, to keep us safe until we reached America. Too much already had been lost.

◎ ◎ ◎

As the long days passed on the sea, I kept myself busy. I helped with the sick and the dying and coaxed smiles out of ragtag children. Taking care of other people had become such a part of my nature that I didn't think twice before offering my hand to strangers. And the more occupied I was, the less I heard the incessant keening in my own heart.

Tom spent his time with the other men, most of them reluctant exiles like himself, who were willing to work for a new life in America but who would have preferred never to have left. The men talked of vast farmlands in the center of America, land where wheat would grow faster and higher than even God had intended, land that they could own and pass on to their sons.

But Tom wasn't interested in land. He was convinced that we would return to Ireland within a year, or two years at the most.

"We'll do what we can for Ireland in America," he said, as we ate our meal of soggy oatcake. "And when we can go home to a free country, we'll be on the first boat back."

"Didn't you notice, Tommy, that the traffic is all flowing this way?" I said. "There's nothing left to go home to."

He shook his head in disagreement. "Plans will be set in motion," he said. "Great plans made by great men. We'll finish what was started in '98." Cheerfully he began to whistle a popular rebel song.

I marveled at his return to boyish exuberance. Had he forgotten that this ship was a refuge from the gallows?

◎ ◎ ◎

I couldn't get Kitty out of my mind. Her white face haunted my dreams. My darling friend, the only one to whom I told my deepest secrets, my yearnings, my fears. And yet she had ached with a secret so dark that it took her life away.

In my bones I knew she was gone. I hoped that the Lord in all His mercy had understood what drove poor Kitty to madness. I wished above all that I had been there that last day. And oh, how I hoped that poor babe had died in her sleep and was waiting to greet her mam in heaven.

At first I found it hard to look at the babies tied in their mothers' shawls. For me each pale face and open mouth was a horrible reminder of what I had lived through in the past few months. But as I got to know the younger women sharing this temporary world of the ship and put other names to the faces, I felt myself beginning to imagine a happy future again. A life with Tom in a place where we could settle down, where laughter and music and love would fill our hearts. And where maybe, some day, we'd have a healthy baby of our own.

On the thirty-seventh day of the voyage, a seagull circled overhead in the cloudless blue sky. News that land was near spread jubilation throughout the hold. "You'd think it was the Holy Ghost Himself flying through," said Tom. It was like sunshine to hear him joke again, after the cold dark weeks on the sea.

In the early morning Captain Threadgood had the three sickest passengers carried up on deck. Then he ordered a thorough swabbing of the hold, an all-out effort to rid the ship of the accumulated filth of five weeks' confinement before the medical examiner made his inspection in the harbor. We sloshed buckets of cold seawater through the berths and scraped up the foul sludge. We washed our necks and faces and whatever of our clothing could be removed without complete nakedness. Skirts and shirts fluttered from the rigging like banners, drying in the sun. Ruined mattresses and clothing were tossed into the sea and floated in a procession behind the ship.

I was relieved to have constructive work to do. If we had done such a cleaning job every week, conditions might not have been so wretched, I thought. But never in my life did I ever intend to set foot on a ship again.

In the early June evening the cry went up that land was sighted. We rushed up onto the deck, crowding as far forward as we were allowed, to glimpse the green island that lay mistily before us. As the ship approached I saw a score of sister ships, most larger, moored at anchor.

"They're waiting for the medical examiner," explained the first mate to the group of passengers who approached him.

"The doctor checks you over and sends the sick ones to quarantine hospital on Staten Island," he continued. "And those that need burying. Always a couple of old ones who hang on just long enough to avoid being buried at sea. Almost as if the sight of America is enough to kill them."

"That island is not New York, then, sir?" asked a young man.

"You have to sail into the harbor, through the Narrows, past Brooklyn," answered the mate. "A New York pilot does that fancy bit. Brings her right into South Street, tight as ducks." He chuckled. "You'll know New York when you see it. Just mind your money and your baggage, and you'll do all right. There's plenty of work for hod carriers."

Tom and I stayed on deck the whole of the last night and through the day, waiting for the glimpse of America. The next afternoon, around four o'clock, the *Constance* tied up at a berth in the bustling South Street seaport. Into the harbor trailed a flotsam of discarded clothing, moldy food, and human sewage, floating on the tide. When the gangplank was lowered, we were among the first to step down it, our legs shaky and weak on firm ground. When we reached the pier, crowded with people coming and going, Tom dropped our bundles and gathered me into his arms. "We've arrived," he said as he squeezed the breath out of me. "Now we're to find Hugh Sweeney in the city of Troy, and we'll be all set."

"How do we get to Troy?" For the first time, America was real to me. An entire country awaited us.

"We sail up the Hudson River on a boat," replied Tom.

"Holy Mother of God, not another boat!" I burst into tears at the very thought.

CHAPTER 22

As Tom held me weeping in his arms, a little fellow dressed in a bright green coat darted toward the bundles at Tom's feet.

"You're off to a good start, I see," said the man. "I'm one of your own countrymen, Jacko Murphy by name, and I'll see that you're taken to the best accommodation in New York." His patter was fast as he reached to pick up the ragged bundles.

"Put it down," said Tom. "I'm not interested in your generous offer—go and prey on someone other than an Irishman, if you truly want to help your countrymen." I stopped my tears to listen.

"Ah, boyo, you're a tough customer, I see," the man replied. "For a small sum I'll give you the name of an honest landlady three blocks around the corner. She'll take care of yourself and your wife, on my word, she will."

"No, thank you," Tom said. "We're being met by friends. Go and find yourself another customer."

The small man took himself off down the pier in search of an easier victim to fleece. It probably wouldn't take him long to find one—the ships were disgorging passengers at a fast clip today.

I sniffled and dried my eyes. "I'm sorry. I won't cry anymore. I'm glad to be on dry land, that's the truth." I bent to pick up my parcel. "So where are we going, Tom? Do you know?"

"My friends in Ennis told me to look for a fellow from the

Irish Immigrant Society," he said. "Not one of those hustlers."
He glanced around the pier.

A little way ahead of us, I saw Kathleen Garvey with her
brood of three children and a young girl who had been traveling
on the *Constance* alone. They were talking with a man dressed in
a dark suit, a tweed cap on his head.

"Excuse me, Mrs. Garvey," I said politely when she noticed
me. "I was wondering if you knew, is this the man from the
Immigrant Society?" I spoke in Irish, so as not to embarrass Mrs.
Garvey if I was mistaken about the man.

The man himself stepped forward, holding out his hand to me
with a smile. "My name is Charles Kelly, of the Society, and I'm
pleased to offer our help," he said in Irish. "You're from Clare, I
can tell. Do you have any English at all?"

"All the English that I want and need," I said. "My husband and
I just got off the boat, and we'll be on our way to Troy tomorrow."

"Could they come with us to your place as well, sir?" asked
Mrs. Garvey. "For a wash and a meal and a change of clothes, as
you said?"

Mr. Kelly was already extending his hand to Tom. "We're
pleased to welcome you to America," he said. I bit my lip to keep
from crying again.

We followed him through the crowded streets to a brick
rooming house a few blocks away. A hundred times the number of
people in Limerick must live in New York City, I was sure. Mr.
Kelly led us through a narrow passage to the kitchen garden at
the back of the house. A large woman in a white apron came
out to greet us, her expression undismayed at our travel-worn
condition.

"Aren't you the nicest group ever? And three young rascals,
too," she said in a cheerful voice. "With a little soap and water,
and a hot meal, you'll be ready to take on the world, so you will."

America was indeed the land of miracles. I was fairly reeling
from exhaustion, but I forced myself to offer her help.

"No, dear, we've got this down to a fair routine," May Butler said. "There's kettles of water and soapy rags in the kitchen, and when you're done I'll find you some clean clothes to wear. Not too many outfits make it through an ocean voyage still wearable." She had a kind way about her that made it seem less like taking charity. Even Tom was able to accept the help without shame.

◎　◎　◎

My new dress was dark green wool, mended and patched at the elbows and cuffs and a little large, but I felt like a queen in it. My curls were black and springy again and combed back from my face. I was a new woman in a new country. Last night I had resolved to put the sorrows of the old country behind me, to lock them in my heart and throw away the key.

With directions from Mr. Kelly and a grateful good-bye to Mrs. Butler, we set out in the early morning for Troy, a small city sprawled on the east bank of the Hudson River, a few miles north of Albany. People said the land was good for farming, flat and rich, but Tom had no desire to return to that life. He would rather take his chances earning dollars in the iron mills.

Much as I dreaded the leaving of dry land again, we took passage on a steamboat traveling upriver to Troy. In the space of a day and a night we would arrive at the city where Hugh Sweeney lived. I still found it impossible to suppress the shivers of excitement that ran through me as the steamboat whistle signaled our departure and the brightly painted vessel began to chug away from the pier.

"Did you ever think we would be doing such a thing, Tommy?" I whispered, holding his arm tightly. His blond hair was trimmed and his face freshly shaven.

"I did not," he replied. "I never thought it would all come to this." His expression surprised me. I had expected hope but saw bitter regret. "I'll curse the British to my dying day, the lying soulless bastards," he said.

I looked at the small group of immigrants clustered together on the narrow deck. They all looked like death warmed over, emaciated and ill-clothed. But they were the lucky ones. They were alive.

Wanting someone to share my excitement, I left Tom to his anguish and went to stand at the rail next to a woman who held a small child in her arms. For only a moment I felt the searing pain in my breast that accompanied thoughts of Kitty and her infant, and then I pushed them out of my mind.

"Are you going to Troy as well, Missus?" I asked.

The young woman smiled. "We've got family in a place called Poughkeepsie." She wrinkled her nose as she tried to pronounce the unfamiliar word. "My brother came out ten years ago and he's just brought us over. He says it looks a bit like home. God knows I'll be glad to see a friendly face, after the way we've been pushed along like cattle everywhere we've been."

I nodded. "We're hoping it will be different over here."

"It can't be any worse," said my new friend. "Poughkeepsie is a far cry from Skibbereen."

Standing at the rail, I was amazed at how the great paddle-wheels churned the water. The engine chugged and puffed, and smoke and cinders flew up from the smokestack. The banks of the river went by at a brisk pace. Past the crowded buildings on the shores of Manhattan Island, northward mile by mile until there was nothing to see but tree-covered banks and rocky crags along the wide waterway. Occasionally a town spread its houses along the shore and up into the soft green hills. It was very beautiful, a place teeming with life and hope.

When we boarded, we Irish were instructed to stay to ourselves on one side of the deck. Other passengers strolled fore and aft of the wheelhouse or sat in comfortable deck chairs. I watched them covertly, trying to understand their American-ness, what made them different from us. At dinnertime they brought out from their cabins great hampers of food, and at that I turned away. No use to awakening appetites that would not be satisfied.

We slept on the open deck that night, huddled against the cool breezes on the river. But the air was sweet and fresh in the morning, and off to the west I could see the hazy shapes of purple mountains. They probably had some unpronounceable Indian name. And I wondered if we would see any of the native red men. Perhaps the British had chased them all from their country, too.

The steamship carried us to a dock at the foot of Troy. The city beckoned above us. Once again we Irish were herded with our belongings into a cramped area surrounded by ropes. We were not permitted to leave the dock with the other passengers.

"You've all got to wait here 'til the doctor comes," said the man in charge of the landing dock.

To me it seemed all too close to the humiliating examinations of the passengers on the *Constance*.

"Begging your pardon, sir, but why a doctor?" I asked, holding the fear out of my voice. To be sent back now would be unthinkable.

"You filthy people brought the ship fever with you," he replied. "There's two hundred lying sick in the fever sheds near the river, and who knows how many of the quality folks in Troy are dying in their own beds from the contagion. The doctor won't let you go into the city if you've got the signs."

I swallowed the words about to burst out and looked around at the passengers. None were the picture of health, but neither did I see the rash or shaking chills that betrayed the black fever's infection.

"There's none sick here," I said.

"And you are a doctor," said the man.

"How long will it take for the doctor to come?"

"What does it matter? Most of you have no place to go but the streets anyway."

Tom stepped in front of me, and I could see that he meant a fight. His black mood simmered just below the surface.

"Don't, Tom," I said. "Let it go. We've come too far now. We'll just wait for the doctor and—"

The man had already turned his back on us. One of the other men said a few words quickly to Tom, in Irish, and nodded toward the American. Tom shook his head and laughed, the tension broken. Whatever was said was not going to be repeated in front of the women and children. But humor made it possible to stand the long hour in the sun until the doctor arrived to check us for fever.

Late in the afternoon Tom and I waited with our bundles on the steps of the boardinghouse where Hugh Sweeney rented a room by the week. If I closed my eyes, I could believe I was back home, listening to the sounds of children playing and quarreling in the street, their mothers calling them in for tea with cadences familiar to my ears. The south side of Troy was Ireland, until I opened my eyes and saw the American street lined with stone curbs and row houses two and three stories high. The houses had glass-paned windows and wide front steps, grander than any I had seen in Ennis. And a few blocks down and around the corner were enormous hotels and dozens of storefronts, their sidewalks crowded with well-dressed people, many of whose faces were a mirror of my own.

The landlady, gray-haired and plump, assured us that Hugh returned from the Troy Iron and Nail Factory by six-thirty each evening, to a supper of bread and tea, which we were welcome to share. And her neighbor Mrs. Halloran had a room to let, if we were interested. Tom had explained that we would have to wait

until we talked with Hugh before we could make any plans. I was
sure the woman knew we had no money left but what Hugh might
lend us—her offer of tea was a kind one.

Hugh Sweeney's face as he came up to the front stoop was
black with grime and streaked with sweat. He had filled out in the
year since he had left starving Ireland, and his shoulders were
broad, his brown beard thick. Tom leaped off the steps, clapped
him on the back, and thumped him on the head with great delight.
Hugh responded in kind, having never expected to see his best
friend again. And here they stood, together, on a street in Troy,
New York.

I hung back, a wave of emotion squeezing my heart. Now it
was my turn to feel the pain of loss, the resentment that I stood
three thousand miles away from the place where I was born, not
through my own desire. I tried to shake it off, make the best of
things, to be glad that we had found an old friend.

But the reunion was bittersweet. Seated on wooden chairs at
a clean scrubbed table, we ate brown bread with butter and jam,
and we drank tea with milk and sugar—luxuries unthinkable a
week ago. Hugh jumped up and shook Tom's hand all over again
when we told him of our wedding in Kilvarna. "We'll go to the
pub for a pint to celebrate on Saturday night," he said happily.

But more than once I found my throat choked with grief as I
answered Hugh's eager questions. The devastation of Kilvarna
sounded unbearable, and Hugh's face grew more somber with
each piece of news he received. When I got to the part about
Jackie and Kitty Shaughnessy, I couldn't go on.

Tom nodded to Hugh in the way that they always had done,
meaning "I'll tell you later," and steered the conversation over to
Hugh's new life in Troy. What sort of work was there to be had?
Could Hugh get him into the iron factory?

There was plenty of work, Hugh promised him, and though it
paid only four dollars a week, it was enough. The skilled ironworkers—molders and puddlers, they were called—earned three

times that much. Hugh aimed to move up in the trade as quickly as he could. The superintendent of the factory was a Scotsman, an engineer by the name of Burden who had a talent for mechanical invention. At this moment he was working on a machine that would turn out horseshoes. "Only in America," Hugh said, laughing. Tom could go along with him tomorrow.

At nine o'clock that night, as twilight turned dark, Tom and I crossed the threshold of our first home in America. It was a single room with a sagging bedstead on the third floor of the Hallorans' house off Fourth Street, smelling of cabbage and grease and strong soap. There was a pump for water in the back garden, and an outhouse for all the boarders to share. A plump black cat rubbed against my ankles as I paused in the doorway. I leaned down to stroke the soft fur, listening for its purr. In America, I was sure, they didn't eat the cats.

And couples made love on real beds, in private rooms with doors. Wasn't life getting better already?

CHAPTER 23

HUGH SWEENEY WAS AS GOOD as his word, and Tom got a job the next day. I knew that Tom found it hard to settle down to a twelve-hour workday in the ironworks, after having the freedom of the roads in Clare. But he did the best he could, coming home covered in smoky grit, too tired to do much more than eat the potatoes that I boiled for our supper. The work was dangerous, physically demanding, and made all the worse by the heat of a Troy summer. But after the first weeks Tom grew tough and wiry, and he was eager to take up the cause of Ireland's freedom again. He began to look for new friends.

I quickly found myself growing restless. If we were going to get ahead in this new country, I wanted to do my share to make it happen. Most of the young women and many of the widows worked six days a week, the same as the men, to keep their families from slipping back into the poverty and hunger that plagued the Irish in the new country as well as in the old.

Mrs. Halloran's three daughters worked for a firm that made collars for gentlemen. It was a new and growing business, these detachable collars, and Troy was the center of their manufacture. Instead of laundering a shirt each day, a gentleman could simply attach a new starched collar and look as crisp and professional as an American businessman should. At least that's what the advertisements promised.

Much of the collar-making was done as piecework, cut and stitched by girls and women in the neighborhoods and delivered back to the shops for finishing. The Hallorans, though, were expert laundresses—starchers and ironers who worked in the shop itself to prepare the collars for final shipment. They earned nearly as much each week as a man could get starting out at the ironworks. When I heard that, I decided to become a laundress.

Ellen Halloran laughed at me when I suggested it. "A little slip of a thing like you! How would you lift the heavy pressing irons at all?"

"I'm getting my strength back," I protested. "I can't sit about like the queen when I could be earning money."

Ellen was just twenty, a tall girl with muscular arms and a cheerful disposition.

"They might take on somebody for the starching," she said. "If you want to learn a skill, you could start there."

"Would you put a word in for me?"

"I will," replied Ellen. "My sister Annie's ready to move up to ironing, so maybe you could take over for her. It's hard work, though, Margaret, I'm warning you."

"Hard work is nothing new to me," I said.

Six of us crowded together in a basement room not more than ten feet wide or long. The air was stifling with the steam from the laundry boiler and the starching tubs, the glowing coals under the plate to heat the irons, and the closeness of the rapidly moving women. A small window at the top of the outside wall provided only a waft of air every now and then.

My green dress was drenched with sweat under my white apron, its sodden hem dragging on the wet floor in the starch drippings. I had pinned my hair up in a knot and rolled my sleeves past my elbows. My hands and forearms were reddened with the water and heat. Ten hours had passed in this room, with a few minutes' break for bread and tea and a visit to the outhouses behind the factory building. Now Lizzie, the youngest Halloran sister, was pulling out the mops from the corner so that she and I could swab the floor at the end of the day. Annie and Ellen Halloran were frantically pressing the last batch of white collars, while Eileen McCarthy waited to box them and add them to the finished stack outside the door. Bridie Corrigan carefully banked the coals with ash, to keep them alive for early morning, when we would start all over again.

Tomorrow was Saturday, when I would receive my first pay packet. The first thing I planned to do with the money was buy a length of cotton fabric to make a lightweight blouse and skirt, clothes that would dry between night and morning. I hated putting on my damp wool dress at dawn—it reminded me of the weeks in the hold of the ship, when nothing was dry and nothing was clean.

At six o'clock we shut the door behind us, climbed the stairs to the outside world, and took deep gulps of the golden air. It was only a short walk to the house off Fourth Street, where Mrs. Halloran would have potatoes, cabbage, and bread with butter waiting with our tea. Now that I was working, Tom and I paid extra to eat our meals with the family. And two or three nights a week Tom left for a meeting at the Lark, a local saloon, just like at home. He had found a group of like-minded men whose desire for revenge and freedom for Ireland drove their efforts for success in America. Over pints of Troy-brewed porter they kept their hatreds and their spirit of rebellion alive. He was happier than I had seen him in a long time.

◎ ◎ ◎

Autumn came, with colors more glorious than I could have

believed, had I not seen them with my own eyes. Hugh Sweeney began keeping company with Eileen Magill, a pretty young woman who sewed collars as piecework. On Sundays the four of us would go to the social afternoons at the church or take a picnic out to the waterfalls on the Poestenkill. Tom and Hugh were moving up in the foundry. Tom was a popular fellow, it seemed, judging by the number of greetings and handshakes he received wherever we went. I felt lucky. The two of us were working, we could save a little money toward the future, and we were settling into the community. I pushed the memories of Kilvarna away from me in the night. And Tom seemed to do the same.

The bad news had spread through the neighborhood and the factories almost instantly. As Tom and Hugh walked alongside the wagon carrying the body of Patsy Fitzgerald, covered with a canvas tarp, the word of an accident at the ironworks brought the women and children out to the street. Three of Mary Fitzgerald's closest friends rushed to comfort the new widow, to be at her side before the scalded flesh of her husband was returned to their home. The parish priest from St. Mary's passed the wagon at a fast trot, alerted by a runner from the factory. Tom, Hugh, and Patsy's eldest son, a boy of twelve who had ridden in the wagon with his father, carried the corpse up the steps into the Fitzgerald house. By that time, the news had reached even the six of us in the laundry room.

Tom was quiet when he came home from the Lark that night. He lay next to me under the blankets, and I could sense the dark stream of anger running through him. I rested my hand over his heart, trying to reach him with a lover's touch.

"This is the worst accident I've seen, and I've seen a few already," he finally said. "It didn't have to happen. The ladle tipped at the wrong moment, and the poor man was half-covered in molten iron. We pulled him away but he just kept on screaming. Screaming until he died." Tom's body shuddered. "And tomorrow they'll put another man in his place. Have you noticed, Margaret, the number of Irish widows and orphans in America?"

It was my turn to shiver. "You're careful, aren't you, Tom?" I whispered, leaning over him.

"As careful as I've got the time and footing to be," he said. "I'd like to keep myself all in one piece. A man with an arm torn off has a hard time earning a living."

"Still, we'd have starved to death if we'd stayed," I said. That was as far as I went. I moved closer to Tom and he opened his arms for me.

"I'm thinking of asking the Widow Fitzgerald if she wants me to keen for her husband at the wake tonight," I said to the other laundresses as we worked. There had been a momentary lull in the morning's conversation about the accident and the other doings of the neighborhood.

"When I lived at home in Clare, I learned the keening from old Nuala Lynch. Maybe you've heard of her." I hadn't told this to anyone until now. Neither had I shown anyone the small stone figure of Brigid, my link to the life before this one.

The swish-swish of the collars in the rinse water did not stop. Nor did the sizzle of Ellen's hot iron meeting the layer of starch on linen. But the silence of women's voices was deafening.

"We don't do that over here," said Bridie, finally, as if speaking to a slow-witted child.

"We've left Ireland behind us," said Ellen.

"We're Americans now," said Lizzie. She was scarcely taller than the paddle with which she stirred the laundry boiler.

I looked around the laundry room at the women who were my neighbors and friends. Women who had locked the tragedy of Ireland in boxes and buried them deep, who did not wish me to rip open the lids and let out the miasma of the dead. Women who feared the keener's wail would invite the banshee to America.

A thick strand in the cord that bound me to Ireland snapped in my heart, a sharp cutting pain. I took a long breath and carefully continued to dip linen collars into the steaming starch. "As I am too," I said at last.

CHAPTER 24

THE IRISH CONTINUED TO POUR into Troy, but in the summer of 1848 they brought with them a new disaster—the cholera epidemic. The dreadful killing disease had swept through the west of Ireland, reducing villages to empty shells, destroying more of the population than had starvation or the black fever. The cholera traveled on shipboard, able to strike a man down in the midst of a sentence as if felled by an ax. Some people survived, but more often the cholera sent its victims to the grave, or to the bottom of the ocean.

The Troy city government turned the fever sheds down by the river into a quarantine hospital for those who arrived already sick. Local doctors volunteered their skills, but there was little that could be done. People who were meant to recover, did. Several of the young doctors gave up their lives in service to the poor.

I was drawn to their stories, printed in the newspaper. I admired their selflessness, their desire to help the less fortunate, their willingness to put the needs of others above their own comfort. Even at the risk of death.

I said as much to Tom one Saturday evening, when he came home from the Lark.

His face clouded over with anger. "I forbid it, Margaret, absolutely," he said.

"You forbid it? Forbid what?" I hadn't exactly formed a plan yet, though I thought I might be able to manage three evenings a week after work at the laundry was done.

"I forbid you going near those cholera sheds. After all we've been through, I will not have you throw yourself away on good works." The couple of pints of porter he had drunk fuzzed his thinking a little, but I knew what he meant.

I couldn't help smiling. Throw myself away on good works? On gambling, maybe, or hard liquor, or bad men, but on good works?

"But the doctors are such heroes, Tommy," I said. "They're working for a cause they believe in. I would like to have a cause to believe in, too, and not just spend my life starching collars. You have a cause—"

Tom thumped his forehead down on the tabletop, covering his head with his arms. "Had a cause," he said in a muffled voice. His body was collapsed in defeat.

Instantly I was beside him, my hand on the back of his neck. "What's happened? What did you hear?"

He raised his head as if it were too heavy to lift. I looked at his eyes and saw the sadness there, the loss of hope.

"The rising has failed," he said. "Failed utterly. The July newspapers from Dublin came in on the packet boat today."

"But I thought you told me John Mitchel had been transported to some prison colony—where, Australia? Did the rising go on without him?" This was the rising Tommy had been hoping for, working for, all these long years.

Tom sighed. "William Smith O'Brien took over after Mitchel was arrested and sent to Tasmania. A descendent of Brian Boru, for Christ's sake—he should have been able to pull off a rebellion!" He covered his head with his arms again, his escape from reality.

"How many men were lost?"

"Only two. The French backed out and the Dublin rising was

aborted because of informers. The entire battle was fought in Widow McCormick's garden in Ballingarry." He groaned in frustration. "A handful of policeman in a Tipperary farmhouse against all the men of Ireland—who *were not there*."

I knew that the rising would have turned out differently if Tom Riordan had been leading the men of Clare. Or Tom as well would have been on his way to Tasmania, or worse.

"A failed rebellion is better than none at all." I tried to comfort him. "Each time we rise, the British are forced to take notice."

"We need money and guns of our own," said Tom. "And the next time we'll succeed."

No more was said about the cholera sheds. Tom threw himself into his work making rivets and bolts, and he expanded his circle of friends. I was given the chance to learn ironing, another step up the ladder of success for Irishwomen in America.

◎ ◎ ◎

"A wedding! A real wedding, with a cake and a new dress? How lucky you are," I said. Eileen and I were walking home from early Mass on Sunday. "I'm so happy for you."

"It's the American style," said Eileen. "Hugh's doing well at the foundry, so he's not looking for a dowry from me. Instead we can entertain our friends and families."

Hugh's intended wife was a lovely girl with clear brown eyes and a handsome figure. Her less-than-intense approach to life made her a perfect match for Hugh, who wanted his life on the south side of Troy to be a smoother road than he'd had. I wondered sometimes about Eileen's own life—what had she gone through to come from Mayo?—but Eileen never spoke of the past. Only the future was important to her.

"We want you and Tom to stand up for us. Hugh is going to ask him. Would you do us the favor, Margaret?"

"I'd be honored. When is the date set for?"

"The third Sunday in October, in the afternoon. I've got to have time to sew my dress."

I too was seized with the desire for a new dress, something to see me through the winter. I decided to ask Tom whether we could spare the money this month. We had enough saved in the little bag under the mattress to get us through the annual winter layoff this year, when the foundries closed for the coldest months. I would continue working, and the wage increase for an experienced ironer would soon be mine.

CHAPTER 25

FROM THE ONE ROOM AT Mrs. Halloran's that had been our home for more than a year, we moved to a small one-bedroom apartment three houses down the street. We had space for Tom's friends to gather in the evening, and an oil lamp provided enough light for me to sew. More often I would read the daily newspaper, absorbing the information that would turn me into a real American.

The collar manufacturing businesses were expanding rapidly, hiring as many Irish women as applied for the laundries. Working with scalding kettles and harsh soaps and starches, the women earned every penny of their wage and more. After the school day was over, boys and girls would hurry through the streets with wagons loaded high with white fabric, cut and ready for stitching by the hundreds of women and girls working in their homes. The pay for piecework was miserably low, but it had the advantage of allowing mothers to look after their small children while earning their living. Widows and orphans were not uncommon in a community where the most dangerous work was done by Irish men.

Tom apprenticed himself to an iron molder, leaving Hugh to churn out horseshoes by the thousands. The molders were the most skilled in the trade, crafting the sand molds into which they poured the molten iron for casting, and it was no small thing to be taken on as an apprentice. Tom's good humor and steady hands quickly advanced him, and in time he would be experienced enough to run a molding crew of his own. It appeared that the cast iron industry would be Troy's other ticket to prosperity.

It was the future that led to the big ruckus between us.

The night before Hugh and Eileen's wedding, I was putting the final touches on my new blue dress, small satin ribbon bows tacked in a row down the side panel of the full skirt. It was beautiful.

"Such finery as you'd never see in a dirt-floored cottage in Clare," I said to Tom.

"Then perhaps you'd better make a dress more suited. How long does a dress last? We'll be going home again in a couple of years."

I dropped the needle into my lap.

"We're not going back, Tom. Our life is here now. And you could be arrested." I should have noticed the stubborn set of his jaw.

"In five years no one will remember or care about the death of a landlord's agent," said Tom. "We can go home again. Why do you think I'm saving every penny? I want to go home and finish what was started. Drive the British out of Ireland and reclaim our own land." He looked at me with a heart-piercing intensity. "Aren't you with me, Margaret? You didn't want to come here— now you don't want to go back?"

"There's nothing left to go back to," I said flatly. "Everyone's gone."

"Kitty's there," said Tom.

"Don't ever mention her name. You must be terribly desperate to use that as an argument."

Tom flushed. "I've devoted my life to the cause of Erin's freedom, and now you are telling me that I can't return. How desperate do you think that makes me?"

"And I ran with you when you fled for your life—because you asked it of me. I gave up my gift of keening so I wouldn't have to keen for you. Now I'm building a life of a different kind, here in America, and I don't want to give it up all over again."

"I never planned to stay here, Margaret. I never told you so."

"The rebellion is dead, Tom. You said it yourself—a scuffle in a cabbage patch. The British are still running the country, and the people are still starving to death. I'm not going back."

Tom rose and carefully pushed his chair in to the table. "I'm going out."

"Fine. See if any of your cronies at the Lark can run a revolution from a bar stool."

"Money and guns," said Tom, and he walked out.

I crumpled the blue dress into a ball in my lap. I would never return to Ireland. Kitty surely was dead by now.

I went by myself to Mass in the morning, since Tom had not come home last night. I walked in with my head high, another woman whose husband was gone. I knelt and stood in automatic movement, and instead of listening to the Latin prayers I counted the wives among the congregation whose husbands had left them to fend for themselves and their children. A few called themselves widows but everyone knew they truly belonged among the abandoned.

What would it mean, a life without Tom? I could hardly breathe when I thought of it. I had been his, and he mine, since before I could remember. How could he leave me to return to Ireland? How would I live with only half a life?

Ellen Halloran stopped me as I passed through the doors of the church at the end of Mass, my fingers still wet with the holy water that I didn't remember touching. Or maybe they were tears I didn't remember shedding.

"Margaret! Are you all ready for the wedding today? Did you finish the trim on your dress last night?"

I looked at her with eyes red from weeping.

"Whatever is the matter?" Ellen gasped. "You look a terrible sight."

"I'll be fine," I said. "I'm just not feeling myself right now. I'll be fine by four o'clock. I will."

Ellen looked at me doubtfully but did not pry. I carried no obvious bruises, and Tom was never rumored to have that nature. She patted me on the shoulder. "Go and have a little nap," she said. "We'll all be back here at a quarter to four."

Numbly I walked down the steps and through the streets to my home. Thoughts repeated over and over again, on every block. How could I go back to Ireland, when I had a future here? How could I bring a child into a world of starvation and oppression, when I had the opportunities of a lifetime here? How could I have a child at all, without a husband?

Obedient to Ellen's instructions, I went straight to the bedroom. I tossed my shoes and shawl in the corner, lay down on the bed, and put my head underneath the feather pillow to block out the light. If I didn't wake up again, I really didn't care.

At one o'clock the front door opened and Tom Riordan quietly stepped into the parlor. He looked as if he'd spent the night on his feet, which in fact he had. He'd walked the length of Troy, along the river banks and back again, out to the falls at the Poestenkill, back to the city streets where he lived. Pacing and thinking, struggling with his past and with his future. Now he had come home.

"Margaret?" he called softly.

Hearing no reply, he thought the worst. She had left him. On the day of his best friend's wedding, his own darling wife had left him.

He threw down on the kitchen table the bunch of flaming rust chrysanthemums that he had bought from a flower seller on Second Street. Their spicy sweet aroma tickled his nose and made him sneeze.

◎ ◎ ◎

The sneeze was so ferocious that I heard it from underneath my pillow. It was such a wonderful sneeze.

"Tom?" I called from the bedroom. "Is it you?"

I heard another sneeze that shook the house.

"For heaven's sake, whatever—" I stood in the doorway. Tom grabbed for a huge pile of chrysanthemums and clutched them to his chest. His face was the same shade of rust red.

"I'll stay with you," he said. "I'll raise money for guns and ship them over, but I'll stay right here in Troy with you."

"You can make more money with iron than with turf," I said. I held out my arms to him.

Tom tossed the flowers on top of my shawl in the bedroom corner and began to remind me, slowly, lusciously, of why we should never part.

At five minutes past four, we scurried into St. Mary's Church to take our places in the wedding of Hugh Sweeney and Eileen Magill. As matron of honor, I was looking much recovered from my headache at Mass that morning. The best man was a little the worse for wear, but that was to be expected from someone who had been seen walking the streets all night.

CHAPTER 26

THE WINTER IN TROY HAD been a hard one, bitter cold, with snow so constant that each day's walk to the laundry and back was a struggle. My boots were never dry. When I stepped out at night from the heat of the ironing room, wisps of steam rose from my feet. In the morning I reluctantly stuck my toes into the damp leather, cold and clammy even through my wool stockings. But at least I had boots, and at least I had a job.

The river froze, and the waterfalls that powered the factories turned into columns of thick white ice. The men in the shops were put out of work for the winter months, as happened most years, and those newcomers who hadn't saved a bit to get by were reduced to hunger again. The charities helped the worst cases, and by the end of March the thaw came.

Tom had spent the time doing what he loved best—organizing the men in Troy who still dreamed of a free Ireland. Sometimes he would go for a week to New York City, to meet with the big men in the secret societies. It was like the old days, but instead of bringing me home a loaf of bread, Tom would pull a length of bright ribbon from his pocket, or a set of pretty buttons. I didn't mind his trips, although I was relieved when he returned safely each time. It was our bargain. Money and guns.

The iron molders' shop where Tom worked would be opening again on Monday, so he'd made his last trip down to the city this week. I expected that he would return tonight on the daily steamboat.

On my way home from work, I stopped off at the butcher shop and picked up a small piece of ham to cook with the potatoes and turnips for our supper. I wanted to celebrate the sure signs of spring—the factories opening again, the melting snow. At home in Clare we would have already seen the early lambs in the fields, and the air would carry that sweet soft mist of spring rain that turned the grass greener than you could imagine. As usual when thoughts of my earlier life intruded, I sighed and reminded myself that starving people were eating that green grass and dying, and wasn't I lucky to be standing in America with a bit of ham in my bag?

The supper was ready, the table was set with two plates and mugs, and I had the water boiling for the tea when I heard the stamp of men's feet coming up the stairs. Not just Tom, then, I thought, with instant disappointment. And I wondered whether there was enough brown bread to go around the table.

The door opened and Tom walked in, smiling from ear to ear, a tall fellow right behind him.

"Look what the cat dragged in, Margaret!" he said, and stepped aside.

I couldn't believe my eyes. There stood Tom's brother Danny, alive and in America. I had left him on the road to Limerick as I went away to join my husband on the run.

"Danny!" I reached up to put my arms around him. "Tom never told me you were coming. I'm so happy to see you."

"Tom himself didn't know," Danny said. "There was a job that had to be done for some people and it meant a free ticket to New York, so I took it. Just the luck I'd run into my brother at the same pub where I had to report."

Danny looked so much like Tom had looked when we left Ireland—thinner than a man should be, jacket and trousers worn to shreds, but underneath it all the fire of hope and youth. My handsome husband, whose hand clasped mine warmly, was thriving in our new life. I desperately wanted the same for his younger brother.

"Sit down, sit down, and I'll get your supper on," I said. "We're eating like the rich folks with a piece of ham on a Saturday night." I wanted to feed this poor lad everything in sight.

"Thank you," Danny said.

"He'll be staying with us for a few weeks." Tom knew our home was always open to his brother. He was the only family we had left. Unless I counted my own brother Jimmy, last seen on the road to Belfast and not heard from since.

"We can make up a cot in the kitchen," I said. "We're glad to have you, Dan." Without thinking, I dropped the boy's name and used the man's. My father's name.

"*Sláinte*," replied Dan, raising an imaginary glass to our health.

I poured the tea, sliced the bread, and dished up the plates. News from Kilvarna could wait another hour.

As it turned out, Dan brought no news from Kilvarna. He had left for Dublin when Tom and I fled Clare, and he never went west any more. It was the worst place in Ireland, he said, and left it at that.

Even though we had a guest sleeping in the kitchen, Tom and I managed a quiet half hour of lovemaking before both of us fell into exhausted sleep. As I stroked the hard muscles of his body and felt the strength in his arms as he held me, I was glad we had come to this new world. Here we had a chance.

On Monday morning I packed our lunch buckets, and Tom went off to his job and I went to mine. A new girl was starting today, and I wanted to be there a few minutes early to meet her.

The line of women waiting to be let into the building was already forming. Still bundled in shawls and mittens, most of the women chattered more cheerfully than they had through the frigid icy mornings this winter. The men were going back to work today, which meant a pay packet on Saturday next. The shop-keepers could be paid some of what was owed, and the oatmeal and sugar and tea would be carried home in quantity.

I noticed the new girl right away. She was a tiny creature, no bigger than a twelve-year-old, standing away from the building and glancing around. Her dress was thin and her shawl not much better. I couldn't see her hair under the shawl, but I could see her rough red hands, bare of mittens, holding the shawl closed against the wind. My heart went out to her. Was this how I had looked when Ellen Halloran had brought me here the first day?

"Are you the new girl for ironing?" I asked her.

She nodded. Her face showed her to be around sixteen, not a child. I was relieved.

"I'm Margaret Riordan, and I'm going to help you get started today," I said with a smile. "What's your name?"

"Cathleen Brady. Pleased to meet you, ma'am."

"And where are you from, Cathleen?"

"I've just come from Ireland," she said.

I laughed. "So have we all, Cathleen dear."

She blushed. "From Sligo, that is. I came to my aunt in Albany, and she sent me over here to find work. I'm small but I'm a hard worker," she said firmly.

The doors opened and the women began to file in. "We'll see what you can do, Cathleen. Today we'll start with—" My words stopped as she dropped the shawl covering her head. Cathleen's bright coppery hair was the same shade as Kitty's had been, back in the days when we were leaping Beltane fires. Tangles of curls, just like hers. I looked away for a moment, my eyes suddenly blurred by tears.

Cathleen didn't notice, swept along in the crowd of women moving rapidly to their places. I shook my head to clear away the past and hoped that someday I could remember my darling friend without pain.

Over the course of the week I learned that Cathleen had lost her family, too, except for the aunt in America, who worked as a maid in one of the fancy houses in Albany. The aunt had sent the money to bring her here, but Cathleen was completely on her own. She shared a room with three other girls in a basement. I thought again how lucky I was to have my husband at my side when I set foot in this new place. Not every woman might want to take the risks of life with a man like Tom, but he suited me fine.

I asked Cathleen to come to the house on Sunday after Mass. I couldn't bear the idea that she would be confined to a dark basement room after spending the week in the steaming sweat of the laundry. Her face lit up as if the Queen had invited her to tea.

"May I bring anything for you?" she asked.

The poor child hadn't even a warm shawl or a pair of mittens. "Only yourself," I said. "That's enough."

I had already knitted a pair of dark green mittens—all but the left thumb, which would be ready and waiting on Sunday.

CHAPTER 27

DAN HAD FOUND A TEMPORARY job clearing away a winter's worth of fallen logs and brush that clogged the waterways near the factories. It was treacherous work. The banks were slippery with mud, and chunks of melting ice clashed and crashed together in the swiftly flowing river. Only the most recent immigrants were willing to sign on for such danger.

On Sunday he and Tom were planning to spend the afternoon with Hugh Sweeney and a few other men from Clare. I was glad of a chance to have some time with Eileen and Cathleen, just the three of us. Eileen was bringing a length of cotton print that she had bought at a good price, enough for a plain blouse, and I had found a skirt that could be cut down to fit Cathleen. If we sewed while we talked, Cathleen could go home with a new outfit for her new life.

Eileen and Hugh walked back with us from the church, and by the time the kettle was on and the bread and butter were laid out on the table, we heard a light knock at the door.

"Could you let Cathleen in, please, Tom?" I asked. He was rising to open the door even before I asked.

"Come in, come in," he said. "Be welcome and make your-self at home."

"God bless," Cathleen said politely. "I came as quick as I

could. The priest had an awful lot to say this morning, and there was a grand rush out at the end. I was nearly trampled to death. The churches here have so many people!"

Tom smiled and glanced over her head at me. She's not like Kitty, his look said. It's only her hair.

The six of us drank our tea and ate our breakfast until the last crumbs were gone. Eileen helped me clear the mugs and plates from the table.

"Do you see the way he's looking at her?" she whispered.

"Tom?" I said with a start.

"No, silly, Danny—like he's never seen a girl before." Eileen giggled.

"But he's going back to Dublin next month. This wouldn't be good at all."

"You never know." Eileen went over to Hugh and handed him his cap. "Don't you fellows have somewhere to go? We women have work to do."

Hugh grinned. "Here's your hat, what's your hurry?"

"Do you need me to lend a hand with something?" Dan asked, looking at Cathleen.

"Not unless you've miraculously learned to thread a needle," I said. "You can all come back for your dinner." The beans and salt pork had been simmering since early morning.

As soon as the men trooped down the stairs, I pulled out my sewing basket. "We've got a surprise for you, Cathleen."

Eileen brought out her pretty blue-flowered print, and I shook out the folds of the navy skirt. "We're going to fit you out properly," Eileen said.

"For me?" Cathleen's eyes were bright. I remembered how I felt when that patched green wool dress was handed to me the first night in America.

"Stand still so I can measure this skirt against you," I said. "And then you and Eileen can cut out the blouse." She was such a tiny thing, it wouldn't take long.

"Why would you do this for me, when we've only just met?" Cathleen asked.

"Because we've both been where you are now," I said, mumbling over the pins held between my lips. *And because you remind me of someone,* I said silently.

The three of us cut and pinned and sewed industriously through the rest of the morning and early afternoon. I heated up my small iron on the stove and pressed the seams, wishing I had the more professional equipment I used in the laundry. Eileen was a rapid stitcher, with all her experience of sewing piecework collars, and Cathleen did her best to keep us supplied with threaded needles and hot tea. I could tell that Eileen liked her, and I was becoming quite fond of her myself.

By the time the men came back, Cathleen was dressed in her new clothes, her cheeks pink with pleasure. Tomorrow she would be back in the laundry again, lugging baskets and boxes of gentlemen's white collars, but today she was among friends, the hardships of Sligo no longer a burden. Just the sight of her made me happy.

And without a doubt it made my brother-in-law happy. In the late afternoon he walked her home–she wearing her new green mittens–and it took much longer for Dan to return than could be accounted for by the distance.

◎　◎　◎

Eileen knocked at the door after supper one night, itself an unusual thing. She had a pale wan look about her, and I wondered what was wrong.

I fussed over her a bit and made her a cup of tea. We sat at the table and sipped from our mugs. Someday, I'm going to have a set of real teacups, with saucers, like the ones I've seen in the shop windows. And a pretty dresser to display them on.

"Do you ever miss your family? Your mam?" Eileen's sudden

question jolted me out of my teacup dreams.

Unprepared, before I could put up the walls, sorrow rushed through me in a flood. "Why?" I said. I turned the question away from me, back to Eileen.

"I just wondered. Lately I'm feeling the loss of my mother, of my sister, of everybody." Eileen never talked about her family in Mayo. "I'm on the edge of weeping all the time. I haven't any appetite at all."

Shades of Kitty. And of my mother. I deliberately thrust down my own feelings, as deep down as I could push them. Please, no, I prayed. I can't go through this again. I can't lose someone else to that terrible emptiness, that deadening void.

"I try not to think about the hard times," I said slowly. "It's only the future that's important. Our lives here. Hugh, and Tom. We can't do anything about the rest."

Eileen sighed. "Maybe it's just been a long winter. I'm so tired all the time, I can barely keep my eyes open while I'm sewing. I was fine a couple of weeks ago, when we made Cathleen's new clothes. Now it seems like it's too much effort to boil a potato for supper."

"Are you having any troubles with Hugh?" I tried to ask delicately, without prying into their personal life.

"Oh, no, he's the best man ever," she said. Her voice lifted, and I knew she was still in love with him.

I looked at her face closely. There was something about her that had changed, rounded. And then I knew. Of course. But a tremor of fear ran through my body.

"I'm not your mam, but I think I know what's wrong. That is, what's not wrong," I corrected myself.

Eileen still looked puzzled.

"I think you're in the family way."

"Oh!" She clapped her hand to her mouth with an audible sound.

After a moment she laughed. "You could be right, Margaret. That didn't even cross my mind. I guess I wasn't paying attention."

"You'll know for sure in a few weeks."

"I'd be so happy," Eileen said.

And I'll try to be happy, too, I told myself. Everything will be fine. This time.

CHAPTER 28

EILEEN'S SECRET HAPPINESS SOON BECAME apparent to everyone. Hugh strutted around as if a baby had never been born in the world before, and gradually I began to release my fears. Having a baby was the most natural outcome of two people being married, and most times their lives did not end in tragedy. Nevertheless, I was not looking to star in the same play myself anytime soon.

The weather was warm and the scent of lilacs filled the air in this last week of May. Tom and I had gone out to the Poestenkill Falls with Dan and Cathleen for a Sunday afternoon picnic. We sat on a blanket under the dappled trees, the roaring of the water a pleasant background. For some time Tom and I had been wondering when Dan was going to return to Ireland, but still I was surprised when Tom asked him the question directly. Especially in front of Cathleen.

"I'm not going back," Dan said.

Tom shook his head as if he hadn't heard correctly.

"Of course you're going back. I'd go back in a minute if—"

"No," Dan interrupted. "You're worth more here. You know what I mean. But I'm not going back to Dublin. There's no future for me there."

"What about the future for the people still starving in Clare? In the rest of Ireland? We're not giving up the fight while there's a British flag flying."

"I'm not giving up. But I'm not going back. I've thought it over and I have another plan."

I glanced over at Cathleen, wondering if this was news to her. She was twisting a blade of grass between her fingers, her eyes on the ground. So she knew, whatever it was.

Tom flushed angrily. "I thought you were a loyal Irishman. I thought you stood beside me. You're my brother."

"I can never be who you are, Tom. I have to make my own way. I'll work for Ireland but on my terms, not yours." Dan's tone was determined.

Tom glared at him. Dan didn't flinch.

I didn't dare intervene between two Riordans. Tom strode off toward the waterfall, his fists clenched. Dan waited a long moment, the conflict visible on his face, and then he followed. I didn't think either of them would hurl the other over the falls, but it took all my restraint to remain on the blanket next to Cathleen.

Silently I began to pack up the picnic. The minutes dragged on.

"I'm sorry, Margaret," whispered Cathleen. "Dan made me promise not to tell. Not until he had a chance to talk to Tom."

I remembered the secrets that I had held for Tom.

"I understand," I said. "I truly do."

She flashed a nervous smile. "I hope it will be all right."

"It will, in the end. The two of them have only each other. They'll work it out."

"Dan asked me to marry him. And I said yes."

The day had no end of surprises.

"So that's why he doesn't want to go back to Dublin," I said. "He must truly love you."

"He does, I think," Cathleen said shyly. "But his plan is to send even more money to support the rebellion."

"And how will he do that?" Another rebel romantic Riordan.

"We're going to California. To hunt for gold."

However Dan explained himself to Tom that afternoon, it was a few more days until the brothers were back on their old terms. On the night that Tom came up the stairs whistling "Oh Susanna," the popular new song about the Gold Rush, I knew he had come to accept Dan's decision.

I was delighted to have Cathleen as my future sister-in-law and sad at the prospect of losing her so soon. She and Dan planned to be married on the last Saturday in June and leave for points west the following day.

Eileen was feeling better now that the first months were over. We decided to make two dresses between us for Cathleen to take on her journey, as well as an apron and a wide-brimmed bonnet suited for the hot sun in the West. Avidly we read the newspaper accounts of men who had made fortunes in gold dust and nuggets picked up from the ground. There were some who mined ten or even twenty thousand dollars' worth in a single week. We imagined Cathleen and Dan sweeping the gold into dustpans with brooms.

The bridal pair were almost delirious with excitement. Three weeks was not a long time to put together a wagon and supplies for a journey lasting perhaps three months and crossing three thousand miles. But they were determined. Having so recently made the voyage across the ocean, perhaps an overland trip appeared less of a challenge to them than it did to me.

I intended to stay in Troy for the rest of my natural life.

The lamplight flickered and sputtered unevenly as I stitched furiously down the seam of Cathleen's pale brown wedding dress. I didn't want to have to fill the lamp again tonight, and this long side seam was all I had planned to finish. The rest could be done tomorrow in daylight, on the Sunday before the wedding.

Tom went to answer the knock on the door, a late visitor but not unusual for us. I thought it was probably one of his friends with an urgent message. I was surprised and then concerned to recognize Hugh Sweeney's voice behind me.

"What's wrong?" I said, laying down my needle. Dread seeped through me in an instant. It was too soon for the baby to come.

"Eileen's bleeding some," Hugh said. "She wants you to come with the midwife, Mrs. Mellowes, if you would, as soon as you can."

"Her house is down around the corner," I said, grabbing my shawl. "When did it start?"

"Only this afternoon. She's been lying down but she's a bit frightened now."

"Go on home and wait for us. We'll be there soon." I clattered down the steps as quickly as my feet could carry me in the dark.

Mrs. Mellowes was the midwife who attended most of the home births in the ironworkers' part of Troy. Some women went to the hospital, but most had neither the money nor the time to lie in for two weeks. Between delivering babies, Mrs. Mellowes also dispensed herbal remedies and practical advice. She was a healer not unlike Nuala Lynch, and I liked her.

Within just a few minutes she and I were standing beside Eileen's bed. The men were banished to wait outside while Mrs. Mellowes gently examined Eileen.

"Your color is still good, dear," she said reassuringly. "You're spotting but it's not a great flood."

My stomach lurched. I wouldn't have made a good midwife. It was death I had been trained for, not the bringing of life.

She felt Eileen's swollen belly carefully, and then she put her ear against the skin. Maybe she could hear a heartbeat. I didn't know.

"I'm going to poke his little rump," she said, "and see if he pokes back." I wondered how she could tell where the baby's rump was, but she seemed satisfied with the response.

"You're still feeling him move around?"

Eileen nodded apprehensively. "I thought he had gone to sleep before, but now he's kicking again."

"That's a good sign, indeed." Mrs. Mellowes patted Eileen's face. "I think you've been doing too much, Mrs. Sweeney. You'll need to stay off your feet for a week or so. And I'll leave you with some tea to drink that'll strengthen you. This little fellow has to be patient, that's all."

I felt as if I could breathe for the first time since we had entered the room.

Mrs. Mellowes smiled at me. "You're looking a little pale yourself, Mrs. Riordan. Are you going to be needing my help, too?"

"Oh no, ma'am. Not me. I was just worried, that's all."

She straightened the blanket covering Eileen. "Get some rest and I think you'll be fine. Your friend will help me make the tea."

I filled the kettle, and Mrs. Mellowes sprinkled a handful of dried leaves into the teapot.

"I should have thought of raspberry tea myself," I said. I recognized the leaves and knew their properties.

The older woman looked at me sharply. "I had heard you were a keener in the old country, but not that you were a healer."

"My grandmother taught me. But the keening isn't wanted here, and I left my supply of herbs behind. I'm so busy working in the collar laundry I haven't had time to gather new ones."

"I wouldn't mind sharing mine with you, and I could use help in gathering and drying this summer, if you're interested. My bones are getting stiffer every year."

"I would be honored to help you, Mrs. Mellowes. Thank you." It was a tiny connection to my old life but it felt good. And this time my best friend would be all right.

My second best friend.

CHAPTER 29

THE WOODEN FARM WAGON WAS loaded with barrels of flour and casks of water, with sides of bacon, sacks of cornmeal and flour, blankets and buckets and pots and pans. A canvas tarp was stretched across the wagon bed, and behind the six mules sat my brother-in-law and his new wife. She might have looked like a pretty little doll in her bonnet, but I knew how strong and wiry she had become. The grueling workdays in the laundry were probably good training for the wife of a California panhandler.

Like thousands of other hopeful souls, they were following dreams of gold. The news of a huge deposit found last year near a river in California had slowly made its way eastward, and now ships were sailing from Europe filled with treasure hunters. Dan and Cathleen were traveling the overland route, joining a wagon train and hoping to reach their destination by October. They had enough money saved to buy miners' tools and enough faith to think that they would actually strike it rich.

I laughed when I saw the full wagonload of goods, thinking of how Tom and I started out our marriage. A different country and a different life.

"Write to us when you can," I reminded Cathleen. "We'll keep you in our prayers and in our thoughts."

She leaned down to squeeze my hand one last time. Tom

slapped his brother's shoulder and then the lead mule's backside. We watched together as they rumbled off in the direction of the ferry landing, which would start their journey west.

"Back to only ourselves again," I murmured. For weeks we had been climbing over stocks of provisions accumulating in our rooms. The place would feel empty without them, and without Dan sitting at the table.

"Didn't I tell you, Margaret? I've invited two young lads from New York to get out of the hot city and stay with us for the summer." Tom sounded perfectly serious.

I searched his face. "You are joking, aren't you?"

"I am," he said. "There's only one."

That one turned out to be merely an overnight guest, sent to collect something that I neither saw nor heard mentioned. A polite young man, with a Dublin accent and a ticket back to Ireland in his breast pocket. I wondered if he was sent to take Danny's place.

I enjoyed spending some Sunday afternoons with Mrs. Mellowes. Hugh was taking such good care of Eileen that I didn't need to worry. I began to let go of the nightmare of Kitty's pregnancy and replace it with a vision of hope and happiness for the Sweeney family.

Tom didn't mind my walks out with the midwife, any more than he had minded the same with Nuala Lynch. It wasn't the same, though, and sometimes I returned in a dark frame of mind, mourning what I had lost. But then I would have to pick myself up and get on with whatever task needed doing. Our kitchen was filled with drying stems of wild herbs and jars of brewing tinctures. Seeing them did make me happy, most of the time.

I earned another promotion in the laundry, and the small increase that came with it was very welcome indeed. Tom and I were putting anything extra aside to save for a house of our own. It would take years, of course, but there was a chance of our getting a piece of property that we would own. Never could we have hoped for such in Clare.

From new immigrants just off the boat we heard rumors that half the villages in the West of Ireland had disappeared, the families fled to America or dead, the cottages tumbled. In my heart I knew they were not rumors. The land had been emptied.

◎   ◎   ◎

Eileen's little boy was born in October. He'd apparently been waiting eagerly to make his appearance, and he came out bawling and kicking. Mrs. Mellowes caught him in her experienced hands and, like a slippery fish, he squirmed and wriggled until she got the blanket around him for a good grip. She bound the cord and cut it with her sharp little knife, and then she handed him to me. I'd never seen an infant so glad to be born.

"What a bold lad you've got here, Mother," said Mrs. Mellowes to Eileen. "He's a little Samson, isn't he?"

Eileen lay back in her bed, exhausted but with a proud smile on her face. "Hugh wants to name him John, after his father," she said. "May I see him, please?"

I handed him to Eileen while Mrs. Mellowes finished the rest of the job. No, I definitely didn't want to add midwifery to my skills. I sat myself down on the bed next to Eileen and put my head down between my knees. Maybe it was the difference between this birth and the last one I had experienced. My head felt light and I thought I might faint.

"Are you all right, Margaret?" Eileen's voice penetrated through my fog.

I lifted my head. She was in better shape than I was, sitting up with the baby at her breast already, his tiny fuzzy head cradled in her hand.

"I will be," I said. "It's just that this is so different—from the last time." Pale baby Bridget and starving suffering Kitty, a widow at seventeen. I did the best I could for them, but it wasn't enough.

"I don't know what you're referring to, but I'm sure it wasn't a birth I attended," said Mrs. Mellowes.

"It wasn't," I said. "It was my best friend back in Clare. In '47." That was the most I could say.

"Then I know what you've gone through," she said.

Oh, but she could not. No one else could.

CHAPTER 30

SOMETIMES THE THINGS THAT YOU think are just dreams turn out to be true. In the bitter cold of February 1850, a letter came for us from California. It had traveled thousands of miles, been carried in saddlebags and pouches, passed through who knows how many hands, and wound up on our table in Troy, in the state of New York.

Tom slit open the paper with his pocketknife. A tiny gold nugget fell out.

"Sweet Jesus," he said. "Did they do it?"

I picked up the tear-sized nugget and displayed it in my palm. "How could they send something like this in the mail?"

Tom laughed. "You are so practical, my darling girl. The point is, they did."

He shook the letter to see what else fell out. Nothing did, so he began to read aloud.

Dearest Margaret and Tom,

Hoping you are well, with God's grace. After suffering from Indians and tornadoes, Dan and I arrived in California with the rest of our party in October. We staked our claim near the South Fork of

the American River, and almost immediately little
bits of yellow gold were shining in our pans. It truly
is the Promised Land.

When we have mined all the gold near the surface,
we're going down to San Francisco for the rest of the
winter. Then we'll come back in the spring to dig some
more. It's hard dirty work, but so is ironing. And iron
molding, Dan wants me to add.

Why don't you come out here too?

Much love,
Cathleen Riordan

"Well," said Tom. "Maybe we should get a wagon."

"Over my dead body," I replied instantly. A tiny nugget of gold was not enough to drag me from my home to a second strange land.

"I was only teasing."

"Maybe," I said. "But if you go, you go alone. I've got a job here and friends and a life. And a husband," I added.

"Do you now?" he said as he bent to kiss the back of my neck. It was Saturday night and we had nowhere else to go. The bath water was heating on the stove.

"Shall we make it worth our while for the bath?" Tom asked.

"Oh yes," I said. "Let's."

Eileen Sweeney had taken to mothering like a duck to water. She had nestled the baby in her shawl, filled him full of her rich milk, and returned to sewing collars when he wasn't yet a month old. Johnny grew faster than any babe I had seen in

Clare. His grip on my little finger was strong from the start, and at five months old he sat on my lap, shook his wooden rattle, looked all around, and laughed. I permitted him a hold on my heart as well.

Tom was away with his cronies in New York City, his last trip of the winter before the ironworkers' shops reopened. Time seemed to speed by in America. How could it have been a year ago that Dan showed up at our door? A year ago that we met Cathleen? At this rate I'd be an old woman before I knew it.

Some days I was worn to pieces by the demands of the ironing room. The collar factories were growing fast, and now I had more than a dozen women who worked under my direction. I couldn't believe there were enough men's necks in all of the country to wear the number of collars we turned out each month. The rage for the collars was spreading down from the bank managers and lawyers to the lowly clerks, I supposed.

Without Tom home for supper, I didn't feel like fussing. I warmed up the oatmeal from breakfast and ate it slowly, disliking the slimy texture and pasty taste.

"My, how you've come up in the world, Margaret," I ridiculed myself. Three years ago a cup of oatmeal was our wedding feast. Look at me now, wishing for chicken soup in my bowl instead of porridge. And then I ran for the bucket and threw up.

A queasy stomach had plagued me all week, since Tom had been gone. I blamed it on my hard days at work, but I was beginning to suspect another cause. And I wasn't sure how I would handle it. Losing my supper so abruptly brought me face to face with the reality. I could no longer ignore the swelling and tenderness of my breasts. My monthly flow had been only a trickle. I would have to admit that I was pregnant.

The voices of reason in my head assured me that this happened all the time. Hadn't Eileen produced a beautiful child, healthy and strong and surviving? And hadn't she returned to her own cheerful self, happy and busy and engaged in her life? And didn't I know a dozen other women my age who were mothers? But the voices of the past screamed out to me still. Danger lies this way. Madness. Horror.

My body began to shake and my throat ached with tears. Alone in my room, surrounded by the shadows of Kitty and Jackie and baby Bridget. Never able to talk about them, not even—not especially—with Tom. How would I get through these next few months?

I wrapped myself in a blanket and huddled in a chair. My eyes burned and my hands trembled and my skin was clammy. I can't do this, I kept repeating to myself. I'm too afraid. I can't do this.

Sometime during the night, the deepest most alone part of the night, I heard myself begin a keen. A keen for Kitty, and for Jackie, and for Bridget, and for all those unfortunates who had gone from my life in the past three years. For Patrick the young Kerry fiddler, for Nuala Lynch, for the people of Kilvarna and the people of Clare and the people of all Ireland. For the ships that never made it to America. For the people who died in the fever sheds. For the people who had found no peace.

I cannot tell what words I sang, or if there were words at all. I keened through my fears and into the healing of my life.

By the time the morning whistles blew at the factories, I was deeply asleep in my chair. I woke to the sound of the start of the day and the voice I heard in my head whispered, you can do it. You are not alone. You can do it.

I can do it. I will do it. I *am* doing it. I'm going to be a mother.

◎　◎　◎

I waited another two weeks before I ventured to tell Tom the news. I thought he would take it better when he was back at work with the iron molders, earning a good weekly wage, than when we were at the lowest point of our savings for the winter. In a way I was surprised that he didn't notice the signs. But instead of morning sickness, the nausea came on me when I left the laundry each evening. I hoped it would be over soon, although Eileen and Mrs. Mellowes both assured me that it was a sign of a healthy baby.

Eileen was delighted. "I thought you never would!" she exclaimed. In her eyes, the baby was already real. She volunteered to care for my infant along with her Johnny so that I could return to my job. I would talk that over with Tom, of course, but it seemed a good plan to me. I was working my way up in the collar laundry, just as Tom was in the ironworks, whereas Eileen was supremely happy to stay in her house and be a loving mother. If she could earn a little money another way, she could give up the piecework sewing of collars. And I would spare myself from being alone in a house with a new baby all day, every day, forever. I wouldn't be like Kitty, at all.

Tom Riordan can still surprise me, even after three years of marriage. I told him after supper one night, in an offhand kind of way, that he was on the road to being a father.

"Now, Margaret, you're not joking with me?" Tom looked me straight in the eye and I blushed.

"No, Tommy, it's true," I said. "We're going to be a family."

"Jesus, that's good news," he shouted. "I thought we never would!"

I hadn't known he'd cared.

PART II

1858

CHAPTER 31

"Jimmy! Where's your father?" I called down the hallway. I set my lunch pail down on the floor next to Tom's. I was late myself getting home from the laundry, and now I had to put a meal together for the children. Tom probably hadn't eaten at all.

"He's at Druids Hall," Jimmy shouted back. "At a meeting."

Jimmy was the picture of his father at eight years old, wiry and fair. He pursued me into the kitchen in hopes of snagging something to eat before supper.

"Be a good lad and run upstairs to fetch the others," I asked him. "Aunt Eileen must be a saint to keep them so late today." In the house we had bought in South Troy, we rented the upstairs flat to the Sweeneys.

"She's not a saint," said Jimmy seriously. "She said a bad word at tea when Danny spilled the milk."

"Did she?" I kept a straight face. "Do you want to tell me what that bad word was?"

Jimmy hesitated. I could see he was caught between a rock and a hard place. If he said the word, he'd be liable to have his mouth washed out with soap—at least that's what I've always threatened. But it would be so satisfying to say it out loud, being merely the answer to a question and therefore no sin involved. Jimmy had recently made his First Holy Communion and was always on the lookout for sins he had to report.

"I could whisper it to you," he compromised.

"No, you can't. A word so powerful has to be said out loud or not at all."

Jimmy considered for a moment. "Then I'll keep it to myself," he said. "I don't want to get Aunt Eileen in trouble."

"Good man. Now go up the back stairs and fetch Danny and the girls."

I sliced a new loaf of bread and put the slices on a plate. Cheese and sweet pickles, with hot sweet tea, would make a fine supper for the children and me. Tom would no doubt have something similar—ale rather than tea—after the meeting at Druids Hall. The iron molders were gathering to form a union.

A burst of children through the door ended the quiet minutes of my day. Seven-year-old Danny, darker and smaller than his brother, ran straight to the table and sat in his place, all the sooner to eat. Jimmy shepherded the little girls, brown-haired Mary Bridget and Elizabeth Rose, to their seats. He lifted Rosie up onto the wooden box that elevated her to table level. At five and three, the girls were still too young for school. They spent the days upstairs at the Sweeneys, where they played with Eileen's children. The arrangement had allowed me to keep my job in the laundry of the collar factory, where at twenty-nine I was already a forewoman.

"Who can tell me what tomorrow is?" I asked, as I buttered bread for the girls.

"My birthday," said Rosie. It was always her answer.

"Easter," said Mary Bridget.

"Easter already was," said Danny in disgust at his sister's ignorance.

"May Day," said Jimmy. "They're putting the flower wreaths on the Virgin Mary at St. Joseph's."

"My, you've become a good Catholic," I said. "Do you know, when I was a girl, we still had the bonfire on May Eve, back in Ireland."

"We could burn the trash in the yard tonight," said Jimmy with enthusiasm. He loved anything to do with fire. He had already determined that he wanted a job in the smelting plant, where the great fires reduced the iron ore to shining molten rivers.

"We could but we won't," I said. Jimmy then lost all interest in the old days of Ireland as he piled another slice of cheese on his pickles.

It was just as well. Those days were gone, a dozen years and three thousand miles away.

The hall was filled with twice as many men as had been present the night before. Working men, iron molders who put in twelve-hour days, willing to listen to the determination and dreams of the handful of their brothers who had—two nights earlier—formed the Iron Molders International Union, Number 2 of Troy, New York. The union had six members on April 28, 1858. Tonight the membership might swell to twenty.

"Most of us here remember what it was like in the old country," began the first speaker, Marty Collins. "When we worked to till our small plots, raised a pig to pay the rent, and yet ended up starving and destitute. The landlords stripped us of everything, our property and our freedom." Rumbles of assent interrupted the speaker. "But we don't hark back to those earlier days, because now we are in America, land of the free and land of opportunity. Am I right?" He looked around at the nodding heads. Then he roared, "Well, boys, we had *better* pay attention, because the factory owners are the landlords of America! They'll take from us every penny that we earn, they'll cut our wages to increase their profits, and they'll turn us into slaves all over again—*unless we have a strong union!*" Collins's words were underscored by whistles and cheers and the stamping of boots.

"We are the cream of the crop in this room tonight," he continued. "The most skilled in the iron trade, the molders who make it all possible. Not a mill could run without our gearing, not a factory would have the machine parts they need if we didn't do our jobs with precision and pride. Even the rich men would fall off their high steps were it not for the strength of our ornamental railings—" He got the laugh he was fishing for.

"But how do we protect our jobs? How do we put a value on the experience and skill we bring to our craft? How do we keep our wages steady? When the owners tell us that their sales are down and their costs are up, so we have to take a cut in pay—how do we say 'NO!'? With a Molders' Union, that's how! United together in brotherhood for the protection of us all."

He waited until the cheers and whistles died down again. "And what will it take to create such a Union? Brotherhood. Commitment. Courage." He softened his voice so the men would have to listen closely. "And is there a molder in this room who does not already possess those stellar qualities? Who does not *already* use them every day in his shop? There is not." The room exploded with sound.

Several more rounds of speeches—from other molders and from an organizer from Number 1 in Philadelphia—drove the men to line up at the membership table. Tom Riordan congratulated each and every molder as the man inscribed his name on the membership roster and handed the initiation fee to Tom. He knew them all, his brothers in the trade. And most of them knew him, in a similar capacity though not so public. Every payday Tom collected donations for money and guns. The Fenians in America were going to be a great support to their brothers in Ireland.

◎ ◎ ◎

The letter arrived first for Hugh Sweeney, bearing a Belfast postmark. A sheet of paper in a wrinkled envelope, addressed to "Hugh Sweeney Ironworker, Troy, New York, United States of America." The foreman of Hugh's department at the Burden Iron Works handed it to him on his way out. "You're not a bloody Orangeman, are you, Hugh?" he asked, grinning.

"I've never been north of Ballyvaughn," Hugh replied, mystified at the postmark. The letter made him unaccountably anxious, so he carried it home in his pocket to open in the presence of Eileen.

"Well, it's not from your mother unless she's moved again," said Eileen. Hugh's widowed mother was living in Ennistymon with her only surviving daughter and son-in-law. Hugh sent them a sum from his pay packet every month, as he had done from the time he left Kilvarna. "Open it, Hugh. Let's see."

The single sheet was in a careful handwriting, only two paragraphs:

Dear Hugh Sweeney,

 I hope you are doing well for yourself in America. I heard from a man who met your sister Mary's husband at a horse fair that you are in Troy, in New York, and that you may know the whereabouts of my sister Margaret Meehan. She is all the family I have left. Someone told me she had run off to Australia with the rebel Tom Riordan but now I guess that is not true. I hope to hear that she is safe and well.

 Please respond to the address below. I am employed in a small shipping firm in Belfast and will be married next month. I would like to share my happiness with my sister, if God wills it.

With the kindest regards of the writer,
James Meehan, formerly of Kilvarna, Co. Clare

"What is Mary's husband doing at a horse fair? Is that how they spend our money?" said Eileen Sweeney before she could stop herself. She laughed and clapped a hand over her own mouth.

"Now, Eileen, stop," said Hugh mildly. "If you had any family left, we'd send money to Mayo, too."

"We have enough family here." She was expecting their fifth child—or fifth and sixth it might be, from the size of her belly. "Won't Margaret be excited, to hear from her brother after all this time? She named Jimmy for him."

"I would think so," said Hugh. "And since she hasn't yet run off to Australia with the rebel, I suppose we'd better deliver the letter."

Eileen said she was all for making a big to-do of the occasion, but it turned out that Hugh was right to simply hand the letter to me as I sat with my mending. Had I been standing, I would have fallen to the floor.

Jimmy's letter clutched in my hand, I left Hugh, Eileen, and Tom drinking tea at the table. I closed the door to the bedroom and knelt down at the oak bureau. In the bottom drawer I kept the ancient stone from Brigid's well, wrapped in a red flannel scrap. Most of the time I barely remembered it was there, a relic from another life before this one. The only link I had to Clare, aside from the living connection of my husband and his lifelong best friend.

Underneath the winter wool blankets I felt around for the knobby little package. I brought it out and unfolded the cloth. The rough stone figure was just as I remembered it. I was an eighteen-year-old girl again, kneeling at the holy well, swirling the stone in the dark water, promising to keep the old ways alive, to continue the keening, if only in my heart.

The drops of water that now soaked the stone were not from Brigid's well in Clare. They were the silent tears that I shed—in sadness for what had been forever lost and in joy for what had survived.

CHAPTER 32

AFTER A DOZEN YEARS, I still wasn't accustomed to the icy cold of New York, although the winter's daylight lasted two hours longer than at home in Clare. Hurrying to work in the dark mornings and trudging home in the gloom as well, each week I looked forward to seeing the sunshine on Sunday mornings as we walked to Mass. Jimmy and Danny, of course, didn't mind the cold—they spent the hours after school sliding down snowy hills on makeshift sleds and playing crack-the-whip across frozen ponds. Real American boys, I often thought, with some amazement. My life had taken such a different turn than what I had imagined when Tom and I first jumped the May bonfire.

Now spring was beginning to take over the city. The first days of April 1861 had brought a mild breeze, and the snow remained only in smudged black piles that grew smaller every day. Bright yellow, white, and purple crocuses glowed in masses of color in front of the Court House. Taking a moment to admire the blooms, I enjoyed a sense of hopefulness, so hard to maintain during the long frigid season when the ironworks were closed and the men idle. Tom had spent his days persuading workers to join the Molders' Union, now over 400 strong, and many of his nights doing who-knows-what for the Fenian Brotherhood. He had a knack for politicking and fundraising, which seemed to be what the Fenians on this side of the Atlantic favored, to my relief.

The foundries down by the river had reopened a month ago, and the winter months of organizing had almost immediately resulted in a vote to strike. The foundry owners hired too many low-wage helpers, Tom said, who were taking away work from the experienced molders and creating dangerous conditions by their inexperience. I had become accustomed to the succession of strikes—some successful, some not—but each time Tom told me of another one, I pitied the wives and children of the other workers. Not everyone was as fortunate as I was in having a forewoman's job in the collar laundry that paid a decent wage all year round.

Our concern over the strike was being quickly overtaken by the worsening reports coming from the South, though. The newspapers implied that a war over secession was liable to break out any day. President Lincoln was doing his best to avert that tragedy, but hope was failing. When Mr. Lincoln had stopped at Union Station in February on his way to be inaugurated, he had given a stirring speech to the crowds. Tom had taken Jimmy and Danny to see the great man, and Danny was still talking about it. He believed Abraham Lincoln was the tallest man in the world, probably over eight feet with his black stovepipe hat. Jimmy had been more impressed by the 34-gun artillery salute.

As I rounded the corner of the street where we lived, I saw a commotion out front of the house next to ours. A crowd of men and women milled about, and I began to run.

Eileen broke away from the crowd as she saw me coming. "Margaret!" she shouted. "Don't worry—no one has hurt the children!"

"Oh my God, what's happened?" I ran toward Eileen but my eyes were searching the crowd for my children. And for Tom.

Eileen reached me and put her arm around me protectively. Her face was red, her hair slipped out of its pins and half-falling down her neck.

"They attacked the wrong house," she said.

For a split second I was standing on the road to Kilvarna, Kitty telling me that the constables had burned my house to the ground. I swayed and Eileen held me firmly.

"Attacked?" I echoed.

Eileen began to steer me toward the crowd in front of my neighbors' house. The Sheehans lived there, a houseful of nicer people than you could ever hope to meet. Who would attack the Sheehans?

I looked up at the windows on the second floor of my own house. My two girls, Mary Bridget and Rosie, waved down at me, surrounded by the younger Sweeney children. The children were safe. What had been attacked?

The crowd in the street parted for me. In the center I saw Jimmy and Danny, and behind them the destruction of the front of the Sheehans' house. The two big windows were shattered, glass in shards on the porch and steps. Great gashes of blackened scorched wood at the sides of the window frames dripped with dirty water. Empty wooden buckets sat in the street. Smoke curled from the sodden mess inside the front door.

My sons were standing in front of me, their faces pale, watching for my reaction. I couldn't take it all in. I said the first thing that entered my mind, the automatic assumption of a mother of sons.

"Are the two of you responsible for this?"

"Jesus, no!" shouted Jimmy, visibly jumping back. "It was the strikebreakers after Dad!"

"They threw flaming bottles that blew up," Danny said. "Only they got the wrong house. It was supposed to be ours."

My brave young sons stood straight, not a lip trembling, giving no sign that they feared the danger our family had been put in—just like their father. I gathered myself together and hugged them. "I'm sorry, so sorry. It's not always easy to be a Riordan." I'd known that for a long time.

Andy Neill from across the way stepped out of the crowd of

neighbors, a big burly man in work clothes streaked with smoke and dirt. "Mrs. Riordan, I saw the horse and cart drive by, going at a terrible speed. Two fellows hurled something out of the wagon, and next thing you know the windows were shooting flames."

I closed my eyes for a second. The situation could have been so much worse.

"Me and your boys got the family out and the fire put down. Someone's gone with a message for Tom Riordan." He laughed without humor. "Although I believe a message is what he's received."

"I can't thank you enough, Mr. Neill. We've been warned about strikebreakers' violence, but it's still a shock. Thank God no one was hurt."

"Thank God indeed. But this won't stop the strike, ma'am. It's just one more example of the ways they try to bully us. I've told the Sheehans that we'll have men here tonight to fix up the house good as new." Andy was a union man, too, as were a number of the men who lived on the street.

"Thank you again, for all your help. Now I've got to apologize to my unfortunate neighbors." What could I possibly say to the mothers whose home was attacked in our stead?

The two Sheehan wives and a dozen children huddled in a dazed group on the small patch between our two houses. Poor family, they hadn't deserved this fright. Jim Sheehan and his brother Mike drove carts for a city hauling company. They weren't union organizers.

I went over to them, distress in my heart.

"You and your family are all right?" I asked gently. They just stood there looking at me, as if I had two heads. "I couldn't be more sorry for this trouble," I continued. "I never expected such a terrible thing—to attack a man's wife and children . . ." Somewhere deep inside, anger was rising above the feeling of shock.

Mrs. Jim Sheehan found her tongue. "We're not union people, Mrs. Riordan, and this isn't our fight. Your husband has put us in mortal danger, and even if the place is fixed up tonight, who's going to promise that we won't be blown to smithereens some other night? Or you and your young ones, either?"

I hated to hear my own fears voiced aloud. During other strikes of the past two years, there had been fights and brawls and attacks on picketers. Sometimes Tom came home bloodied and bruised, but it had never touched our home until now.

"I don't know what to say to comfort you," I admitted in all honesty. "I can only pray that the strike will end soon."

"And I'll keep praying for you," said my neighbor. "But tonight we'll be discussing where to find another house to rent. Your Tom Riordan is a threat to the street—aye, the whole city block." Her usually smiling mouth was set in a bitter line.

I swallowed any defense or protest. Instead I offered them the hospitality of my house. At the very least I could make tea and bread and jam for the children.

"No, thank you," said the other Mrs. Sheehan. "As soon as our men get here, we'll be removing to my sister's house. You've caused us enough trouble for one day."

My temper flared at last. "A working man should be able to protest unfair conditions without his home and family being attacked! This is America."

The women said nothing but turned away from me.

Eileen came up and took my hand. I was shaking with anger. "There's nothing else to do but wait for Tom, Margaret. You may as well sit down with a cup of tea to brace yourself. Our union star is going to be in a rare state."

But in fact, once the work was underway to repair the damage to the Sheehans' house, Tom was almost cheerful. To his way of thinking, attacking the wrong house proved that the owners were bringing in strikebreakers from other towns to do the dirty work.

That meant they were getting desperate to settle the strike. As the threat of war loomed, the iron foundries needed the skilled molders back on the job, he said.

What about the danger to your children today? I wanted to ask my husband. *Are you so single-minded that it's the union, first and foremost?* But I held my thoughts to myself. And as we were settling into our bed late at night, Tom told me quietly that he had posted armed guards around the house. There was not a trace of cheerfulness in that remark.

A week later, the Confederate troops fired on Fort Sumter in North Carolina, and the Rebellion began. Immediately people in Troy tried to outdo one another in showing their support for the Federal Union—I had never seen such a display of patriotism, coming as I did from a land of oppression and poverty. The bombardment took place on Friday the twelfth of April, and by Monday the Stars and Stripes were hoisted on all the public buildings and churches, and on many of the shops and businesses. Mary Bridget and Rosie begged for red, white, and blue ribbons for their hair, which I bought for them at the milliner's shop owned by Mrs. Ludlow. She could scarcely keep the ribbons in stock this week, she said, and her bolts of red, white, and blue cotton had sold out on Tuesday. I could hardly believe my eyes when I saw respectable women downtown dressed as if they were flags themselves.

Volunteer enlistment offices were being set up around the city. Tom came home each night to glumly report the number of union members who had joined the Second Regiment of New York Volunteers. The younger ironworkers were eager to fight for the honor and glory of their adopted country—and the word "Union" was taking on another meaning entirely these days. Preserving the Union against the attempted secession of the

Southern states was a goal worthy of sacrifice, everybody said. Even the Sunday sermons talked of nothing but the war.

The molders' strike began to seem less than patriotic as the workers volunteered to go off to Camp Willard to train for duty. We suffered no more attacks from strikebreakers. And the foundry owners settled with the union—who compromised by allowing apprentices to join as members, rather than accept the non-union helpers—before the first regiment of troops was seen off from Union Station in May.

I was thankful that my own boys were too young to join up, and Eileen's son John was not quite thirteen. All of us prayed that the Rebellion would be put down within the year. Surely a few slave-holding states in the South couldn't hold out long against the army of the United States of America.

Tom and Hugh and the men in the iron trades worked long hard hours during the first months of the war. The horseshoes turned out by machine at Burden's were so coveted by the Confederates that they ambushed Union supply wagons to get them.

"Whatever those rebels steal, we'll make twice as many the next day," Hugh bragged. It seemed to me that people took the war very personally here.

Tom was more involved in trying to keep the trade unions from disappearing entirely, since so many of the members were either in uniform or working long shifts to keep up with the wartime production. He was having more success with recruiting for the Fenian Brotherhood, it seemed, which may have had something to do with the old hatreds still simmering. To Tom and his Fenian friends, the fact that England was still discussing cotton trade with the Confederacy marked her all the more as the enemy, now in America as well as in Ireland.

Jimmy and Danny followed the reports of the war with great

enthusiasm. Jimmy had a job selling the afternoon edition of the *Troy Daily Times* on a corner down by River Street, so we were always up on the latest news. As soon as the bundles of papers were released, Jimmy would stand on his corner and call out the headlines. "By Telegraph! This afternoon's report on the Rebellion!" And people would rush out of the offices and factories to scoop up a copy. When the news told of an important victory for the North, Jimmy would catch a few extra pennies in tips tossed in the air.

Last fall two men from Troy had sponsored an inventor named John Ericsson to design a new ironclad battleship, which the government approved. Its enormous iron hull plates were made in the Albany Iron Works down by the river. Jimmy could rattle off the height and weight of the plates to the inch and the ounce and bore me to tears with detailed descriptions of exactly how the plates were constructed, and how the turret containing the guns could rotate, and why a boat made of iron could float.

I was pleased that at least he was reading the papers he was selling, but I didn't pay much attention to how important everyone thought this odd-looking ship was going to be. I was busy trying to manage the starchers and ironers during the day and my two growing daughters at night. It wasn't such a bad time, though—the girls and I joined in the campaign to knit socks for soldiers, so every evening we'd sit and click our needles and tell stories.

The *U.S.S. Monitor*, as the ironclad was named, steamed down the east coast in early March 1862 to engage the enemy. When the news came that our sturdy ship had driven off the Confederate ironclad *Merrimac* after a five-hour battle in Virginia, saving the fort and the wooden fleet, the city was beside itself with pride.

On a Saturday evening two weeks later, we all bundled up in our shawls and warm jackets to celebrate the victory of the *Monitor* and honor the men who made her plates and rivets. We stood on a street corner as about four hundred of the ironworkers from two of the foundries marched through the city in a torchlight procession. We had never seen such a display in our lives, and at first Rosie hid behind my skirt, peering out. These few hundred men, through their sweat and strong backs and tireless arms, had created the iron rivets and hull plates that saved the day. A wagon rolled past carrying a large picture of the battle scene, lit by the eerie flicker of hundreds of flaming torches. The marchers were whooping and shouting and laughing. The crowds along the streets were whistling and clapping and cheering.

So many of the ironworkers, catching sight of Tom standing tall and fair on the corner, raised their fists in salute that I turned to him and asked, "Did you have something to do with the *Monitor,* too?" It wouldn't have surprised me.

"No," he said. "Those men are my Fenian brothers. The Irishmen of Troy make a grand sight, don't they?"

He returned the salutes of another group of workers as they passed by. "And here in America we'll never forget the old country. Or the fight for Irish freedom."

No one could ever argue the point that Tom Riordan was anything but steadfast.

CHAPTER 33

THE AIR WAS UNUSUALLY CHILLY for the second week of May. Yesterday the newspaper had remarked on the possibility of snow. I started off to work on Saturday morning in a gust of wind that propelled me down the street a little faster than I was expecting, as if an invisible hand were pressing against my back. I was glad it was Saturday and an early dismissal—all week I had been longing to get into the bit of garden patch in back of the house, to uncover the tender green of my winter-hardy herbs and turn over the damp cold soil that would soon hold the seeds of string beans and cabbages. The growing season here was nothing compared to the soft, long summers of Clare, but we didn't have to worry about the blight, either. And I could buy all the potatoes we wanted at the market down the street.

Tom had gone off to the foundry hours earlier. I left the girls eating their breakfast of oatmeal porridge, with a list of household chores to finish before I returned home. The two boys were still abed, but no doubt they would go off and do whatever boys did on their day free from school. Jimmy had to sell the early afternoon edition of the paper down on River Street, and sometimes Danny went with him for practice. When Jimmy moved on to the ironworks as an apprentice next year, Danny would take over the job.

Thoughts of my family and my garden kept me going through the increasing wind until I reached the collar laundry. I was prepared to help the other women finish up our orders for the week as quickly as we could, the sooner to get our pay packets and return home. We all put our attention to the work and the morning sped by.

Just after noontime the air inside our room began to smell of smoke. Not the ordinary whiff of burning coal that kept our irons hot, or the acrid scorch of a collar left unattended too long. This was a heavy, dense, ominous presence. My breath caught in my chest, for a factory fire was a certain disaster. I looked around at the women to see if they sensed the danger I did. But for the moment most of them seemed merely curious.

"I'll go out to see what that smoke is about," I said. " 'Tis probably nothing at all to concern us."

Our laundry room was on the street level, and the instant I opened the door into the hallway the smell grew stronger. Two of the other forewomen were also on their way to the door, looking as worried as I felt.

"The smoke seems like it's coming in from the outside," one of them said.

"It does, doesn't it?" I replied. "But something huge must be afire for all that smoke."

We pushed open the door and stepped onto the sidewalk. People were shouting and running toward the river. The air was thick with smoke but I could see where they were pointing. My hands flew up to my mouth to cover a cry.

The railroad bridge from Green Island to Troy was on fire. The whole length of the covered wooden bridge was engulfed in an inferno, flames whipping fifty feet in the air. Never could I have imagined such a scene. The blazing structure dominated the sky, sending billowing clouds of smoke and burning cinders east-ward toward the city. Even in the few moments I stood there, I saw great flaming timbers of the bridge tumble down to the river below.

"Holy Mother of God, save us," murmured the woman next to me. "The bridge has gone up like a tinder box. Whatever will be next?"

I couldn't stand here gaping while the women in the laundry were wondering what was happening. I went back to tell them the awful news. Not five minutes later we were closing down the ironing room to go home to our families, whether the owners approved or not. It was close on to one o'clock anyway.

Streams of workers poured out into the streets, some heading in the direction of the fire. I felt no desire to go any nearer the flames myself, so I started walking south toward home. One of the horse-drawn fire steamers passed me at full speed, clanging its bell, and I began to sense a growing urgency among the business-men and shop owners I passed. Many were hurriedly piling boxes and trunks outside on the sidewalks, arranging for carters to take them to a place of safety. When a flaming cinder fell from the sky directly in my path, I suddenly realized the reason for their worry. If the fire on the bridge wasn't contained, the whole city could go up in flames. I stepped on the cinder to put it out and told myself I'd better keep my wits about me.

Within a few minutes, I was walking through what seemed like a cannon bombardment. The gale-force winds hurled thousands of burning embers onto the streets and roofs of the city. Right before my eyes I saw a roof burst into flames that within seconds engulfed the building. The neighboring house was ablaze almost instantly. Horrified, I tried to walk faster, picking my way through the crowds of frantic residents who were loading wagons and carts with whatever they could carry from their homes.

Still the wind kept up its deadly assault of firebrands, and on every block the houses were burning. The heat and smoke and ash made it hard to breathe. I wrapped my shawl close around my face. Thank God my children were safe at home on the south side of town. And the foundry where Tom worked was nowhere near this terrible place.

When I reached Sixth Street, I couldn't help but shudder at the sight of the Presbyterian Church, burning to the ground. Its spire was a pillar of flame against the smoke-black sky. Only last week I had stopped to admire the daffodils and hyacinths along the walkway, and now it appeared a vision from hell. Sadness rode along with my fear.

Looking down the streets toward the river, I could see nothing but fire and smoke. Great crashes sounded as buildings collapsed, and dust rose up in clouds. For the first time I wondered if I ever would make it home. I'd left the laundry more than an hour ago.

The area around Union Station was impassable, the railroad depot itself a fiery mass in the midst of several blocks completely ablaze. I ran as fast as I could to find a safer street, but the heat and smoke were almost overwhelming. The deafening roar of the fire was punctuated by shouts and warnings. I saw an injured man being taken away on a wheelbarrow, and a little further down the street a cart and horse were swallowed up entirely by a sudden burst of the flames. The driver leaped to safety, but the scream of the horse was a terrible sound. On the next street a panicked family barely made it down their front steps before the burning roof of their house caved in upon itself. The poor, poor people, my heart kept wailing. Fleeing their homes, leaving behind all that they valued and had worked for, escaping death with only the clothes on their backs—in my deepest memories I knew how they felt.

Another corner brought me to the block of the millinery shop, where I often stopped on my way home. The fire was raging behind me as I spotted the owner, Mrs. Ludlow, in front of the store, shutting the door. As I ran toward her, the maple tree on the other side of the street ignited, along with the apothecary shop. The sound of exploding bottles added to the din.

"Mrs. Ludlow!" I called out. "Do you need any help?"

Her trim figure was shaking as she peered through the haze of smoke. "It's beyond hope, I'm afraid," she said. "I've just locked up and taken my best box of scissors with me. Seems silly to lock the door, doesn't it, Mrs. Riordan?" Her voice quavered.

I touched her hand. "It's not silly. Maybe the fire will spare your shop and you'll come back to find everything safe." Unlikely, but it seemed the most hopeful thing I could say. Another explosion blew out the windows of the apothecarys shop, and glass shards landed at our feet.

"We've got to be away from here now, though, Mrs. Ludlow." I linked my arm through hers and began gently tugging her along with me. "Right away, right now."

"I can't think of where to go," she said. "Everything I have is here." Her footsteps slowed.

"Then you'll come home with me until we find a place for you to stay," I replied cheerfully. "Now let's hurry, and I'll make you a cup of tea as soon as we get there. It's only a few blocks further south and east."

"Thank you for your kindness, Mrs. Riordan. Perhaps I might just stay for the tea. A good cup always straightens me out in times of trouble."

It would take more than a cup of tea to put this trouble to rights, I thought. But I was glad to help out where I could. A man could fight fires with buckets and wet brooms, but a woman—the chattering in my mind stopped cold. Suddenly I knew with certainty what Tom was doing right now, and I couldn't suppress the shiver that ran through me. Of course he would be on the fire lines, probably as close to danger as he could get himself. That would be Tom Riordan's way.

Continuing to lead Mrs. Ludlow at a quick pace through the streets, I silently said a prayer for Tom's protection. St. Brigid was also the patron saint of silversmiths, and maybe she would extend that to ironworkers as well.

On the next street we turned down, three houses in a row were on fire. The families stood in the street, counting heads to make certain that everyone was safe. Passing by, we had just offered a word of sympathy for their loss when a terrifying scream split the air. A young mother who had carried her baby in a blanket to safety stood frozen in horror, screams ripping from her throat. She held out the bundle in front of her with stiff arms.

No one moved for a long moment. I recognized in her white face and dark eyes the look of unbearable shock, and I ran to grab the baby from her before she dropped it. I was too late. The bundle hit the street and bounced. As the woman screamed, the blanket fell open to reveal not a baby but a small pillow.

"My baby is burning inside!" the mother shrieked. "My baby is burning. Help, please help! She's burning!"

Such a wave of memory surged through me that I thought I was going to be sick. The world buzzed around me, filled with the young mother's unending screams. A pillow rescued from the fire by mistake, instead of a small baby. A baby thrown into the fire, mistaken for a sack of oatmeal by a madwoman in Ireland.

The woman's screams pierced my heart. I ran toward the house.

"Don't go back in there! It's too dangerous!" someone called after me. But the mother's shrieks became a keen in my soul, a lament for Kitty and wee pale Bridget.

I rushed through the front door, holding my shawl over my face. The walls were ablaze around me, the heat like a smelting furnace. I could barely see through the black smoke. No wonder the poor woman carried out the wrong bundle.

I entered a hallway not yet devoured by flames, hoping to find a baby not yet dead. Please, please, please.

A small room opened off the hall, and through the haze I could see a child's cot. The roar of the fire was ever louder, throbbing and breathing like a live thing, and I threw myself toward the cot. On the mattress lay three small forms, none of them visibly a baby, but I gathered them all into my shawl, close against my breast, and ran for the door. The flames were licking at the hallway.

I tried not to think, I tried not to breathe. I kept my eyes fixed firmly on the path to the front door. By some stroke of luck the ceiling hadn't fallen and the smoldering floor still held.

I only had to squeeze between two heaps of blazing furniture and we would be safe at the door. I glanced down to find the hem of my skirt glowing bright with flames. All the more reason to make this a quick trip out. Clutching my bundle, I darted between the fiery piles toward the door. I was out the door and down the front steps before I felt a small wriggle against my breast and the tiniest of baby sounds. Only then did I start to cough and cry.

Someone smothered the fire on my skirt, and an older woman took the baby and two pillows from my shawl. "Surely a miracle," she said as the baby opened her eyes. "It's a brave woman you must be."

"Where's the mother?" I asked. I heard no screaming, but why wasn't she here to embrace her baby?

"Alas, they've taken her off to Troy House in a wagon. She went mad with grief."

"But her baby's alive! Doesn't she know?"

The older woman shook her head. "You were in that house for so long that we fairly gave up hope. And nothing would stop her screaming."

I hadn't redeemed one baby to pay the price of another mother in a madhouse. I straightened up and spoke in a stern tone. "Send a man off to stop that wagon before it goes any further. There are better uses for a horse and cart today, God knows, than to drag a poor mother away from her babe. She'll be fine when she gets over the shock." I glared at the woman until she nodded.

"Yes, ma'am, if you say so. I guess my son could catch up with them pretty quick."

"Thank you so much," I said. "Now I've got to be seeing to my own children."

Mrs. Ludlow joined me as I turned to leave. To tell the truth, I had forgotten she was accompanying me. I had lost track of time and place for a while.

"Oh, Mrs. Riordan, what a splendid thing you've done," she said.

"I'm happy it ended so well." This time. And maybe, in the balance, my dear lost Kitty and her baby would rest easier—at least I could hope for that.

◎ ◎ ◎

The great fire continued to rage through Troy all afternoon, destroying everything in its path. When Mrs. Ludlow and I passed near the Methodist Church at State Street, she decided to stop in to see if she could be of any help to the minister and his wife. She promised me that they would find a place for her to stay the night. I wished her well and told her that I'd come by for new skirt fabric as soon as her shop was reopened. I could have whatever I wanted at no charge, she said, in appreciation for what I'd done. I thanked her warmly, but I couldn't actually believe I had rushed headlong into a burning house to save a baby. And I thought I might not mention it at home. It might bring up discussions of the past that I didn't want to have.

I must have been a bedraggled mess when I came through my own door at last. Mary Bridget, practical girl, went to heat the water and get towels and soap. Rosie stared at me and finally said, "Ma, you're black and smoky like a railroad man. Did you go straight through the great fire?"

"I did, and it took me a long time to walk home," I explained. "All the firemen are pumping the steam engines, though, and they'll put out the fire soon."

"Aunt Eileen told us we had to stay here, but the boys went out to sell papers," Rosie said. "They'll bring one back and we can read all about it."

Once again I sighed with the worry of being the wife and mother of Riordan men. Nothing would keep them at home if something exciting were happening elsewhere. It must be in their blood.

◎ ◎ ◎

All evening the sky glowed hazy orange and the smoke drifted from the ruins of the city. Around eight, Jimmy and Danny came in with their pockets jingling with coins, having sold out every copy of the paper's several editions.

"You didn't even save one for your own mother?" I asked. I was that relieved to see them.

"Well, I can tell you everything that was printed," Jimmy said. "Up to the minute. But to do that I'll need something in my stomach."

I fixed them some tea and ladled out the soup kept warm on the stove. But Jimmy couldn't keep back his excitement at what he had seen today. He rattled off every story about the fire in the paper, as if they were headlines.

"Eight orphans were crushed to death at the Troy Orphan Asylum—"

"Oh no, don't—" I began in dismay.

"And then in the next edition the matron said all the children were safe," he continued, stuffing bread into his mouth. "That sold a lot of papers."

"And an old man choked on the smoke in the street and fell down and was burned," Danny said. "And a lady went to rescue her baby in a house and never came out again. But hardly anybody else was killed."

"A miracle," I murmured.

"The fire was started by a spark from a locomotive on the bridge." Jimmy went back to reciting headlines. "Over five hundred buildings burned to the ground. Churches and schools and houses and factories and even the railroad station—"

"That I saw with my own eyes," I said.

Both my sons stopped the spoons on the way to their mouths.

"You were *there*?" Jimmy said. "But it was too dangerous! It was a *conflagration!*"

"How else do you think I got home from the laundry? Believe me, it was a trip I'd never want to make again."

"Ma's skirt got burned up in the fire," Rosie added. "She must have been right in the middle of danger."

"I'm glad I didn't know you were out there," my elder son said. "I thought you were safe at home with the girls."

"Likewise," I said. "And I'm still worrying about your father."

"Oh, he's all right," Jimmy answered. "He stopped over to where we were selling papers on River Street and said he'd be home when the embers cooled down. The Fenians are patrolling the streets to watch for trouble."

The next day we walked up to look at the destruction. Acres of the city truly appeared as a scene from hell. Smoke drifted from the cooling piles of rubble. Partial walls of brick and stone rose jagged above the blackened desolation of the streets. Seeing it, I'd expect that the people who had suffered such tragedy would simply abandon the place and move on, as we had left the tumbled down cottages in Clare.

But this was America. Already the newspaper's extra edition was announcing generous donations for the rebuilding of the city, new locations for burned-out businesses, and reminders that the local workforce deserved preference in contracts for demolition and construction. It wouldn't be long before the city would be back in business, better than before. One letter-writer even suggested that Troy become a "Monitor city," rebuilding its houses of iron plate. Tom and I had a good laugh over that one.

CHAPTER 34

TROY, BIRTHPLACE OF UNCLE SAM, had sent hundreds of her sons to fight in the Union Army. Burden's Iron Works had manufactured the thousands upon thousands of iron shoes required by the horses of the Union cavalry and the mules pulling the supply wagons and munitions. And the iron plates protecting the *Monitor* had been cast nowhere else but in Troy. For all the glory, it seemed there should have been more reward for the ironworkers than wages devalued by inflation and the threat in 1864 of discharged soldiers returning to flood the job market.

Likewise the collar workers suffered from the wartime inflation and the competition for jobs. The collars and cuffs made in Troy were becoming more popular every month across America, and yet the average laundress was earning only three to four dollars a week—sweatshop wages. But the widows and wives and daughters were desperate to keep their jobs, being often the only support of their families.

I had my own struggles with the War Between the States, as it had come to be called. I didn't worry that Tom would go off to war—between his union work and the Fenian Brotherhood, Tom was up to his neck in causes.

The problem was with Danny. That quiet dark boy had inherited his father's temperament, and the desire of his life was to run away to be a drummer boy. Thirteen years old and volunteering for death, I told him over and over again. Why couldn't he follow his brother into the rolling mills, where he could get the skills to earn a decent living?

Danny was stubborn. He had a dream of himself carrying the Union flag across some battlefield in Virginia or Pennsylvania, a vision of bloody glory that frightened me into talking to the priest.

I went to the rectory of St. Joseph's Church, the parish of the ironworkers, whose contributions had paid for the soaring steeple and whose pride in its construction was not misplaced. I had made an appointment for five o'clock, costing me an hour's pay.

Father Aloysius Keegan was a substantial man, some said well on his way to becoming Monsignor Keegan. He welcomed me into his office. I was the wife of a generous parish benefactor, a man who never forgot the needs of the oppressed country of his birth. Father Keegan's involvement in the Fenians in Troy was a secret that even his confessor did not know—and I probably shouldn't have. Old hatreds die hard, even among priests.

"And how may St. Joe's be of help to you today, Mrs. Riordan?" Father Keegan asked encouragingly.

"It's about my son Danny, Father. I don't know what to do, and I'm hoping you might be willing to talk to him." I felt at a disadvantage in his polished office, but I told myself that a good piece of our pay packets had gone to provide the heavy drapes and the carpet on the floor. The least the priest could do was to forbid my son from going to war.

"What seems to be the problem?"

How often priests had said those words. Were they ever still surprised by the answer?

"Danny wants to join the army. He's only thirteen, but he's set his heart on being a drummer boy. He sees himself carrying a flag across a battlefield." I felt foolish saying the words, but there it was.

"And I presume you would prefer that Danny stay here in the safe arms of Troy?"

I restrained myself from glaring at him. "I'd prefer he went to the mills like his brother, yes, Father, if that's what you're asking."

"Danny is a small little fellow, isn't he? Takes after his mother? Not the tall man like Tom Riordan?"

"What's his height got to do with it?"

"The army has certain standards, even at the hoped-for end of a brutal war. They've run through enough drummer boys already, I imagine. A short drink of water won't be likely to carry the day."

I blinked at his frankness. "I don't think I could tell him that, Father. I was hoping you would offer a more . . . constructive suggestion."

A sudden light gleamed in the parish priest's eye. "Have you considered the seminary for young Daniel, Mrs. Riordan?" he asked casually. "Such a need for priests to minister to the growing Catholic population."

The look on my face told him that I had not. Unquestionably, had not.

"The attraction of a 'uniform,' the discipline, the comradeship of men—not so very different from the military if you think about it. Except all in the service of God," he said. "Perhaps the life might appeal to Danny. Perhaps he might have a vocation."

"I really don't know," I said.

"Ask Danny to come and see me after school on Monday," said Father Keegan. "We'll straighten this out and you won't lose your son."

I left the rectory with mixed feelings. How would I feel if Danny went off to be a priest? Why did it feel nearly as much a sacrifice as if he went to be a soldier? I decided not to mention my visit with the priest to Tom. He had enough on his mind with the impending strike.

◎   ◎   ◎

The whistle sounded as another long shift at the collar laundry came to its end. I felt the usual ache between my shoulder blades, the result of lifting the hot flatirons from stove to ironing table and back again, hundreds of times a day. But I counted my blessings that I had chosen to be an ironer rather than a starcher or washer. The caustic soaps and bleaches that the washers used were irritating to the skin, and the new starching machines reached such high temperatures that the women frequently were scalded.

Ironing was more skilled and better paid. I had become a master of the different shapes and weights of iron required by each style of collar and cuff. As forewoman of the department I trained the new ironers, supervised the work, settled any problems among the girls, and encouraged them to do their best work, as quickly and efficiently as they could. They were the elite of the industry, I told them. They put the finishing on the work of hundreds, even thousands, of other women, who cut and sewed and trimmed and turned and bleached and washed and starched to keep their families fed and roofs over their heads. They weren't in service in a household, doing the private laundry or cleaning up the messes of the privileged—they were working women, earning wages the same as the men. They couldn't have done that back in Clare or Killarney or Waterford or any of the other places the women had called home.

Still, the wages weren't stretching as far as they had before the war. The cost of basic necessities had grown much faster than the pay packets. The ironers were not alone in this difficulty— families in parishes all over Troy were struggling to make ends meet. The winter had been bitter this year, and I saw painful reminders of the poverty that we had fled in Ireland. There was no famine here, but there was hunger, especially among the newest immigrants, who swung picks and shovels to earn their bread.

Tom had the right idea, I believed. Organize the skilled workers—those whose work the manufacturers could not easily replace—and the wages would be on the rise for every worker. The Iron Molders Union had just asked for a fifteen percent increase in members' pay, and if the owners did not comply the men would strike in March. If the men went out, the families would depend more heavily on the women's work. All the more reason that the collar women should be paid their fair value.

I wished the other departing ironers a good night and took a last look around the room. The finished collars were stacked in boxes, the worktables were neat, and the floors were swept. We had such a good crew of women.

Pulling on my knitted wool gloves, I began the walk home. My girls would have the potatoes boiled and ready for supper, and there was still half a bread pudding left from Sunday dinner. Tom had a rare evening at home tonight, and it would be nice if we could spend it together.

"Mrs. Riordan," called a woman's voice behind me. I regretfully left my thoughts about how best to enjoy the evening with Tom and waited for the woman walking toward me to catch up. She was young, about twenty, and looked familiar.

"Mrs. Riordan, might I have a few minutes of your time?" she said quickly.

Now I recognized her. The girl was Kate Mullaney, an ironer who worked in another firm—a bright, well-spoken young woman. I smiled warmly at her. "As many minutes as you need, Miss Mullaney."

"I'll walk with you on your way, so as not to slow you down," she said.

We picked our way along the icy streets, to all appearances two ordinary collar workers heading on home, chatting about the homely interests of women.

"A labor union of our own?" I repeated. I was instantly convinced of the rightness of Kate's idea.

"I've been developing a plan to organize the laundresses," Kate explained. "I'd like to tell you about it and enlist your cooperation. I'm hoping that the women in all the laundries will work together, like the iron molders did—"

I interrupted. "You know it's dangerous work, to go up against the manufacturers. You could be fired just for talking about a union. And our women have to be willing to bear the hardships of a strike, to take the abuse of the public and even the other workers." I had been through it all with Tom.

"I know," said Kate Mullaney. "I believe we can do it." She was young and strong and determined.

I stopped in front of our painted frame house. "We're at my doorstep, Miss Mullaney. Please come in and have some supper with us. My husband is home tonight and we can talk unions until we're blue in the face."

"I won't impose on you for too long, Mrs. Riordan," said Kate. "But if you could get the women in your shop to support the union, a lot of the others would follow."

Kate Mullaney stayed so late that Jimmy walked her home to be sure she got there safely. Kate's mother had the lamp burning in the front window, as usual. So many nights Kate was out on business until midnight. And she still had to be at the laundry at six in the morning.

"It's going to be hard going, Tommy," I said, lying next to him in the bed, warm under the covers. It was after midnight and we had drunk enough tea with Kate Mullaney to float a ship.

"The Molders Union will help you," he promised. "This could truly make a difference. There's no women's union any-where in the country. You'll catch the owners by surprise."

"I told Kate that she could hold some of the meetings here."

"We're a hotbed of intrigue in the city of Troy, aren't we, Margaret? The molders, the Fenians, and the ironers beat a path to our door."

"Aren't they mostly one and the same? The molders are married to the ironers, or their sisters and daughters are ironers— it's the same families cropping up over and over again. The Fenians are the quieter bunch."

"When the time comes, all the world will hear from the Fenians," said Tom. "We've never stopped working for Ireland's freedom, and we never will." Even lying flat in bed he had the words on the tip of his tongue. Then one of his pet peeves came to mind and he sat bolt upright. "I cannot understand how John Mitchel could have escaped from Tasmania and joined the Confederate Army. How can a man who fought Ireland's enslavement by the British turn around and support American slavery? Has the man no sense of the absurd?"

I knew I shouldn't tease him about his former hero but the opportunity was too much to resist. "Maybe when they told him he could be a general for the Rebels, he mistook the Cause."

"Ah, Margaret, that's pathetic," said Tom. "You can do better than that."

"It's been a long day," I said.

CHAPTER 35

A MURMUR HERE, A WHISPER THERE. Kate Mullaney and I and Kate's friend Esther Keegan spread the idea of a union through the laundries. Women met in the evening at our house, at St. Joe's after Mass, anywhere that a small group would not raise too much attention.

The younger women, in their teens and twenties, were more likely to support the union, with its almost certain outcome of a strike. They had less to lose than the older ones, who were mostly widows with families to support. I could see the fear in their eyes when I spoke to them, women whose wages barely covered the essentials of rent, food, and clothing for their children. Women who would slip quickly into destitution, even in America.

About three hundred women worked in the commercial laundries, and by the middle of February, I must have talked to every one of them. My daughters complained that they never saw me—I was getting to be as bad as their father with the meetings and the secret organizations. I hugged them and explained that I was working for their future, so they would have fair wages and better conditions when they began their own jobs in the laundries.

"We've decided to become teachers instead," Mary Bridget said solemnly. Rosie nodded her head in agreement, her brown curls tortured into braids that she clearly had done without help from her mother.

"Oh. Well, teachers might need unions too."

"Then you can organize one for us," Rosie said. "You might not be too old by then."

I laughed. I was a lot younger than my own mam was at thirty-five, it seemed, but my daughters wouldn't see it that way. I quickly brushed off the shadows that gathered when I thought of that hungry life in Clare, of my mother's death and the keening of Nuala Lynch. I didn't tell those stories to my children. I never would.

"It's a fine dream to be schoolteachers. I would be proud of you both."

"And I'm never going to marry," continued Rosie. "I'm going to wear nice dresses and have my own books with pictures in them."

"I might get married. But only if a nice boy asked me." Mary Bridget couldn't name one nice boy of her acquaintance at present, so it seemed a long shot.

"You've got your whole lives ahead of you, my sweethearts. You don't have to decide today." I hugged them again, aware of how lucky I was, and grateful. It was more important then ever to preserve their future.

A rumor spread from washing tubs to starching machines, from bleaching kettles to ironing tables. "They've beat us to it!" said the laundresses. "The sewers have walked out today. Four thousand women are on the streets of Troy, demanding a wage increase!"

It was an exaggeration on that day in February. When the sewers' request for a raise in rates was turned down by the group of manufacturers, the women in one shop on River Street left their machines and went out. But within two days the women from many of the other shops had gone out as well. The fifteen collar companies in Troy were crippled in their busiest season.

The manager of our laundry called an emergency meeting of all his forewomen. He stood before us in his tailored suit and jabbed his finger in the air.

"I don't want to have any of this nonsense here," he said. "Keep your girls at their work and don't let them talk among themselves. Those women who left their sewing jobs are going to find that there are plenty of Bridgets and Marys to take their places. The manufacturers will not put up with this kind of blackmail, I can tell you that." He glared at the women standing in a semicircle in front of him. I tried not to feel intimidated when he kept his eyes on me longer than on the others.

"If I hear any whisper of union talk—the slightest mention—that worker will be out of here faster than a greased pig. And her friends with her. Do I make myself clear?"

We nodded. Threats like these were familiar echoes of the landlords' agents and the rent collectors at home in Ireland. But this was Troy. In silence we filed back to our departments. The bolder ones winked at one another as we parted.

The sewers held a massive meeting to determine their course of action. They did not invite the laundresses but kept to their own—more than half the striking sewers were native-born Americans, who did not care to forge links with the Irish immigrants. A couple of men from the Iron Molders Union attended to offer their support, but Tom said it was politely and firmly declined. The women assured them that the owners would see their responsibility to treat their workers fairly and would do the right thing.

The union men shook their heads at the women's innocent trust in their employers. But after two and a half days, the owners capitulated and gave them the requested wage increase. The sewers happily went back to work, not a union maid among them.

But their success inspired Kate Mullaney to put her plan into action the next day.

At noon on the twenty-third of February, the collar laundresses walked out. Close to three hundred women from fourteen laundry firms put on their shawls, picked up their lunch pails, and headed to the streets.

The newly formed Collar Laundry Union met with the membership that afternoon to work out our demands.

Kate Mullaney and Esther Keegan ran the meeting with good humor and efficiency. They helped the members to draw up a list of demands, balancing the needs of the washers, starchers, and ironers who were in attendance.

"We all want a wage increase of twenty to twenty-five percent," Kate finally summarized after much discussion. "All in favor, say aye."

I looked around the room at the women, all shapes and sizes and ages. With one strong voice, including my own, we overwhelmingly approved the demand. For the first time in our lives, we voted as members of a union. Most likely it was the first time any of us had voted at all.

The safety of the women who worked with the new starching machines was the other item that made it to the top of the first women's union meeting agenda. And the offer of advice and financial support from the Iron Molders International Union, Number 2 of Troy, New York, was gratefully accepted.

A delegation of women presented the union's demands to each of the laundry owners. The proprietors, after discussing the demands among themselves, responded that they could not afford to meet the increase in wages unless they passed the cost back to the collar manufacturers, which they were unwilling to do.

"Why was it so easy for the sewers?" I asked Tom at home that night.

"They had strength in numbers, I think. And they weren't organized into a union, either—the one-time demand could be gained but there was nothing planned over the long run. Just tell the strikers to hold on, Margaret. It will be worth it in the end."

I spent the next four days walking from house to house in the neighborhoods where the laundresses lived, while Kate and Esther handled the union negotiations, drawing on the molders for advice about offers and counteroffers. Part of my job was to ensure that no woman's family suffered beyond endurance during the time without an income—the molders had provided a sum of money from their own strike fund for emergencies. We had no idea how long the strike would last.

It seemed strange to be walking out in the daylight hours, on a weekday. But a strike was not a holiday. This was deadly serious. I mounted the steps to the next house on my list, where a washer named Alice Fahey lived.

Following the landlady's instructions, I knocked tentatively on the door of the room at the top of the house. The door was cracked and badly fit into the frame. From inside I could hear the sound of a child wailing.

Alice Fahey opened the door, the baby in her arms squalling and red-faced.

"I'm Margaret Riordan, from the union," I introduced myself. The reality of it was still sinking in. "I came to see if you needed anything, Miss Fahey." Or maybe it was Mrs. Fahey? The union list wasn't clear.

She invited me in to the crowded room, where two young children sat on the bare wood floor and damp laundry was draped over the chairs. I was reminded of the room where Tom and I had lived for the first year of our marriage. Even in poverty it hadn't been so cold and cheerless as this one.

"I'm watching my sister's children while she goes out to clean," Alice Fahey explained. "We share the place together, since I'm alone and her man went back to Tipperary after leaving her with this little one. The shiftless coward." She looked down at her niece or nephew—I couldn't tell which—with affection. "She's cleaning while I'm on strike, just to keep the money coming in."

"If you need something to keep the children fed, just let me know. That's one of the benefits of union membership."

"We can manage, if it doesn't go on too long," said Mrs. Fahey. "Use the money for them that really needs it."

I thanked her and walked down the three flights of dark stairs. The laundresses were proud, strong women. They had brought the best of Ireland with them in their souls.

On my way down Second Street, I saw Kate Mullaney crossing in front of me. The young woman carried a sheaf of papers in her hand.

"Miss Mullaney!" I called. It wasn't polite to go shouting someone's first name after her down the street, as if calling a cow.

Kate recognized me and hurried toward me.

"We've done it," she said, her voice trembling with emotion. Her eyes were shining with the joy of success. "They've agreed to the increase and a safety review. We can all go back in tomorrow!"

"Congratulations, Kate. You've made a grand beginning!" I hugged her.

"We must get the word out to return. Have you the energy to organize a meeting for tonight?"

"Tom said we could meet at the Molders' Hall whenever we had the good news to announce—I'll start the message around, for seven o'clock."

My heart was light as I left to spread the news that the strike was over. I laughed to myself when I thought of the clever slogan that someone had suggested for the Collar Laundry Union banner— "Never iron while the strike is hot!"

Perhaps I would use that in my own speech tonight.

CHAPTER 36

I had gotten used to the men in my parlor. Really it was silly to call it a parlor, since it wasn't used for ladies visiting but for men plotting rebellion—and occasionally for women organizing strikes. Since the end of the war there had been a regular parade of veterans marching through the house. They came sometimes for union business but more often for the cause of the Fenians. The Irishmen who had fought for the Union in America were anxious to continue the fight for freedom in their native land.

When the 1866 Fenian national convention was held in Troy, Tom had brought home half the city every night. After working the full day at the laundry, I had brewed pot after pot of tea for the strangers filling the house. Tom was in his element, reunited with his fellow rebels, singing the songs and raising the money and shipping the guns that Ireland needed to rid herself of the British oppression. James Stephens, founder of the Fenian movement, came to New York after escaping from British imprisonment, and Tom had been proud to hand him a generous sum of cash for the needs of the lads back home. Where that much cash had come from, I didn't know— the Iron Molders Union had been locked out by the owners on

St. Patrick's Day, and the Collar Laundry Union had donated a thousand dollars to the molders' strike fund in support. Perhaps Tom and his Fenian brothers had a secret way of collecting money for the Irish cause—if it had been late summer, I would have guessed the horse races at Saratoga.

A knock sounded on the back door. "Come in!" I called out. The quiet of a Sunday afternoon in May was delicious—after dinner the girls and Jimmy were off to visit friends, and Tom was meeting with a few of the molders to try to resolve the lockout, which had gone on for too long. I hadn't expected a visitor, but when the door opened and Eileen Sweeney entered, I was happy to see her. Without even asking, I got up to put water on for tea and Eileen sat herself down at the table, for once without a child on her lap.

"What's the grand occasion, Eileen? You've come yourself without the Sweeney mob."

"I wanted to talk to you in private, Margaret. Tom's not around, is he?"

I assumed it must be something to do with female problems. Even though the pharmacies in Troy dispensed pills and potions for female troubles, I still relied on the herbs that my grandmother had taught me to brew and Mrs. Mellowes had helped me to find in America. After the last birth Eileen had needed building up, and she was looking much better now.

"Tom's off at some meeting or other, even on Sunday." I rinsed the teapot with scalding water and measured in the black tea leaves. Eileen watched me pour the boiling water into the pot and set it down before she spoke.

"I've heard something very disturbing, Margaret, and I want to tell you, if you don't know it already." Eileen's tone was serious.

"About Tom?"

"And Danny." Eileen nodded.

"What about Danny?" Nothing could be wrong with Danny—he'd been at seminary since September. He wrote home every week. I waited on Eileen's words, not breathing.

"I overheard Hugh and Tom talking about a Fenian uprising, and your Danny is involved in it. He's leaving the seminary to join the men from Troy in a raid on Canada."

"He wouldn't!" But I knew in my heart that he would.

"I didn't think you were aware, or you would have stopped it. Is Tom himself leading the raid?"

"I don't know, but I'll find out. The secret societies are not so secret as they imagine."

Eileen poured the tea into the cups and spooned in the sugar.

"Is Hugh a part of this?" I asked.

Eileen shook her head. "Not actively. He's so busy running the saloon that he doesn't have time for the Fenians—but he gives them a place to meet and hatch their plots, I'm sure. The more they shout about how they'll overthrow the yoke of England and create an Irish republic, the thirstier they get. And that's good for business." Hugh had left Burden's Iron Works and bought the Lark Tavern from its former owners. His genial personality was a benefit behind the bar, and the business was thriving.

It wasn't that I was angry at a Fenian action. I myself had heard rumors of a ship being built with American funds, armed with American guns, to sail across the Atlantic and roust the Queen's soldiers from Erin. No, I was angry that my efforts to divert Danny Riordan from his desire to join the Union Army had merely served to direct him into another war.

"Thank you for telling me, Eileen. I'll deal with this when Tom gets home." I sipped my tea as if I tasted it. What was the man thinking of?

◎　◎　◎

"He's just a boy, Tom. How could you even *think* of including him in this dangerous plan?" The tips of my ears were flaming red with anger.

"It wasn't my idea," said Tom in defense of himself. "Danny heard about it from someone—maybe even Jimmy—and insisted on joining up."

"So Jimmy is in on this too?"

"I didn't say that," said Tom.

"Oh, indeed you did."

Tom tried another tack. "We've been having this same discussion for twenty years, Margaret," he said. "The struggle for freedom does not come without a measure of violence. Armed rebellion is the only thing the British will listen to—why do you think we are standing in a free country in America?"

"We agreed on money and guns, Tommy. That did not include sending our sons off to fight for Ireland."

"When I was their age, I was out in the streets of Clare with Daniel O'Connell, agitating for repeal," said Tom, in the manner of fathers everywhere.

"And did we get freedom, Tom Riordan?" I looked him in the eye. "No. We got exile."

To Tom's credit, he did not flinch. But he could make no reply to the story of our life.

"Don't go, Tom." I softened my voice to show him the love beneath the anger. "And don't take our boys. Any of them. Please."

"The Fenians will do what they must," Tom said. "Most of them were Yankee soldiers. Now they want to strike a blow against England, in support of the Republican Brotherhood."

"Money and guns, Tom. Give them money and guns. Not our blood."

◎ ◎ ◎

By the middle of May, when the lilacs bloomed, the striking
molders went back to work. The solidarity of the unions was
spreading to other trades, and the benefits were moving out into
the community. The unions established a cooperative grocery
store, a workingmen's clothing store, a library. Even a debating
society was being formed, although why the men needed a formal
club to do what they all did anyway was beyond me.

One evening at the end of May, Jimmy did not come home
from the foundry. Tom and the girls and I ate our supper without
him, the table seeming oddly empty—Jimmy never missed a
meal. Tom left for the Lark immediately afterward.

I waited up until after midnight when Tom returned.

He shook his head when he saw me standing fully dressed,
my hair still up in pins, prepared to receive the priest or the police,
or both.

"I'm sorry, Margaret," he said. "Two hundred men from Troy
have left for Canada and Jimmy went with them."

"You were supposed to stop him."

"I thought I had," said Tom. "Danny listened to me. But
Jimmy made his own decision and left. I didn't know." Tom had
never been rendered so powerless in his life.

"What can we do now?"

"We just have to wait," he answered.

The telegraph office in downtown Troy was mobbed with people
waiting for the hourly bulletins on the progress of the Fenian
raid on Canada. Through the windows we could see the teleg-
rapher in his shirtsleeves at the machine, and when a particu-
larly long message was coming through, we pressed forward

toward the glass, as if we could translate the strange clicks ourselves.

One of the Canadian newspapers was providing updates every hour, live from the battlefront. With my Jimmy in the midst of the troops, I wasn't sure that I truly wanted such immediacy. If the worst happened, how would I take the news here on a public street corner? But thus far there had been no list of casualties, no black-bordered telegram sheets pinned to the wall.

I was as surprised by the sudden attack as the Canadian armies at Fort Erie apparently were. The Fenians—whose estimated numbers ranged from thousands to hundreds, depending on who was doing the estimating—had massed on the Canadian border near Buffalo, in their shirts of Kelly green. Their mission was to capture Fort Erie and use it as the first hostage in negotiations to force the British government to declare Ireland a republic. The long-range plan was to continue the takeovers of Canadian outposts until Britain had no choice but to agree to the Fenians' demands.

In the crowd around me I recognized at least one member of nearly every Irish family of my acquaintance. They couldn't all have sons as foolhardy as mine, I thought.

Tom was not at the telegraph office. He must be getting his news privately, delivered to the meetings where he had been closeted since yesterday, when we first heard of the attack on the fort. I was torn between my responsibilities at the laundry and my overwhelming need to be there in person if any news came through the telegraph office. I ran back and forth on the streets of downtown Troy all day long. We knew that the Fenians under John O'Neill had held Fort Erie through the night of June 1, and the next day we got the blow-by-blow descriptions of the defeat of two volunteer Canadian armies, at Ridgeway and at Erie.

Whenever the news of success was posted, the crowd would shout and cheer. The Fenians' bold plan seemed to be running like clockwork, and the people of Troy liked nothing better than a well-oiled machine. Irish pride was bursting at the seams. It was hard to resist the leap of imagination that cast the Irish in America as the saviors of all Ireland.

As the hours passed on the third day, I began to feel a dread rising within me. Surely a few hundred ironworkers and ex-soldiers couldn't so easily bring about the freedom for which thousands of Irish men and women had fought and died over the centuries. It would be a wonderful thing, but it wasn't the usual turn of events that described the luck of the Irish.

Someone tugged on my sleeve as I stood there waiting, and I turned to see Rosie, her young face showing a troubled frown.

"Ma, you've got to come home. Dad sent me to fetch you."

"Is it Jimmy?" I put my hand to my throat.

Rosie shook her head. "We don't know anything yet about Jimmy. Come on, Dad wants to tell you some news." She took my hand and led me through the crowd, away from the telegraph office.

We were nearly a block away when we heard the crowd roar. Another telegraph message must have come through. I started to turn back but Rosie dragged me forward. We ran all the way home.

Tom was pacing at the door when I arrived out of breath and out of hope.

"I got an advance telegram," he said. "The rising is over. Old Mother England has a very long reach. American gunboats blockaded the Niagara River today and stranded half the Fenians in Canada. The rest of the men are on the Buffalo side—there's hope they can escape into the neighborhoods and disappear."

"Where is Jimmy?"

"I don't know, Margaret. If he's across the river in Ontario, he's been arrested."

I squeezed my daughter's hand and smiled at my husband. "Jimmy is coming home. I'm sure of it. He's my son and like me he would never set foot on a boat to Canada—not even for Irish freedom. My Jimmy will never see Ireland unless God gives him wings."

Tom looked at me skeptically. "I want to believe you. I hope you're right. Do you still have the Second Sight, do you think?"

"I told you twenty years ago, Tom Riordan, I'm a keener, not a seer. Don't you ever listen to me?"

"I do, Margaret dear, every word. Always."

PART III

1905

CHAPTER 37

I was comfortable enough in the straight wood chair that my grandson Tommy, Mary Bridget's boy, had placed under a shady maple tree. Around me swelled the hubbub of the Sunday picnic organized by Mr. Connolly and the other labor activists as a fundraiser for the union treasuries. Children rolled hoops across the grassy lawn, dogs chased each other and their tails, and serious-looking men and women gathered in conversation near the tables loaded with bread, ham, and cakes. They were discussing the threatened labor strike, I assumed. At seventy-six years old, I couldn't hear as well as I used to, although my other moving parts worked just fine. I hoped that when James Connolly spoke I would be able to catch every word. The man was a marvel at rousing a crowd.

Even twenty years ago I had still been active in union work. But in July 1905, I knew myself too old to join this new organization, the International Laundry Workers' Union. It had ties to the American Federation of Labor and the international labor movement, which accounted for the presence of James Connolly, a socialist come over from Dublin. He sold life insurance to the Irish families in Troy, as well as giving them dreams of a life where all workers would be fairly treated and no children would go hungry.

Today I was merely an honored guest at the picnic, like the Civil War veterans who paraded on Independence Day. An old woman whose young memories stretched back to a hungry and beautiful land and whose life had been spent in a collar factory.

It was a different world now, and a different century. What would these young people think if I told them that back in Ireland I had known an old woman who lived in the tomb of a king? It was not often that I allowed myself to recall the old days. I doubted that any of my grandchildren even knew the name of Kilvarna.

My son Jimmy brought a glass of lemonade in one hand and a pint of black porter in the other. He offered them both to me with a grin.

"Sweeney's Tavern donated three barrels of porter today," he said. "Don't you want to drink to the memory of Uncle Hugh and Dad?"

"I'd have to crawl home on my knees if I drank that. And you'd better be careful that you don't have to."

"Oh, Ma," said Jimmy. "This is only my third, but who's counting? Shall I bring you a bite to eat?"

"How long is it until Connolly speaks?"

"Another hour or so. You've got plenty of time. Are you lonesome here by yourself? I could send the girls over to keep you company."

I looked over at Jimmy's three grown daughters enjoying themselves with their coworkers. They had the Meehans' blue-black hair and small bones, whereas Jimmy favored the Riordans.

"No, leave them be," I said. "I'm fine here. A small slice of cake wouldn't go to waste, though."

Jimmy went off to fetch it. He looked from the back very much like his father had, tall and fair, with muscular shoulders even in his fifties.

Though Tom has been gone for more than fifteen years, I will never get used to the loss. He worked as an iron molder until the very instant he fell to a heart attack. When they carried him home from the stove works that morning, the ancient keening rose in my throat without warning. My wailing voice cried out from my heart and my soul, begging him not to leave me. But my children, who had never heard the keen, called for a doctor to control my "hysteria." Once more I turned my grief inside, the keening silenced in America.

Father Dan Riordan—now Monsignor—had celebrated the Mass for his father. Tom's funeral was a Fenian's dream, with pipers and drummers and a huge contingent of the Ancient Order of Hibernians following the procession from St. Joe's to the cemetery. They joined the hundreds of union marchers in honoring Tom's tireless work for their causes. Among them were scores of members of the secret Clan na Gael and the Irish Republican Brotherhood, which I knew had received a generous portion of Tom's money over the years.

I still missed him, of course, every day that I drank tea by myself in the dark predawn mornings. I couldn't shake the habit of a lifetime of arising early, even though I no longer packed the lunch pails and went off to the collar factory myself. I made the tea and oatmeal porridge for Jimmy and his family, then settled myself in my chair by the front window, where the day would go by outside. Truth to tell, it was a boring life. Not like the old days.

Jimmy must have wandered off with his porter and forgotten the cake. No matter. I closed my eyes for just a moment, and when I awoke I was surrounded by a family of children. Four girls and a little boy, trailed by their mother. The oldest girl had long brown hair plaited in braids and round intense brown eyes. She reminded me of Rosie at that age.

"I'm sorry we woke you, Mrs. Riordan," she said. "We thought perhaps you were dead."

"Nora!" exclaimed her mother.

"Her eyes were closed, and she sat so still," Nora said. "I was worried, that's all."

"I'm not dead yet," I said, shaking myself awake. "Good afternoon, Mrs. Connolly. It's a pleasure to see you all here."

"I apologize for Nora's frankness," said Lillie Connolly in a soft voice.

"Not at all. I'm looking forward to living long enough to hear your husband's speech this afternoon. It's such important work he's doing."

"It is, isn't it," interrupted Nora. "Daddy writes such wonderful speeches—"

"Come along, Nono, we mustn't disturb Mrs. Riordan any further," said her mother. "The program is about to begin."

"Perhaps you might like to visit with me some afternoon, Nora," I said impulsively. "We can share stories about Ireland." She was such a bright star of a girl—I would enjoy her company.

"I am homesick sometimes," she said. "I love our little house here, with the fruit trees in the orchard, but I miss our friends in Dublin and Belfast."

"I've never been to either city, though my brother lives in Belfast. You can tell me all about it. And I can tell you about the ancient heroes of Ireland—the warrior queens, too."

"Thank you, Mrs. Riordan," said Mrs. Connolly. "Nora would enjoy that, I'm certain. I'll send her around next week at your convenience."

"That would be lovely." I settled back into my chair to listen to James Connolly, whose writings and speeches on behalf of the oppressed working classes were both brilliant and inspiring. Troy was lucky to have such a skilled organizer to work with the unions—though the newspapers referred to him as "the great agitator." Tom would have loved the man's speechmaking.

Nora Connolly spent many afternoons that summer in my front

parlor. I was surprised at first at the quickness of the little girl's mind. She was only ten but well ahead of other girls her age in her understanding of the world. She was her daddy's shadow, Nora told me, going with him to meetings and helping the cause in every way she could. She had learned to stuff envelopes for political mailings before she could button her own shoes.

Nora was no stranger to hunger, either, I discovered through the sharing of stories from Belfast and Dublin. She and her father had visited some of the poorer neighborhoods in Troy, where conditions rivaled the worst slums of Dublin during the long winter when unskilled laborers were out of work. Something in the way Nora described the people, a compassion unusual in a girl so young, told me that life in tenement neighborhoods like these was not unfamiliar. I felt fortunate that Tom and I had learned the skilled trades early on, that our own children and grandchildren had grown up without suffering real hunger or destitution.

I never told stories about the Great Hunger, not even to Nora. But one golden afternoon in August, as we sat together on the porch of my house, I told Nora about the old keener Nuala Lynch, about the ancient Irish poetry of lament that passed from the old women to the young. Nora begged to see the stone from Brigid's well, to hold it in her hands just once.

"I'll get it out for you next time," I promised. "It's in the bottom drawer of my bureau, wrapped in an old scrap of petticoat."

"I'll go and find it for you," Nora offered.

"No, it's late now, and your mama will be wondering what's happened to you."

"Oh, please, please, please," she begged. Nora could be very persuasive in getting what she wanted, a trait that always stood her father well.

"Come on, then, have a peek," I said, rising from the chair to go inside. "It's the only thing I brought out with me from Ireland."

Nora followed close on my heels. "And you never went back home?"

"No, never. I didn't want to sail the ocean again," I said. "My home is here now, in Troy."

"My daddy says we'll be going home someday, when the time is ripe," said Nora. "I don't know when that will be—but it's not yet."

I tugged open the bureau drawer, with Nora's help. Carefully I unfolded the red scrap of flannel, marveling at how well it had stayed for all these years. I don't believe I ever showed the stone to my granddaughters. They thought of Brigid as a chaste saint in a nun's habit, not the fiery source of energy that this rough stone image brought back to me.

Nora put out her hand and I gave her the stone.

"It's warm," she said.

"Maybe from the heat of my hands," I said.

"It's a special kind of warmth," she insisted. "Like inside your heart."

"You're a very astute young lady, Nora Connolly," I said. I'm sure she had no trouble at all understanding the word.

She handed the stone from Brigid's well carefully back to me and gave me a quick little hug and a smile. Then she flew out the door to make up for lost time.

When I rewrapped the stone to return it to my bureau drawer, I pinned a scrap of paper to it. "For Nora," I wrote, as clearly as I could. My hands were trembling and my chest felt tight. Perhaps a few minutes' rest would put me right.

EPILOGUE

Jimmy Riordan gave the stone from Brigid's well to Nora Connolly, as his mother had wished. He didn't know what the fuss was about—it was just a piece of stone from the old country. But five years later Nora tucked the ancient stone into her traveling bag to carry on board the ship that would take them to Ireland. James Connolly had a new job—to organize an Irish workers' union in Belfast—and the Connollys were eager to go home.

When James Connolly led the Citizen Army in the ill-fated Easter Uprising of 1916 in Dublin, his daughter Nora led her own group of volunteer nurses from Belfast to Dublin—Margaret's great-niece Grace Meehan among them. What happened to Nora and her father—and how Nora gave the stone from Brigid's well to Grace Meehan—is a story for another book.

ACKNOWLEGMENTS

So many generous people have helped me over the long course of my work on this book that I can't hope to thank them all here with the individual gratitude that each deserves.

I have been truly blessed with the support of three friends, all writers. Cait Johnson is my soul sister and my best friend—always there, always a gift. Harriet Schwartz is the "just do it" friend who said, "Why can't you go to Ireland?" when I despaired of finishing the research. Karen DeMauro has helped me beyond measure, in such beautiful ways.

Gail Dell, Janine Stanley-Dunham, Lyndee Stalter, Ashling Kelly, and Maureen Rant read early drafts and gave insightful comments. Shelly Angers read the nearly final draft and began the publicity wheels turning.

I'd like to thank Bill Campbell for sharing his historical videotapes; Professor Angela Bourke in Dublin for answering my questions on keening; Dr. Michael Lippman for information on gunshot wounds and cholera, and for being my beloved friend; Meghan Nuttall Sayres for the audiotape of one of the few keens recorded; the Rensselaer County Historical Society; the Troy Public Library; the Clare Heritage Museum in Corofin, Clare; and the Famine Museum at Strokestown Park, Roscommon.

Other people have helped in various ways. Nora Connolly O'Brien and Margaret Brennan Collins, both gone now, encouraged and inspired me. Mary Sweeney of Doonagore Farmhouse welcomed me to Clare, and within ten minutes her mother-in-law was telling me she had danced with my father's cousins in

Kilfenora. Dawn Christenson fed me at her restaurant when in my mind I was starving through the Famine. Ellen Marble first told me about Kate Mullaney. Alyssa Martin reviewed the draft from a young woman's perspective, and Sue Martin's in-laws shared their memories of an Irish family in Troy: Patricia McGowan Turner, Mary Ellen McGowan Martin, Colleen Buckley Moss, and Joan Martin Horning. I'd like to especially thank Tom McGrath, owner of Tipperary of Tara, a splendid shop, for all his help in negotiating the ins-and-outs of the Irish community in Troy, both yesterday and today.

The people at Medallion Press have been wonderful. My editor, Pam Ficarella, understands the Irish American experience as I do, although she has the advantage of a canonized saint in her family, Oliver Plunkett. My appreciation goes to Helen Rosburg, the publisher, and to Leslie Burbank, Connie Perry, Jamie Morgenroth, and Adam Mock.

My mother, Beverly Shaw, was an enthusiastic companion on our trip through Ireland with Pat and John Preston and is ready to go again. Bill Shaw, my late father, taught me the love of Irish history and music, along with ideas of rebellion. My son, Nick Tantillo, offered creative help with plot details and designed my website www.mauradshaw.com.

My husband, Joe Tantillo, has become an honorary Irish-American over the thirty-plus years we've been together. No one else would have searched out Famine fever hospitals and their mass graves, photographed rusting soup kettles, and tracked down the holy well of Brigid on a beautiful Lughnasad day with such good cheer. He is my partner and my love.

Sláinte. To your health.